CHRIS
BEYONI
WOULD
LIMITS OI FANTASY.

MEL

his lust for power was transcended only by his ravenous hunger for Christina's passion.

ZENYA

a silent mystic, shrouded in ominous darkness, he drew Christina into strange, primitive worlds of eroticism.

MARGARET

a psychic groupie eager to experience the intimacy of the circle, suddenly controlled and terrified by the passions that engulfed her.

NICHOLAS

his Jaguars, his social connections, his bizarre sexual obsessions could not silence the voices that haunted him from beyond.

MASTERSON

reclusive until he was naked in the circle of yearning, he would touch Christina and receive a message from beyond the grave.

Also in Arrow
by Blakely St James

CHRISTINA'S CHALLENGE
CHRISTINA'S CONFESSIONS
CHRISTINA'S CRAVING
CHRISTINA'S ESCAPADE
CHRISTINA'S NEED
CHRISTINA'S PARADISE
CHRISTINA'S TOUCH

CHRISTINA ENCHANTED

Blakely St James

ARROW BOOKS

Arrow Books Limited
62-65 Chandos Place, London WC2N 4NW

An imprint of Century Hutchinson Limited

London Melbourne Sydney Auckland
Johannesburg and agencies throughout
the world

First published in Great Britain 1987

Printed and bound in Great Britain by
Anchor Brendon Limited, Tiptree, Essex

ISBN 0 09 951710 8

For Nancy Smith

CHAPTER ONE

I used not to believe in the occult, or astrology, or ESP. When I followed the advice of a mystical friend and started talking to my plants, they wilted. When I tried to pick up the secret thoughts of my lovers, all I ever heard was radio static. When I had my astrological chart drawn, it told me I was a modest, undemanding person whose simple tastes were easily satisfied. Me, the heiress who throws tantrums if her breakfast croissants aren't properly warmed, or her Liebfraumilch is a few degrees below cellar temperature. So I dismissed mysticism . . . until what happened to me on my vacation with Mel.

Mel is a young; ambitious lawyer whom I met at a gallery opening in New York. Most lawyers are a bore; when they're not telling you how much money they're making (which is usually trivial, anyway, compared to the dividends I earn from my own investments), they're describing their latest tax loopholes; and frankly, this kind of thing is not just incomprehensible, it's tedious as hell.

But Mel was different. Oh, he enjoyed his large income, and he had a taste for the finer things in life. Fine things like Lamborghini sports cars, dinners at the Four Seasons, the Metropolitan Opera, and beautiful women such as me (well, that's what he said, and I wasn't modest enough to argue with him).

And he happened to be fantastically good-looking. When I first saw his face I thought he was an actor;

he looked like a younger Paul Newman, complete with curly blond hair and blue eyes that fixed on me with a mixture of sincere interest in me as a person and pure lust for my body (a mixture I have always found hard to resist).

Within days, Mel and I were enjoying a wonderfully passionate, expensive love affair in New York. And it wasn't hard to persuade him to take a week away from his law practice and go somewhere with me, just the two of us, alone together. And London was where we ended up.

Of course, I'd been in London more times than I could count. It's one of my favorite cities and I feel at home there, so I wasn't expecting anything out of the ordinary. I certainly had no inkling that this getting-away-from-it-all was going to metamorphose into my getting into something else—something strange and frightening—deeper than I could possibly imagine.

We stayed at the Ritz, which set us back a couple hundred dollars a day before we even dialed room service, but it was worth it. The grand old building on Piccadilly had just been totally renovated, and they'd saved the best of the old, side by side with the new. The place was littered with antiques—a Louis XV rosewood writing desk in our room, for instance, and a fine old Victorian fender around the fireplace, which of course was in working order if we'd chosen to ask the staff to haul up some coal (hardly necessary, with the ample central heating). And at the same time each room had an enormous new modern bathroom with shower stall, bidet, and giant bathtub as well.

On the last night of our visit I was stretched out in that bathtub letting Mel wash my back, using an ample tablet of the Ritz soap embossed with a suitably regal crest. Thus far, it had been the perfect vacation. When we hadn't been in bed making love in front of the giant mirrored doors of the built-in wardrobe, we'd been out hitting every nightspot in town, and tracking down the best restaurants, and seeing the occasional historic landmark in between times.

No hint of the occult yet. I didn't know it, but that was still to come.

Lying in that pool-sized bathtub, I realized I didn't want to go home. "I suppose you can't spare another week?" I murmured to Mel.

He rinsed the soap from my shoulders, then turned me over in the warm water, so I was lying looking up at him. He ran a wet fingertip down my nose.

"Christina, I can't spare another day, let alone a week," he said. "I'm a law partner, not a playboy."

"Maybe you'd consider changing that vocation?" I looked up at him with large appealing eyes.

He laughed. "Playboys don't earn. They spend. And unfortunately, Christina, unlike you, I have no inheritance to support me."

"Money!" I scoffed. "Is that all you care about?"

He started rubbing the washcloth across my breasts slowly, working up a fresh lather. His hand moved lower, till the soft, creamy soap was massaging around each nipple, and I felt familiar stirrings of desire. "No, money's not *all* I think about," he said.

"Money and sex, then."

"Are you complaining?" He dropped the washcloth and started using his hands, very gently, his fingertips caressing my breasts through the rich, smooth lather. I arched my back and pushed my breasts up and felt the nipples stiffen and my skin tingle with a sudden wave of warmth. "No," I said, "I'm certainly not complaining."

I reached up to him and pulled his head down toward me and we kissed long and deep, very intimately, his tongue pushing into my mouth and his hand slowly clenching on my breast. He was so quickly aroused; there seemed no limit to how often he would want to have me. And I felt the same way about him. We'd already made love twice that day, once when we'd woken up, and again a couple of hours ago, after dinner. And now we both needed it again, urgently.

His lips left mine for a moment and he moved back just far enough to be able to stare into my eyes as his hand shifted from my breast, down under the water, between my legs. I rolled half toward him and parted my thighs. The water sloshed and churned. His finger pushed straight inside me and I gasped and wriggled my hips and clutched at his shoulders, forgetting that my hands were wet and he was still wearing the Liberty shirt he'd bought that afternoon. It hardly seemed to matter—he didn't notice—he just stared at me and said in a very low, determined voice, "I want you, Christina. I want you *now*."

At the same time, his finger pushed down onto my clitoris, a little sharply, making me gasp with a mixture of pleasure and surprise.

I sat up in the bath, my face flushed, my breathing coming quickly. I reached over the side and undid the fly of his pants and pulled his hips up toward me. His cock came out hard and ready; I closed my warm wet fingers around it, looked up at him for a moment, and then started sucking him. His cock swelled more and seemed to fill my whole mouth, the head of it pushing a little way down my throat. I moved my head up and down while I held him by the hips, and I heard him groan with pleasure and need. His cock felt so warm and alive and beautiful, and I knew if I sucked him for just a minute longer I could make him come; but of course we didn't want that to happen yet.

I released him, sat back in the bath, and smiled at him. He was breathing heavily, his fists clenched, his eyes bright. His cock was sticking out firm and red and all wet where I had sucked it. It pulsed gently in rhythm with his heartbeats.

"If you don't get out of that tub and get yourself dry inside of one minute, I'm coming in there with you," he said. And I could tell he meant it.

Well, even the biggest bathtub is no substitute for a comfortable bed. So I stood up and grabbed one of the enormous towels and started quickly rubbing the water off my body. He watched me, and I realized that the spectacle was turning him on even more; so I started taking a little longer over it, especially when I dried my legs. I lifted first one leg up onto the side of the bath, as I dried myself, and then the other leg, completely exposing my vagina to him. I looked down at it, pink and moist and inviting beneath the golden pubic hairs. I looked up at him and saw him staring. And then he grabbed the towel out of my hands, threw it aside, pulled me to him, and embraced me so that we were pressed face-to-face, standing up. He kissed me so hard I felt as if he were physically joining himself to me, so that I no longer existed separately from him. And his cock probed between my thighs and rubbed against my labia and I shivered and hugged him harder against me.

His fingernails dug into my back and his clothed body rubbed against my nakedness. His hips ground impatiently against mine. "Come on," he said. "Into the bedroom."

"But I haven't finished drying myself."

"It'll evaporate. As steam!"

He took my hand and hauled me after him, though in reality I hardly needed to be persuaded into it. I was just as hungry for him as he was for me. We tumbled down together across the bed and I started pulling at his clothes, eager to feel his body under my hands.

His new shirt lost one of its buttons. His shoelace became knotted, so I just grabbed and pulled hard and got both his shoes off without undoing the laces. Then his pants, and then he was naked and on top of me, holding me down, his warm breath on my face. "Put me inside you," he whispered.

I reached down for his cock, held it a moment, loving the feel of its hardness and strength and sense of power. And then I guided it between my legs. For a moment I teased him, rubbing the head of his penis between my labia, holding myself almost out of reach. I felt his hips move impatiently and saw the muscles tense in his arms as he held me more tightly. "You want me?" I whispered. "You really want me? Really?"

He didn't answer in words. He just kissed me, so violently, so desirously, there was no possible doubt. I couldn't wait any longer myself, then, so I moved the head of his cock down to the soft, wet way into my body and raised my hips, and he thrust in, all in one motion, filling me and making me cry out.

I almost came right then, clutching him on the bed, my legs wrapped around behind him, holding him inside me, while my hips rolled and jerked and his hands clenched on my breasts and he went on kissing me while he fucked me.

His thrusts speeded up and he slumped down onto me and I was able to look to one side and see us in the mirrored wardrobe doors (thoughtfully, discreetly provided by the hotel management). I saw Mel's body pressing me into the soft bed, his hands grabbing at my breasts, fingers digging into the soft flesh. The bed rocked under us and I saw his body writhing over me, his hips pounding against me, the muscles rippling under the skin of his back. He looked so sexy and powerful and I looked so frail and yielding, and the sight of us in the mirror was like an aphrodisiac. My orgasm hit me before I even knew it was coming; suddenly I was lost in the bright flowering bursts of pleasure and heard myself crying out, very loudly, yet as if from somewhere else.

He paused then and lifted himself a little way off me. He was perspiring and breathing hard, his curly hair all tangled, his face red with exertion. "That was quick," he said.

"Don't stop," I gasped.

His cock was still hard and deep inside me. He moved his hips from side to side, just a little. "I have no intention of stopping. Not for a while yet."

He kissed me, more gently this time, sensing my need for just a pause in the passion, after my orgasm. That was one of the things I liked most about him—he had such empathy for my moods and needs. But at the same time everything he did was to please himself, as well as me. An ideal lover!

But the gentle, tender kiss was just as sexy as his other kisses, and already I felt myself becoming aroused again. And he felt it too. He started moving his cock in and out of me, slowly at first but gradually increasing the tempo.

"Watch us in the mirror," I said. "That's what made me come so quickly just now."

So we squirmed around till we were both lying stretched out full-length, with the big soft down pillows pushed out of the way, and the covers kicked off the bed onto the floor. Mel rested most of his weight on me, his body seeming to touch mine at every point, and we lay breast-to-chest, cheek-to-cheek, looking at our reflections. He began fucking me, moving only his hips, and his buttocks rose and fell and the bed quivered under us. He stroked my golden hair, watching himself do it in the mirror. He ran his hand down my body, still watching. "Beautiful," he murmured. "You're so beautiful, Christina. Here I am, in bed with a beautiful, sexy, hungry woman."

I arched my body up against him. "Not just hungry," I said, "insatiable."

He didn't need to be asked twice. He braced himself and started fucking me hard, his hips thudding down, the bed shaking under me, his hands holding me firmly by the shoulders. He gasped and grimaced with a wonderful mixture of tenderness and angry passion, and his cock thrust into me till I felt it would fill me completely, my whole body. I pulled up my knees to let him in still deeper, till it even hurt just a little, but I still wanted more. I ran my hands over his chest, feeling all the muscles, the skin hot and slick, and then down to where his cock was pushing in, so strong and unstoppable.

I jerked my hips up and down impatiently, as if to provoke him and urge him on still more. He sensed my mood and saw what I wanted, grabbed my wrists and pinned my arms on the bed above my head, the two wrists crossed over each other so he could hold them there with just one of his hands. I pretended to struggle as he held me there, stretched out under him, so open and available. He went on fucking me, surveying me with eyes that told me I was his, all his, an irresistible delicacy, a pure delight that he would take and enjoy any way he wanted to, for as long as he wanted to. I felt as if I were giving myself to him totally, and that itself turned me on. With his free hand he caressed my cheek, then ran his fingers through my hair and turned my face first to one side, then the other, as if he were savoring my beauty. Then his hand moved lower—his other hand still holding my wrists above my head—and he felt my large round breasts, gently at first, then more roughly, watching my face. I twisted my body helplessly under him and moaned, in pleasure at my own helplessness, in ecstasy at the things he was doing to me. He pinched my nipple between thumb and forefinger, not hard enough to really hurt, just enough to make delicious tingling sensations race across my skin. And then he moved his hand down between my thighs, while he continued to fuck me; and he started rubbing my clitoris with every thrust into me.

My breathing was coming in sobs now. I was holding myself back from orgasm, but it was getting harder for me to keep control. Every touch of his finger and push of his cock took me higher. I started writhing on the bed, moaning, sometimes glimpsing myself again in the mirror, stretched out under his powerful body. I sensed his own passion building as his thrusts speeded up, then speeded up still more, to a frantic pace. I closed my eyes and felt myself caught up in the storm of our lovemaking, buffeted by it, so that I hardly knew where I was. And then I felt him tremble, and his thrusts became erratic, and I heard him groan, and I knew he was coming. I pulled one of my wrists free and reached down and pressed his hand hard onto my clitoris. I let go of my last shred of self-control. I abandoned myself totally and came with him. He fell down onto me and we clutched each other and pressed our hips as hard as we could against each other. I actually felt his cock jerking inside me as it spurted semen, while at the same time I was wrapped up in my own moments of pure pleasure, overwhelmed by him and his lovemaking.

For a while afterward, we just lay there. The only sound was our breathing. The hotel was so totally quiet—the quietest hotel I'd ever stayed in. You could imagine there was no one else within miles. There was just an occasional faint murmur of traffic from the windows overlooking Piccadilly.

And then, just as I felt I was coming back to reality, the phone beside the bed started ringing.

I opened my eyes and found myself looking into Mel's face. He looked just as surprised as I did. No one in England knew we were staying at the hotel; only his business associates in New York knew our location.

"You answer it," he said after the third ring. "If it's one of my partners calling transatlantic, I don't want to talk to him."

I hated having to disengage myself from his warm, strong body, but I couldn't ignore the phone. Somehow its unexpectedness made it sound important.

So I rolled over on the bed and reached for the telephone before it could ring for a fifth time. I grabbed the receiver, put it to my ear, and rolled back beside Mel.

There was a lot of static on the line. That was typical of British phones, of course; but this was even worse than usual. Somewhere behind a mass of crackling and hissing sounds a voice said, "Is this Miss Van Bell?"

"For me," I whispered to Mel, feeling even more puzzled, because absolutely no one was supposed to know where *I* was. The whole point of our vacation together had been to get away from everything.

"Who's this?" I said into the phone.

He said a name that sounded like "Enya" behind all the other noises. Then he asked again if I was Christina Van Bell. He had a slow, monotonous voice, like someone chanting. I felt, for no definable reason, a shiver of apprehension go through me.

"Yes, this is Christina Van Bell," I said as decisively and clearly as possible. "What do you want? How did you get this number?"

"I have a message . . . your sister . . ."

The shiver hit me again. This was becoming positively bizarre. My sister had been dead for five years. "Who the hell *are* you?" I demanded, losing some of my cool.

I felt Mel's arm go around my shoulders and saw him look at me questioningly, but I was trying so hard to hear the voice on the bad telephone line that I couldn't pause to fill him in on what was happening.

"But here is the message," the distant voice was saying monotonously, persistently. "A person named . . . Schmidt . . . sum of money which . . . embezzled . . . her share of the inheritance." Suddenly the line was clearer for a moment. "A very large sum, your sister has told me."

"You're out of your tree," I shouted back. "My sister's dead! Is this some practical joke?"

". . . absolutely serious and . . . no other message . . . go now . . ."

"Wait a minute. Who are you? *Where* are you?"

More static on the line. "Downton Castle . . ." More interference.

"Downton Castle? Where's that, here in Britain? And what was your name?"

The line got even worse, as if a waterfall had suddenly started, growing in volume. I thought I heard whoever it was confirm that he was indeed calling from Britain; then he hung up.

I dumped the receiver back on the phone. I stared at it for a moment. Then I picked it up again and punched the buttons to speak to the hotel operator. The funny British phone made clicking noises inside itself, there was a long pause, and then suddenly a clear, polite British male voice asked if he could help me.

"Who just called this number?" I asked.

"You just received a telephone call from outside the hotel, madam?"

"Yes. Didn't it go through your switchboard?"

A pause. "No, madam."

I began to feel I was losing my grip on reality. "Then how . . . ?"

"With our new phone system, people can ring a room number directly from outside the hotel, madam."

"Oh."

"Will there be anything else . . . Miss Van Bell?"

They were so damned efficient. Already he'd had time to check my name on the records against the room number.

"No, nothing else," I said.

I hung up and turned to look at Mel. He was staring at me. "What the hell was all that?" he said.

"Something very weird," I said. I lay back on the bed, pulling one of the big soft pillows behind my head. There were still residual warm feelings in my body from our lovemaking. I wanted to savor what was left of them.

He lay down beside me. "You sound strange."

I told him the content of the phone conversation. He didn't believe me. I repeated it. He looked as if he still didn't believe me.

"You're sure you don't know anyone who'd do this as a stunt?"

"Maybe, but they don't know where I am. And anyway . . . I'm thinking back. See, my parents died six or seven years ago. That was when I came into the family fortune. But it was to be split evenly between me and Fran—my sister. You know how long these things take; the legal formalities went on for a whole year, while everything was valued and death duties were paid. And then, just when it was sorted out, Fran died in a car crash, and it got even more complicated. And the thing that comes back to me is that there *was* a lawyer involved, representing her estate, named Schmidt. Five years ago, more or less. And I can't think of anyone in the world who'd know that, other than me."

There was a long silence. "If the phone line was that bad," Mel said thoughtfully, "the guy could have said anything, and you would have thought you heard him say Schmidt."

"No, it was clear at that point."

I didn't like the way our conversation was going, driving a wedge between myself and Mel, destroying the warmth we had just shared. On the other hand, I couldn't shake the sense of creeping strangeness and confusion. I've never liked mysteries, especially ones that I'm unable to solve.

"All right," said Mel, "it comes down to one of three possibilities. One: this guy who called you has some kind of blackmail on you, and he's starting off by showing he has some inside information."

"That doesn't make sense!" I protested. "I've done nothing to be blackmailed for, and he didn't make any demands, anyway."

"All right. Two: he's a friend of yours or mine, calling from New York, pulling some stupid stunt. One of my friends could have discovered your name somehow, and I left word where I'd be staying."

"You couldn't have told them your room number. You didn't know it in advance. And the call was dialed in direct."

"All right. Three: the hotel staff were doing it as some weird British joke."

I looked at him. He looked at me. Suddenly I laughed and grabbed him and hugged him. I kissed him. "Oh, Mel. You're so funny."

"Funny?" He looked nettled. "What's funny?"

"You're so *logical*. Relentless. Such a lawyer. I love it."

"Well, it's better than being screwed up and crazy, isn't it?"

"I'm not screwed up and I'm not crazy, so I wouldn't know. Look, I'm not going to talk about it any more tonight. Tomorrow maybe I will find out if there *is* a Downton Castle. If it's close to London, I may even go and check it out and follow you back to New York a day late, just to satisfy my curiosity. But I'm not going to let this spoil our vacation, and I won't let it spoil your mood, either." I rolled up close and pressed against him, so my breasts were pushing against his chest. "Doesn't that feel more important? More logical, even?" I smiled teasingly.

He laughed and embraced me. "I won't argue. No, you're right, let's not allow a crank call to spoil our evening."

We kissed, and I felt I'd gotten the matter out of the way—out of Mel's mind, at least.

But later, after we had turned out the light, I found myself staring at the delicate plaster moldings in the ceiling, lit faintly from streetlights outside the windows. I found myself sleepless, snuggled against Mel's warm body but not feeling comforted or secure. As I say, I hate mysteries. I like to feel I understand everything around me and can control my own life and my own world.

The voice on the phone had destroyed my sense of control. Because the voice *had* said "Schmidt." And thinking back, I realized I had never liked that man; and there had been some suspicion that not all of my sister Fran's share of the inheritance had been accounted for.

My stolen week with Mel was suddenly over. I

knew I had to track down the source of that phone call, for my own peace of mind.

Tomorrow I would begin my own little investigation —and I would follow it wherever it led me.

With that thought I fell into a restless, tormented sleep.

CHAPTER TWO

Ten nightmares later, I decided it would be more pleasant to stay awake than continue trying to sleep. That damned phone call had gotten to me, throwing me off balance and unnerving me. And when something like that happens, I have an automatic response: I get mad. And when I'm mad, I do something about it.

Mel was still asleep beside me. I peeked at my watch —9:30 A.M. No need to waken him yet. After all, it was the last day of his vacation, and he normally didn't get a chance to sleep late.

I crept out of bed and stepped silently across the room to the stack of magazines and tourist guides we'd accumulated during the past few days. I started thumbing through them, scattering the brochures and journals across the long marble-topped coffee table in front of the fireplace. I thought maybe I would find a reference to this Downton Castle.

Ten minutes later I felt even more frustrated, because the castle wasn't listed in any of our guides to Britain. Then I had an idea. I picked up our copy of *The Tatler,* a supersnobbish magazine that I remembered was full of ads for pieces of expensive real estate, including a couple of mansions and stately homes.

I crept back to the bed with the magazine, picked up the phone, and carried it off with me into the bathroom. With the bathroom door shut I could talk without waking Mel. And I didn't want him to hear me, because I knew if he did, he'd tell me I was being crazy, taking all this trouble trying to follow up what was some kind of crank call.

I looked up the phone number of *The Tatler*'s editorial office and dialed it. Soon I was talking to a man with such an upper-class accent, it sounded as if he was being strangled by his starched collar. At first he tried to get me off the line. However, I managed to mention I was an heiress from one of America's more famous families, and I said I was staying at the Ritz in Piccadilly, and the gentleman on the phone suddenly became much more helpful. It's always useful to be able to trade on snobbery. He was only too ready to help me as soon as it was clear I was Someone Important.

Had he ever heard of Downton Castle? He thought perhaps he had. He went and consulted some reference source, then came back full of information for me. It was a privately owned castle in Wales, not open to the public. It overlooked the Teme Valley (wherever *that* was). He remembered that *The Tatler* had run a full-page advertisement for the castle just six months ago, because it had been up for sale, for a few hundred thousand pounds. Nice little place, he said, on twenty-six acres, with eight reception rooms, fourteen bedrooms, nine bathrooms. Someone had snapped it up right away.

I asked if he'd heard who the new owner was.

His gossip dried up at this point. He said he understood the new owner was from one of the Arab countries. That was all he knew. But if I wanted to speak to the estate agent who had sold the castle . . .

I told him no, not necessary, and I assured him I would make a point of recommending *The Tatler* to all my rich American friends when they visited London.

By the end of the phone call the man was quite ingratiating. And I think he'd gotten the idea I was glamorous, and he was trying to work around to asking me out for lunch. I hung up before he could get *that* far.

I crept back into the bedroom and leafed through our atlas of Britain till I found the Teme Valley. In Herefordshire, on the Welsh border. A four-hour car trip out of London, at least.

"What are you doing over there?" said Mel, sitting up in bed, yawning, looking at me with a frown on his face.

I closed the atlas and went back to bed. I was still naked and I couldn't help noticing that his eyes paid close attention to my body, even though he'd only just woken up.

I got onto the bed, knelt down beside him, and kissed him good morning.

It had been intended as a brief kiss, but kissing Mel often turned out to take longer than expected. This was one of those times. His hands closed around my full breasts and cupped them, pressed them, held them squeezed up against me. His tongue slipped tentatively between our lips and touched, fleetingly, the tip of my tongue; and suddenly I felt a wave of arousal.

I managed to pull free. I had something to say. "Mel—"

He glanced quickly at his watch. "Our plane doesn't take off till one o'clock," he said. "We've got time." And he took my hand and guided it under the covers, and I found my long, slim fingers touching his cock, already hard and hot.

"But, Mel—" I protested again.

He smothered my protest with another kiss, and despite my intentions, I found myself giving in. My hand explored around his cock, touching, stroking it very delicately. I pressed my breasts up against the tangle of curly golden hair on his chest. I felt his cock strain and swell under my fingers.

"How did you ever learn to be so irresistible?" I murmured to him, nuzzling and nibbling his neck, then kissing down to his nipples, and then pressing my cheek to his belly, watching my own hand on his cock.

"You're the irresistible one," he said.

"No. You." Then I squirmed lower and opened my mouth wide and closed my lips around the end of his cock. I wriggled my tongue under it, and massaged it with my lips, and sucked hard on it, and he sighed and fell back on his elbows, looking down at me.

"You don't need to . . ." he began.

For a moment I released his cock from my mouth. "I want to," I said. And I did.

I started sucking him again, more urgently now. I put my hands behind his hips and pulled him up toward me and took him very deep, as deep as I could, till I couldn't breathe. I held him there, feeling him stiffen and gasp. I sucked on him so hard, as if to draw the very essence out of him; then let his cock slide halfway out of my mouth; and then did it again.

One of my hands crept around to his balls and held them lightly, fingertips stroking through the hairs and across the sensitive skin down there. He groaned and said my name, and he reached down and touched my face and my lips, so that he could feel, with his fingertips, his cock sliding deep into my mouth.

I drew his other hand around to my breasts and pressed his palm against my nipple. He groaned and his hand clenched. He wriggled his hips. I bobbed my head up and down, up and down, still sucking him as hard as I could. I sensed he was almost there.

"I want you, Christina," he murmured then. "I want to make love to you."

He drew his cock out of my mouth. I was aroused myself now, and if he wanted sex with me, I wasn't about to argue.

He took my face between his palms and kissed me long and deep. My lips were wet where I had been sucking him. It was a heady kiss. We subsided on the bed together and his body pressed down onto mine. I felt overwhelmed by him, his muscular frame, his male smell, the scratch of his whiskers on my cheek, the clenching of his hand on my shoulder.

Still kissing him, I felt down for his cock and found it standing out very hard and hot. I ran my fingers up and down the shaft, which was still moist from being in my mouth.

He paused in his kissing me. He looked into my eyes. He was breathing heavily. The light caresses of my fingers on his penis were having their effect. He groaned with pleasure.

He moved one of his hands down and started caressing my thighs, while he went on looking into my eyes. His touch was delicate, and it made tingling sensations come to life in my skin. I felt my vagina getting warm and wet. I was hot with desire for him, and he knew it. He started tantalizing me, running the very tips of his fingers across my labia. The fleeting touches made me shiver and squirm on the soft bed. I grabbed his wrist and tried to press his hand up harder between my legs, but he held back, smiling at me.

He rolled onto me, so that I was stretched out under him and his weight was holding me on the bed. He kissed me again, hard and purposefully. He moved his hips, and his long, strong cock pushed in between my thighs. The top of it rubbed across my vagina. I wanted it inside me; I wanted to feel him filling me up.

He reached down and held his own cock and moved it to and fro, brushing the head of it just between my labia, giving me little shivers of pleasure and desire. I lifted my legs and wrapped them around behind him, trying to urge him into me, but still he held back. At the same time, he was giving me little tantalizing kisses, touching my lips with just the tip of his tongue, brushing his mouth fleetingly across mine. I knew he was as aroused as I was—we both wanted it—but at the same time we both knew how sweet a pleasure it was to delay the moment until it became an almost unbearable craving.

He allowed just the first inch of his cock to push into me then. It penetrated into my wet warmth. I hugged him to me. My arms and legs were wrapped around him. My breasts were squashed up against him. "Fuck me," I whispered in his ear. "Oh, Mel, fuck me!"

And still he teased me, pretending to pull back out of me, then pushing in just a little farther, and then pausing again and moving his hips tantalizingly.

I wriggled against him. My skin was so soft and warm against his. My body was so open and willing. I dug my fingernails into his shoulders and kissed him passionately, thrusting my tongue into his mouth. Then I almost shouted at him, "Mel! I want you!"

Finally he let himself go. His cock plunged in, deep. He wrapped me in his arms and hugged me up against him, possessing me totally. His hips thrust hard. I heard myself crying out with excitement and pleasure. He began moving in a frenzy of quick, deep thrusts. I gasped and clung to him.

For a moment I opened my eyes. His head was beside mine; he was kissing my neck while he made love to me. I was able to see over his shoulder. I looked up at the ceiling of the room, with its elegant pattern of plaster moldings. I saw the morning light falling softly across the white satin drapes at the window. I felt the gentle touch of the pure down pillows and bed linen against my cheek.

And then his movements became even more desperate and demanding, and the sensations overwhelmed me in a glorious wave. I closed my eyes and gave myself up to it all, and then I came. I think that the sight and sound of my coming was what set him off, too. We were both caught up in the glorious moment, and it seemed to go on a long, long time.

Gradually the delicious sensations subsided. I relaxed my hold on him. He rolled over so that we were lying side by side. Then he kissed me very tenderly.

His cock came out of me. Mel rolled over onto his back, totally satisfied. I kissed his cheek, then his chest, and then I took his penis gently in my hand and kissed it and licked it, feeling I was absorbing the very essence of my lover.

Then I moved back beside him and kissed him again, so he could taste his own salty semen on my tongue.

Then I lay cuddled beside him, enjoying the sense of calm and relaxation.

"When you do that, you always seem to enjoy doing it," he said quietly.

"Of course," I answered.

"Other women sometimes make it seem like a favor," he went on.

I laughed softly. "That's their problem." I reached down and stroked his cock. "If I really like a man, I'll want him in every way. And I'll expect him to want me in every way, too."

"Ah, Christina." He kissed me. "You're unique." He was quiet for a moment. I was half-afraid he was going to make a declaration of love, which would have embarrassed me, because I wasn't entirely sure how I felt about him yet. Instead, though, he laughed. "I was just thinking," he said, "all we need now is another insane phone call."

That brought me back to reality. "Mel . . ."

"All right, I know. We'd better get moving if we're going to catch our plane."

"No, that's not it. Mel, I'm going to stay on in Britain another day or two. I'll catch up with you in New York."

Our faces were very close together. I could see every tiny detail of his expression. I saw surprise, followed by uncertainty, and then control took over. He was a warm man, and a kind man, but careful; he tried to let very little show. "How come?" he said casually.

I disengaged myself from his embrace and sat up on the bed. "While you were sleeping, I did some research. There *is* a Downton Castle—the place that that kook last night said he was calling from. All I want to do is go there and check it out. I don't like the idea of some weird guy knowing personal things about my life. I don't like mysteries. I can't go back to New York till I've settled it."

He was quiet for a moment. Then he shrugged. "Whatever you say. You know I can't do it with you. I have to get back."

"I realize that."

He touched me under the chin. "Well, look after yourself, all right?" He stood up then and started toward the bathroom.

"You're not going to argue with me?" I said, feeling surprised.

He paused and looked at me. "When you've decided to do something, I'm not ever going to try to stand in the way," he said, with a faint smile. "You're the kind of woman, when you've made up your mind, no man is going to change it. Not even a bright young lawyer." And with that he went into the bathroom and shut the door.

I had to admit he was right. And I had to admire his common sense.

At the same time, I suddenly felt very alone. Maybe I had wanted him to argue with me, and beg me to go back to New York with him. Now I was already feeling cut off from him, on my own in Britain to follow through on my little plan. I imagined Downton Castle, out in the middle of nowhere, bleak and cold and strange. It reminded me of one of the nightmares I had had. Suddenly I shivered, as if some presence had come into this quiet, warm hotel room and settled over my nakedness.

I shook my head angrily, refusing to allow any of that kind of craziness into my thoughts. I got up and went to the wardrobe to select the clothes I would wear.

A couple of hours later I drove with Mel out to Heathrow Airport in the car we'd rented during the past week. I'd made arrangements to continue the rental for a couple more days in my own name, and I'd obtained maps of the route out to Wales. We had checked out of the Ritz and all our bags were in the back.

Mel stopped the car in front of the international-departures building. "No second thoughts?" he said, giving me a look that was slightly amused, but slightly troubled at the same time.

I felt embarrassed. "I know it sounds silly," I told him, "but once something gets under my skin . . ."

"I understand." He kissed me gently on the forehead. "Just come back home real soon," he said.

"Of course I will."

"And if there is some guy at this so-called castle who did make that phone call, bear in mind the laws about harassment." His eyes were suddenly serious. "And call me collect, if necessary, if you need any help at all."

I hugged him. "You're wonderful."

Another kiss; then he got out of the car and pulled his bags off the backseat. "Let me know how it turns out," he said. Then he waved, and the last I saw of him was his tall, muscular figure striding in through the automatic doors of the airport building.

I moved across to the driver's seat. I stared at the instruments for a minute, determined not to allow my sentimental feelings to get the upper hand. Good heavens, I ought to be used to taking care of myself by now. I was a capable, strong-willed woman. True enough.

I readjusted the driver's seat and started the car. It was a Rover 3500, one of the largest and more luxurious British cars, almost as comfortable as a Rolls, and more modern. I tuned the radio to Radio Three, which was playing some orchestral music—Brahms, I guessed. It had a sense of tranquillity to it, anyway.

I spread out the maps on the seat beside me, made sure that my dress wasn't wrinkled where I was sitting on it, and then accelerated away from the curb.

I figured I should be able to track down this mystery castle by sunset and sort out what, if anything, the owner knew about me and my past.

CHAPTER THREE

The first part of the journey was effortless, along the M4, a divided highway as wide as any American interstate. And much faster: the posted speed limit was seventy. I cruised around eighty, and the Rover just drifted along, eating up the miles.

I guess because the driving was so easy, I didn't have enough to occupy my mind, and I was able to feel more vividly how isolated I was now that Mel was out of the country. There was nothing on the radio to take my mind off it. So, finally, I stopped at a roadside-service area for some coffee.

The British coffee was terrible, of course—always a little bit worse than anyone would imagine it could be. I got back into the car feeling more discontent than ever, and headed for the entry ramp back onto the highway.

That was when I saw the hitchhiker. He was the shy type who doesn't actually stick out his thumb to ask for a ride, just stands there looking hopeful. He was in his early twenties, with wire-framed spectacles and the kind of striped muffler that British college students wear. He looked studious and totally harmless, standing there in his raincoat with a battered suitcase beside him on the muddy ground. I decided to risk stopping for him.

I lowered the window. "You want a ride?"

He blinked at me, as if he were waking up from

some private dream. He saw the large luxury car, and then he saw me. He obviously didn't believe it.

"Well, do you want a ride or not?" I asked again.

"Oh. Yes. Certainly. I'm going to Bristol," he said.

"Well, I don't know whether that's on my way or not. I'm going to Wales."

"All right, you can drop me before you cross the Severn Bridge." He opened the car door. "I'm afraid my suitcase is a bit dirty."

"That's okay, it isn't my car. Dump your case in the backseat and get in." I sensed he needed to be told what to do to get him moving.

He sat down beside me and slammed the passenger door. I accelerated onto the highway, and out of the corner of my eye I saw him carefully putting on his seat belt.

"You're a student?" I asked him.

"At Bristol, yes."

"What do you study?"

"Lepidoptera."

"Huh?"

"Moths. I study moths." He gave me a look as if to say: Don't laugh, there's nothing funny about it.

Wonderful, I thought to myself. There I had been nervous about giving a ride to a hitchhiker, in case he might turn out to be a homicidal maniac. And now he turned out to study moths. And he'd probably bore me for the next hundred miles, talking about it. His kind of company was worse than no company at all.

"What kind of a job do you aim for, with a degree in moths?" I asked, for the sake of asking.

"Well, I expect to work for one of the pest-control corporations."

"Oh. I get it. You spend all this time learning about the insect world, so you can get a job finding better ways to kill them. Right?"

He gave me a funny look. "You're American, aren't you?"

"Sure. What about it?"

"Nothing." He looked away.

Now I was beginning to feel pissed at him. With that damned British reserve, I couldn't figure what he was thinking—but I had the nasty feeling it was something unpleasant. I stared at the highway thoughtfully. I decided I had to make some kind of *lasting impression* on this repressed example of British youth.

"Is it true that British college students aren't interested in girls?" I asked him casually.

That jolted him. "What?"

"The magazines in America are always telling us that British kids are sexually repressed, there's no action on campus. Is that right?"

"Well, I wouldn't say that," he answered. He looked uncomfortable. I was feeling better already. In fact, I wondered how far I could go.

"Well, what *would* you say, actually?" I asked, imitating his accent.

There was a pause. "I expect college life in America isn't very different from universities here," he said.

"Yeah? So there's a lot of casual sex? I mean, how about you?" I gave him a frank look.

"Really, I don't quite—"

"Well, do you have a girl? Do you screw around? You know, that's why I picked you up back there. I was feeling kind of horny and you looked cute." I tried to keep a straight face while I said this.

Now he just stared at me in amazement. I winked at him. Finally he got himself together enough to say, "Actually, I'm engaged to be married."

"But I'll bet you wouldn't mind cheating a little," I said. I took one hand off the wheel and rested it on his knee.

"I think you'd better stop the car and let me out," he said. His voice had risen in pitch.

"Why? Don't you think I'm sexy?" I gave him a resentful look.

"It's not that . . ."

"Look, just tell me. Aren't I attractive to you?"

"I . . . yes, you're very attractive, really, but if it's all the same to you, I'd be more comfortable—"

"I can't stop," I interrupted him. "You're not allowed to stop on British motorways, are you? Only in an emergency. And anyway, you'd have a hard time getting a ride here on the open highway. Come on, what's your name?"

"Arnold."

"Come on, Arnold. Don't be a stuffed shirt. Relax. Let's have some fun." I slid my hand up his leg and started massaging his cock through his baggy English trousers.

He tried feebly to resist, and then he just sat there staring at my hand as if he couldn't believe what was happening to him. "You're crazy," he said.

"No, I just like the direct approach," I told him. "Uninhibited and free, you know? We Americans are like that." My fingers clenched harder around the shape of his cock under the fabric.

He shook his head. He was beginning to lose his cool, I could tell. "What do you want from me?" He looked at my face. He seemed to be getting nervous. "Sex, or what?"

"Whatever feels right." I shrugged, as if I didn't have a care in the world.

"But who are you? What is all this about?"

"Well, you see, I just said good-bye to my boyfriend," I improvised quickly, "and I was feeling lonely," which was true, "and I've always wondered what British men are like in bed. I'm quite wealthy—I'm an heiress—and

I lead a very easy, sophisticated life. I've done it all, I've been everywhere, I've tried everything. I take my pleasures where I find them, Arnold, and I guess I just found *you*. I mean, when I saw you standing there beside the highway, I couldn't resist." Inside, of course, I was laughing. But toward him I tried to come off completely sincere. "After all," I went on, "you did tell me I'm attractive. I'm sure you wouldn't mind if we . . ." I trailed off and gave him a suggestive look.

He stared down at my hand, where I was still massaging insistently between his legs. "Nothing like this has ever happened to me in my life," he said slowly. He sounded quite dazed.

Under my fingers I felt the shape of his cock growing just a little bigger and harder. "Well, you'd better make the most of it," I told him, "because probably nothing like this will ever happen again in the *rest* of your life, either."

"But . . ."

"What's the matter, don't you like surprises?"

"I don't . . ."

I noticed a sign by the side of the highway, for an exit a mile ahead. I shifted lanes and slowed the car slightly. "Tell me," I said, lowering my voice a little. "Tell me, how big are you?" I looked quickly into his eyes.

"What?"

"How big are you, you know, down here." I clenched my fingers around his groin.

That unnerved him. He just stared at me. He swallowed hard. He didn't seem able to think of anything to say.

"I guess I'll have to find out for myself," I said and groped around for the zipper. I half-expected him to put up some resistance, but he didn't. He just sat there gawking.

I found the zipper and tugged. Bit by bit I opened his fly, still steering with my other hand and guiding the car into the exit lane ahead. I felt inside his pants, touched his cock, and managed to pull it out. I glanced quickly sideways and saw it. It was semierect, and already it looked big. In fact, this skinny, pimply student was amazingly well endowed. He was huge!

I had to hit the brake then as we left the motorway and sped down the exit toward a traffic circle. Arnold grabbed the armrest in one hand and covered his cock with his other hand as we went around another car and then took the traffic circle at speed. I think he was afraid of being seen naked; at the same time, he was afraid I was going to crash.

I saw a small road leading off the circle, and straightaway I headed down it. There were tall hedges on either side, and the road was narrow and twisting; reluctantly I put both hands on the steering wheel, to take the car around the curves.

"I'd say you're about nine inches," I told him conversationally.

"What?"

"Your cock. It would be about nine inches when it's really hard."

He stared at me again. I smiled back at him. I was really enjoying myself, shocking him. I felt amazed at how far I had gone already, but at the same time I wanted to see how much further I could go. There seemed to be no limit to what I could do.

"Here's the place we need," I said then. I braked hard and brought the car almost to a stop. Then I made a turn off the road, between two big wooden posts, into an open gateway to some farmland. I stopped the car before it could roll onto soft ground. There, surrounded by the tall hedges, with a field of wheat in front of us, we were quite secluded from the world.

I turned off the motor and relaxed in my seat. I looked at him. "I think I'd like you to undress me," I said.

Despite himself, he looked at my body. The material of my dress was thin and didn't conceal much. I saw him take in the fullness of my breasts and the little bumps that my nipples made in the fabric. He swallowed hard again, and I thought I noticed his cock grow slightly larger, where it was still poking out of his fly.

"Here," I said, leaning across, so that I came very close to him. "Let me unbuckle your seat belt for you." I deliberately pressed my breast against him and let him smell my perfume. Then I released the seat belt and stroked my fingers casually along his cock, which was getting bigger every minute.

"Now," I told him, "just undo the zipper at the back of my neck." I gathered my long hair up and turned so that the zipper was available to him.

I felt his fingers fiddling with it. His hands seemed to be shaking, and I congratulated myself for having gotten through to him so easily. Well, on the other hand, maybe it wasn't really fair, unnerving the kid . . . and yet, after all, I had to be some kind of special treat for him, didn't I? How often would someone like him be seduced by a glamorous woman out of nowhere?

He managed to undo the zipper. I turned back to face him. I started wriggling the dress down over my shoulders, bit my bit. I made it into more of a performance than I needed to, enjoying his stare of amazement. My breasts wobbled from side to side as I moved, and I shifted my shoulders suggestively. Finally I looked appealingly at him. "Won't you help me, Arnold?"

He nodded dumbly.

I took his hand and pressed it against the garment, so he could feel the softness of my body underneath. Then I guided him, easing the dress down and over my breasts, till they popped out into view. Quickly I put my hand behind his head and pressed his face into my cleavage. "Kiss my tits," I told him.

His lips touched my skin tentatively.

"The nipples," I whispered. "Kiss my nipples."

Nervously he obeyed.

"Suck on my nipples," I murmured. "Yes, that's right!" With my free hand I reached down and found his cock and stroked it. It was so huge; I wondered if he would get so excited he would come just from the sight and the feel of my body.

"Suck harder," I told him. "Yes . . . now gently . . . flick your tongue over the skin . . . now just caress your lips lightly over the nipple . . . oh, that feels good."

While he was doing it all, I stared out through the car's windshield at the field of wheat, dappled in sun. White puffs of cloud were drifting across the sky. Somewhere, some birds were singing. It was idyllic. The trees bent and shook their leaves in a gust of wind. Arnold's mouth worked busily. I thought for a moment how nice it would have been if Mel had been there with me. We could really have had fun together. But, well, this college student was certainly helping to alleviate my feelings of loneliness.

He raised his head from my breasts. His cheeks were flushed. His glasses were askew. Gently I took them off him and laid them on the ledge under the windshield. I took both his hands then and pressed them to my naked breasts. Instinctively his fingers curled, and he held the soft, full swellings of flesh.

"Nice?" I asked him softly. "Do you like my body?"

He nodded dumbly. But he didn't look happy.

"What's the matter?" I asked him. I toyed with his cock while I spoke.

"I don't . . ." he began. "I mean, I don't think we should . . ."

"Should what?" I stroked his cock and tickled his balls. "Tell me, Arnold."

"You'll think this is stupid, but I promised my fiancée . . ."

"That you'd be faithful to her?" I smiled faintly. My fingers ran little circles around just the head of his penis, and I felt it strain and twitch under my touch.

"Yes," he said.

"She's the only woman you have ever had sex with?"

"Yes."

I realized then what I wanted to do. "So we'll bear that in mind," I said easily. I squirmed up in my seat and pushed my dress down farther, out from under me, and off completely, down my legs. Carefully I took it and put it in the back of the car. Then I turned back toward Arnold, displaying my body. I wore no panties. I was completely naked. I took his hand and guided it between my legs. "Touching me isn't being unfaithful," I said.

He bit his lip. He stared at my body. Then he looked away. And then despite himself he looked back at me again. He was making me feel *so* desirable; I loved it.

I guided his hand up against my vagina. "Touch me," I told him. "Go on. There's no harm in it." I opened my legs wide.

Hesitantly his finger found my clitoris. I smiled. "Gently at first, till it gets wetter . . . that's good." And at the same time I went back to stroking his cock, lightly, tantalizingly, not forcefully enough to make him come.

He was breathing quite heavily now and was obviously very aroused. I put my other arm around him and pulled him against me. His head slumped down against my breasts. I felt his cheek pressing against me. I felt almost motherly toward him.

He went on touching my cunt for a couple of minutes. I felt my body beginning to glow.

"Now," I whispered softly, "go down on me."

He gave me an uncertain look.

"What's the matter," I said, "don't you like to do it?"

"Yes, I suppose so," he answered unconvincingly.

"Come on." I shifted around, pulling one leg up and stretching it out across the two seats, so that my thighs were spread wide and he was between them.

Still he hesitated.

"Go down on me," I told him, this time sounding more determined. "Go on, kneel on the floor." I nudged him. Reluctantly he obeyed. "Now. Kiss me here." I touched my own clitoris. "Kiss me here and tell me how sweet it tastes."

I still wasn't sure if it was his conscience, his morality, or his private set of hang-ups making him hold back. I didn't really care. I just wanted him to do it. I had decided I didn't want him to actually make love to me; it would be too intimate, and I didn't think he'd be a great lover, no matter how big his penis happened to be. And he'd probably have a premature orgasm anyway, and it would be a mess. This was much better. This was just what I wanted.

I urged his head down between my thighs. I held his face in my hands and wriggled my hips toward him. And then his lips touched my labia. The contact was delicious.

"With your tongue, now," I told him. "Push it into my cunt. Yes! Wiggle it around. And now lick my clitoris. Lick it. Harder. Ah, that's the spot. Ahhh . . ." I luxuriated in the warm, sensual waves emanating from my groin. I half-closed my eyes and stared out at the rippling wheat field and the beatific landscape. I stroked my hands through Arnold's hair as he tongued me. It was blissful.

And then something odd happened. Where he had seemed diffident about it originally, suddenly he seemed to start getting into the whole act of going down on me. His hands went around behind my hips, so he could pull himself more strongly to me. His mouth closed on my vagina and he sucked and licked it hungrily. He moved his head in little circles, massaging the sensitive areas with his lips. He nibbled and tongued me and did it for all he was worth.

I loved it. I couldn't get enough of it. I wriggled on the seat and made little motions of my hips. I gasped and groaned and urged him on. "Make me come," I whispered to him. And then, louder: "Make me come!"

He doubled his efforts. It all built up in a great wave of pleasure. I locked my fingers together, put my hands behind his head, and pulled his mouth up against me as hard as I could. The bursts of pleasure became more intense. Suddenly I cried out as the orgasm took me, vivid and sweet and altogether delectable.

I sighed then and relaxed in my seat, feeling warm and languorous and quite fulfilled. My breathing slowed down. All the tension had drained out of me. I saw Arnold, sitting on the floor of the car, with his face all wet. He was gasping for breath.

"Here." I helped him back up onto the seat beside me. "You were wonderful. That was really delightful." I kissed him on the cheek.

He was still fully dressed, in his raincoat and everything. He rubbed his wet mouth across his sleeve. "It was all right?" He looked at me nervously.

So eager to please! "It was just fine," I told him. "Now it's your turn." I felt for his cock. It wasn't as large as it had been, but his erection hadn't faded away completely.

"You don't have to," he said.

"Oh, but I *want* to. Don't worry," I told him, "you'll still be able to tell your girl that you haven't had sexual relations with any other woman." I stroked his cock. Already it was getting stiff again.

He slumped in his seat. I squirmed around and got up on my knees. I leaned over into the back of the car, located one of my traveling bags, groped inside, and found what I needed. A bottle of hand lotion.

"Here," I said, returning to him and squirting some of the lotion onto his cock. "This'll make everything feel much nicer."

I suppose in a way it was my apology for not going down on him in return for the oral sex he had given me. But I really didn't want to, and I didn't think he expected it, anyway.

I snuggled up against him and started masturbating him quickly. My hand made liquid, sticky noises in the lotion. I poured a little more on.

He groaned. I saw him clenching his fists. He eyed my body hungrily. "Touch me," I told him. "Touch my breasts."

His fingers brushed my skin tentatively.

"Hold them," I told him. "Go on. You can hold them harder. As hard as you like. Dig your fingers in if it feels good."

He groaned again and his hands clenched on my boobs. He arched his back. His cock strained and pulsed.

I masturbated him as fast as I could. "When you come, I'm going to let you come on my tits," I told him. "Would you like that?"

His eyes widened as if he had never heard of the idea. He gasped.

My fingers clenched on his cock. It was so hot and so huge. It jerked in my grip. The veins stood out. And then he came. Great gouts of semen spurted up and out and I pressed close, so the milky liquid landed where he was still holding on to my breasts with his own hands.

I pulled one of his hands away and rubbed the mound of my breast over the head of his cock, which was still spurting little trails of jism. I pressed his cock against me until his orgasm was completely over. Then I rubbed my fingers through the semen, spreading it across my skin. "It's supposed to do wonders for the complexion," I told him.

I got back onto the seat beside him. He was staring at me speechlessly. "You okay?" I asked.

He nodded vaguely.

I found some Kleenex and handed him a couple of the tissues. "Here, you'd better mop up some of that lotion on your cock. You don't want it to stain your clothes. It might give your girl the wrong idea. You don't want her asking awkward questions."

He flushed with guilt then, and that brought him out of his stupor. He wiped himself and quickly tucked his penis inside his pants. Suddenly he seemed embarrassed to be exposed to me.

I mopped the jism from my breasts. Then I reached into my bag and found some cleansing lotion and used that. Then, finally, I picked my dress off the backseat and wriggled into it.

He looked almost disappointed to see my nakedness covered up. "No one's ever going to believe this when I tell them," he said.

"So don't tell them." I smiled brightly at him.

He stared at me some more. Now that the little moment was over, I realized I just wanted to get back onto the highway and make up for the lost time. It had been a gas, seducing him. It had been wonderful having my orgasm there in the car, overlooking the English landscape. I had gotten rid of my feelings of isolation, and I'd had fun, and I'd satisfied my hitchhiker friend and given him something to remember me by. Now it was time to move on.

I started the car and backed into the little road, then drove along it, returning toward the traffic circle, where I could get back onto the motorway.

"That's . . . all?" he said. He didn't seem to be able to catch up with the pace of events.

"I'm afraid that's all I have time for, Arnold," I told him. "But it was great, wasn't it?"

He sort of laughed. "I still think you're crazy. Are they all like you in America? All the women over there, I mean."

"No way. Arnold, I regret to tell you, I'm unique. A girl in a million."

I reached the traffic circle and slowed the car. I was thinking carefully.

"You know," I said then, "maybe we should split up at this point. I mean, it was the kind of purely sexual moment that can't be improved upon. If we talk now, it'll just spoil the experience. Don't you agree?" I stopped the car.

He stared at me. "You mean you want me to get out here?"

"It's quite a good place to hitch another ride, isn't it?"

"Oh, yes. Yes, I could get a lift here all right, I expect." He stared reluctantly at me—at my breasts, to be exact.

"Some of life's pleasures are brief. And this has been one of them." I smiled sweetly.

"All right. Well, I suppose I'll never see you again."

"Never," I agreed.

"How about if I ever get to America, I could phone you . . ."

I marveled at the change in him. Half an hour ago he'd been full of reserve, avoiding my touch. Now he was unable to tear himself away. "Be realistic," I told him. "Think of your girlfriend. Your fiancée."

He thought of her. The idea didn't seem to appeal to him very much. But then he sighed and shrugged. "Right you are," he said. Obviously he was used to being philosophical about women. He grabbed his bag off the backseat and opened the passenger door.

I waited while he got out. "Good luck," I called to him.

He didn't look very friendly. In fact, now he seemed pissed at me. I suspect he realized I had taken advantage of him in some way.

"Let me tell you something," he said, just before I slammed the door.

"What's that?" I asked him.

"My name's not Arnold. I lied to you." He said it belligerently, as if to tell me he'd made a fool of me.

"All right, mystery man," I said, "see you around." I slammed the door.

"And I think you're . . . you're a sex-starved whore!" he shouted suddenly as I accelerated away from the curb.

I laughed. I just had time to turn and give him a cheerful wave, and then I was taking the car around the traffic circle, and he was receding behind me, out of sight.

I was still laughing to myself when I drove onto the motorway and accelerated into the fast lane. The whole episode reminded me of my own college days, when I'd acted out all kinds of wild desires and wicked fantasies and driven most of the boys crazy, because they never knew what to expect from me.

It was nice to know I could still act a little irresponsibly and bring those impulsive ideas to life.

A pity that Arnold, or whatever his real name was, hadn't been broad-minded enough to enter into the spirit of the thing and just have a good time, instead of getting all excited and then angry at me for driving away. He'd probably take it out on his fiancée.

Meanwhile, I was behind schedule, and I really didn't have time to play any more games.

As I drove, I brought my mind back to the purpose of this car trip: the phone call that had aroused my interest to the point where I simply had to find this place, this Downton Castle, and investigate the mysterious voice that had told me creepy things about my dead sister.

That made me feel more sober and determined. I stopped briefly to check my gas-station map (I had large-scale ordnance-survey maps with me also, of the area of Wales I was interested in, but I wouldn't need them till I was close to my destination). I saw I was close to the Severn Bridge that my hitchhiker friend had mentioned. The bridge linked England to Wales, across a broad river.

I drove on. I took the correct exit and followed the highway across the bridge and into Wales. Immediately the landscape looked different. I found myself among bleak, craggy hills dusted with snow. A few miles farther on I had to leave the motorway and follow a two-lane blacktop, snaking up and around the peaks, doubling back on itself—and on the map this road was marked red, as a major route. What were the minor ones like?

The weather had been mostly sunny. But now, here, it was threatening. The sky was crowded with lumpy cumulus, and I drove through a sudden shower of freezing rain that hit the windshield like handfuls of fine sand.

I put my gas-station map away and opened one of the large-scale sheets. The scale was one inch to a mile; it showed every contour and detail of the landscape. I had circled a little black dot that was labeled Downton Castle on the map. As the afternoon faded into evening, and the clouds massed together in the sky, I came within reach of my goal.

The last bit of the journey was on a graveled road about three inches wider than my car. I switched on the headlights to make myself more visible, and sounded the horn as I rounded each bend between the hills that crowded the tiny road. A fierce, gusty wind blew across the landscape, rocking the car and flattening the tall grass.

And then I reached a hillcrest, and as I looked at the valley below, I saw the castle.

I stopped the car. Ahead of me, on the horizon line formed by the next range of hills, the sunset was a neon-red extravaganza, a long, wide line below the dark clouds, like a gaping, bloody wound. Directly below, its battlements picking up the red hue of the sky, stood the castle.

It was a real honest-to-God castle. With towers and turrets and a massive gateway. The trees all around it were thrashing in the wind. The tall, narrow windows of the building were rimmed with snow. The private drive that led to it was a thin thread of black among the white-dusted, frozen grasslands.

Another burst of freezing rain hit the car like grapeshot from a cannon. It made me jump. I blinked and looked again at the castle, as if expecting it to vanish; but it was still there, sprawling and huge, the gray stonework looking solid and forbidding. I tried to imagine what kind of person would buy and retreat to a place like that. An Arabian gentleman, the guy from *The Tatler* had told me. Maybe he just used it as some kind of summer retreat—although the landscape looked as if it had never seen a summer, ever.

I started the car, put it in drive, and headed cautiously down the hill. Frozen gorse and bracken scraped past either side of the car. The wheels bumped over ruts and deadwood. I eased the Rover between two massive stone gateposts, then took it along the drive that led to the castle's forecourt.

The towers loomed up dark against the mad, liquid red of the sunset. The headlights of my car swung around, and for a moment, picked up in their glare, I saw a startled rabbit in the middle of the driveway. It bolted for cover in a flurry of frozen snow.

There was a wide area around the castle's main entrance. Other vehicles were parked there. I checked them out: two Jaguars, a Rolls, a Mercedes, and a Cadillac. Either the castle's owner was a car nut or he had rich friends. That made me feel a little better; the cars were a sign of twentieth-century life.

But as I parked my Rover beside them, I noticed that they were all thick with snow. It had drifted around their wheels and lay in an unbroken blanket across their windshields.

None of the cars had been used in at least a couple of days. Whoever was in this castle had been there for a while.

I turned off the Rover's engine and put on my long camel-hair coat. I glanced at myself in the mirror. I looked a little pale, but immaculate. I tied a scarf around my throat and practiced an expression of disdain and determination. I looked more confident than I felt.

I pulled on my calfskin gloves and opened the car door. The wind hit me and almost made me lose my balance. It stung my face and made my eyes water. I slammed the car door, locked it, ducked my head down, and stepped across the forecourt toward the massive entrance of the castle.

I climbed some stone steps whose snowy carpet was unbroken, as if no one else had come that way in days. Shielded from the wind by the bulk of the building, I brushed my hair out of my face, composed myself, and then pressed an old porcelain bell push set in a plaster molding beside the entrance.

Somewhere deep in the building I heard a bell ring. It was a deep-toned ringing, like a fire-alarm bell. It echoed away as I released my pressure on the bell push.

I waited, clutching myself against the cold.

I heard slow footsteps approaching across what sounded like a stone floor. A chain was drawn aside behind the oak planks of the front door, and it opened slowly on its ancient wrought-iron hinges.

By this time I was ready to come face-to-face with Dracula. But instead I looked and saw, in the dying red light of the sunset, a little man who was six inches shorter than I. He was thin and wrinkled, in his seventies, I guessed, and he looked at me with tired, rheumy eyes. He was wearing a simple gray uniform and white kid gloves.

"Miss Van Bell?" he said hesitantly.

That threw me. I stared at him. He stared back at me. Eventually, I just nodded.

"Please come in," he told me and opened the door wider.

I hesitated. Then I got myself under control and walked boldly in. I'd always believed there was a rational explanation for everything in life. No exceptions to this rule. So there had to be a rational explanation here.

I found myself in a vast hallway with a vaulted ceiling embossed with elaborate patterns and hand-painted with heraldic crests. There were dark, ancient oil paintings on the walls. The floor was of black-and-white stone tiles. Dim light radiated from imitation-candle electric bulbs in a wrought-iron chandelier hanging on long chains from the ceiling.

"Allow me to take your coat, miss," said the servant.

The hallway was almost as cold as the landscape outside. "I think I'll keep it on, thanks," I said, looking around me with what I hoped was an air of casual, bored indifference. "How did you know my name?"

The little withered man's expression never changed. "Just a guess, miss. I was told to expect . . . a number of people, possibly, including yourself. If you'll come this way . . ."

"Who told you to expect?" I stayed standing by the door, my hands in my coat pockets.

The old servant turned back and blinked at me. "Mr. Zenya, miss."

That was the name the man had used on the phone. So I was in the right place, no doubt about it.

"I'd like to see this Mr. Zenya." I still didn't move from where I stood.

"Of course, miss. He is interested in meeting you, likewise. You can wait in the reception room . . ."

"I'll wait right here."

He paused. "Well, as you wish, miss, but Mr. Zenya may be a little while, he is in his private rooms, where he cannot be disturbed. It would be more comfortable in here for you. There's a fire." He gestured through the first doorway off the cavernous entrance hall.

What the hell, I thought. No point in suffering unnecessarily. And no reason why I should let this place, and this old wizened man, give me the jitters. No *rational* reason for it at all.

So I walked quickly across the tiled floor and through the door that he was holding open.

The reception room was huge and richly furnished. A log fire blazed in a grand marble fireplace. Indian carpets covered the floor. Medieval tapestries and oil paintings of English landscapes were hung on the walls. The furniture was equally valuable: a potpourri of antiques, from a beautiful draw-leaf mahogany table to an elegant chaise longue by the diamond-paned windows.

Well, I thought, it was worth coming here just to see this.

"Mr. Zenya will see you here, miss," the servant said. "I'll tell him you're here as soon as I can."

The old man started out of the room, closing the door behind him. I was feeling edgy, despite my determination to be rational. It was just a little too strange, a little too much of a setup. "You can leave the door open!" I said suddenly, too loudly.

The servant paused for what seemed a long time, looking at my face, as if reading me. I didn't like that; it gave me the creeps. For the first time I thought I detected a change in his expression, a tiny rictus at the corner of his mouth, as if, deep inside, he were laughing at me. Then it was gone and his lined face was as impassive as before. "As you wish, miss," he said, and shuffled out.

I swallowed hard, trying to get my wits back together. But it was a losing battle. I had been thoroughly unnerved, and I felt on edge and jumpy, not knowing what to expect next. I walked around the large room, with its smell of dust and dampness hanging heavy in the air despite the blazing, crackling fire. I perched myself on the edge of an armchair near the flames.

One of the big logs in the fireplace suddenly subsided with a crash and a flurry of embers. I was on my feet before I realized what had happened. My pulse was fast and my hands were clenched.

I cursed silently, made myself relax, and sat back down. Belatedly I checked that none of the embers had been thrown out of the fireplace onto the Indian carpet. I was beginning to feel warm. I started taking off my gloves, and pretended not to notice that my hands were unsteady.

The wind rose outside the castle. It literally howled. There was a cascade of tiny little fluttering, tapping noises on the windowpanes, and I jumped again, till I realized it was just the sound of specks of frozen rain against the glass.

I stood up, feeling restless. Behind all the little noises there was an awful silence about the place, a deadness, like a pool that would absorb and drown any real sound. I was conscious of a faint ringing in my ears. I could actually hear my own heartbeats.

I decided I needed a drink. Maybe the old servant could get me one. Scotch would be good. I turned to the door . . .

And froze. Without my hearing it, someone had entered the room. He was standing there, just inside the door, watching me.

I flinched. Then I got myself more under control and just stared for a moment.

He was very tall—over six feet—and he wore a dramatic robe, shimmering gold in the dim room lighting. It covered him from his neck to his toes. It was embroidered with multicolored figures and forms, mystic beasts, symbols and icons. It looked Egyptian, like something a pharaoh would wear. It was regal, and dramatic, and imposing. And there was no denying that it suited the man who was wearing it.

He was sallow-skinned, black-haired, and he had the darkest, most intense eyes. They stared at me steadily, thoughtfully. His hair was long, gleaming with highlights. He had a thick mustache, concealing his exact expression from me.

We stared at each other for long moments, neither one of us moving. Then suddenly, breaking the spell, he stepped forward. He put out his hand, his arm extending from the folds of his golden robe. Behind his mustache he smiled, his eyes gleaming as he watched me still.

I took his hand. His grip was firm and dry; his skin was smooth.

"I'm sorry I kept you waiting," he said. His voice was low-pitched but almost musical in its tones, faintly touched with an Arabian accent, but more obviously sounding as if he'd been educated at Oxford. I felt uncomfortable under his scrutiny and still shaken by his entrance and all the events that had led up to it. "It is Miss Van Bell, isn't it?" he went on. "My name is Zenya."

"So I figured," I said. My throat was dry and my voice sounded funny. I deliberately turned and stepped closer to the fire, just as a way of breaking eye contact and playing for time.

"So tell me," he went on, "what brings you out here."

I turned quickly. "*What?* Are you serious?"

We stared at each other again. He was absolutely enigmatic, and I realized that he was harder to judge than any other man I'd ever met.

"I'm here—I tracked you down in this godforsaken place—because of your damned practical-joke phone call last night," I said. "And you know it."

Another long pause. Then he nodded. "But no joke, Miss Van Bell," he said, with what sounded like total sincerity.

"And how do you know who I am? And how did

you get my phone number at the hotel?" My voice was becoming shrill now, as all the repressed tension and anxiety came out. "Who the hell are you, and what right do you have waking me up in the middle of the night with . . . with screwball messages from my dead sister?"

"My apologies if I *woke* you," he said with a hint of irony, as if somehow he knew I had not been asleep when he'd called. "But the message was important." He shrugged. "Why else would you have taken the trouble to come all this way to find me?"

"You haven't answered my questions," I replied weakly.

He stepped closer to me. I was already as near to the fire as was comfortable; I couldn't retreat from him. I felt him physically invading my personal space, and it made my skin prickle. He had an intimidating presence. He reached out and touched my arm. I was still wearing my coat, but his touch seemed to go through it, and I jumped the way a person jumps who is being woken from a dream.

"Your questions are important questions, Christina," he said very softly. "But the answers are not easy. You would find them hard to believe. Since you took the trouble to find me, I hope you will take the trouble now to stay a little while and learn more. It is true, I half-expected that you might arrive here; but of course that choice was yours alone to make. Whether you leave now is your choice too. I do not influence people, or give advice; all I have to give is information. Knowledge."

I tried to fight off his amazing charisma and grapple just with what he said. It was hard. "Are you claiming you're a psychic?"

"All I claim is that I have information. Perceptions. Anything else you must judge for yourself."

"My sister's dead, you know that."

He nodded.

"What did you do, pick up a message from her in a *séance?*" I tried to sound sarcastic, but it didn't work. Because I, the great unbeliever, the skeptic who had never even experimented with a Ouija board, was already halfway to believing that this man *did* have something. Not only was it the only explanation for the facts; I *felt* it.

"I do not like the word 'séance,'" he was saying. "It reminds me of old-fashioned ideas, of table-tipping, and voices, and mediums who were usually fakes, taking money from gullible people who wanted to communicate with their dead relatives. No, we do not have séances here."

"What *do* you have?"

He let go of my arm. The release of his hand was almost as disturbing as when he had first touched me. Now I felt suddenly on my own again, isolated. He stepped back and gestured around at the room, the whole castle. "I invite you to stay and see for yourself. There is no other way. We have a number of guests already—you saw the cars outside?—and some spare rooms still. You would be welcome, for one night, at least."

I felt tantalized, frightened, eager, excited, all at once. It was one of the most unusual offers I'd ever had. At the same time, I realized that I didn't just find this man hard to interpret, I actually was scared of him. Normally, with my personality, my wealth, and my looks, I feel more than equal to any man. This was one of the few times when I was absolutely out of my depth, and I didn't like it.

"What do you do, rent out rooms?" I said, trying feebly to make some joke of it, to cover my indecision and nervousness.

He smiled at me, as if he understood everything, knew all that was going on in my head and was telling me not to be foolish, not to be nervous. "Those who stay here are my guests," he said softly. "I have great independent wealth. Money is of no interest to me now."

I swallowed. I shrugged. "Fine," I said.

He nodded, as if my decision was predetermined—as if I had never had any choice in the matter at all. "Dinner will be served at seven," he said. "Jenkins, my servant, will show you to your room. And welcome, Christina, to my house."

Then he was gone, and I was left standing by the fire feeling dazed and disturbed and wondering what Mel would have made of all of this, if he had been here.

But already Mel seemed very, very far away.

CHAPTER FOUR

Jenkins, the little wizened old man, insisted on carrying one of my bags. I gave him the lighter of the two and carried the other one myself, following him up an imposing staircase of polished oak.

We reached the second floor. "Through there is the east wing," he told me, indicating a massive white-painted door with a big brass lock on it. "Mr. Zenya's rooms. He insists on his privacy in there. The guests stay in the west wing. This way."

He led me along a wide hallway. Near the end he stooped and opened a paneled door and flicked a porcelain switch that looked as if it had been made by Edison himself. Still, it worked, more or less: the room was at once flooded with dim yellow light from a lamp beside a dressing table and two lamps on tables either side of an enormous four-poster bed.

Jenkins set down my suitcase and led me around the bed to a smaller door. "In here, miss, you have your own shower and toilet." He sounded disapproving, as if this kind of modern luxury offended his British belief in keeping a stiff upper lip. To my surprise, when I looked in the door I saw a newly fitted modern bathroom, all white tile and chrome.

"Mr. Zenya had one put in for each of the guest rooms," Jenkins said, and sniffed.

"Very nice," I said. I pointed to another door in the opposite wall of the bedroom. "What's through there?"

"Ah, that's a connecting door, miss, between your

room and the next guest room. We keep that door locked, miss."

"Why? To stop ghosts from getting in?"

His lined face didn't change its expression. "No ghosts here, miss."

"It was just a joke." I walked to the window and pulled aside the heavy maroon velvet drapes. Through the leaded panes I saw the last trace of the sunset. Otherwise the landscape was all stormy and laden with gloom.

I drew the drapes back over the windows. "Any way to warm up this room a little?"

"Electric fire there, miss." He went over to a little heater and plugged it into the wall for me. "We generally don't light a real fire"—he nodded at the large empty fireplace—"because of all the bother."

"I see. Right, well, thanks, I'll try to make myself at home." I glanced around, at the four-poster bed, the antique lamps, a large Victorian armoire, the ceiling so high it was almost lost in the dimness, the walls decorated in faded regal wallpaper and the inevitable oil paintings in massive gilt frames.

"Anything else you wish for, miss, just ring the bell." He indicated an ancient bell push beside the bed. "Dinner at seven." He consulted an antique pocket watch. "It's just past six o'clock now."

He shuffled out, at last, and closed the door behind him with a heavy thud. I sat on the bed and tried to warm myself in front of the electric heater. I had just got to the point where I dared to take my coat off, when someone knocked.

I called, "Come in," and the door was opened by a tall, slim woman in her twenties, with shoulder-length chestnut hair and a bright, alert expression. She was wearing stylishly fashioned jeans and a blouse that looked French. "Hi," she said and gave me an open, friendly smile. "I heard you being shown up here, so I thought I'd come and introduce myself, since it looks like we're going to be neighbors. I'm Alexandra."

"My name's Christina," I told her. "Pleased to meet you. You sound American."

"Yeah, just like you." She walked over and sat down on the bed beside me, moving with simple self-assurance, very casual, no affectations at all. "What part are you from? I'm from Boston myself."

In a way her directness put me off. On the other hand, it was good to talk to someone from my own country, from a world I understood. "I have a house in L.A. and an apartment in New York," I said. "I like to move around."

"That's nice. What brings you to Downton Castle?"

I hesitated. "Curiosity, I guess."

Alexandra laughed. "Just like everyone else. I'm a guest here too, you understand."

I nodded at the locked connecting door. "You're staying in the next room along?"

"No, I think that room's empty. I'm across the hall. Isn't it just wonderfully quaint? And all authentic, you know. He deliberately kept it that way, apart from the new bathrooms."

Her enthusiasm grated on me for some reason. Perhaps because she sounded so bright and cheerful and . . . young. "So what goes on here, exactly?" I asked, impatient for some information. "Does this guy Zenya run a black-magic cult or what? Who is he?"

Alexandra avoided my eyes and smiled as if at some private ironic joke. "I guess you'll find out soon enough."

"What's wrong with finding out now?"

She looked at her hands, clasped in her lap. "I wouldn't want to say anything that Zenya wouldn't want me to say, that's all." As she spoke the man's name, I detected a faint flush in her cheeks. Then she shrugged, as if she were shrugging off my questions. "You'll find that the food's good."

"Wonderful. Any other useful information?" I stood up, turned my back, walked over, and opened my suitcases. "And are all the guests as helpful as you?"

Alexandra laughed loudly. "I know I must seem to be unnecessarily secretive," she said, "but, well, you've only just arrived, haven't you?"

"That's right. How long have you been here?"

She hesitated and frowned. "It's hard to say—five days? Four days? I'm not sure."

She talks as if she's on an acid trip, I thought to myself. A nice kid, but weird. I held up a dress. "Is this the kind of thing I should wear for dinner?"

"Oh, anything will do."

"But I'm not an 'anything' person," I told her. "If anyone else is going to be formal, I'll be formal."

"Well, let's see, there's Nicholas—Nicholas Weston, the young British politician, have you heard of him? He's always wearing three-piece suits. Actually he looks kind of sexy in them."

"Is he your lover?" I figured an insultingly direct question might get more of a clear-cut response.

"No." My question seemed not to faze her at all.

"Tell me who else is staying here," I said.

"There's Mr. Masterson. He's from Texas, an honest-to-God old-fashioned oil millionaire. It's his Cadillac outside. And there's Stella, of course. She lives here with . . ."

"With Zenya?"

Again Alexandra smiled oddly. She nodded.

I dumped my clothes back in the suitcase. "Hell, I'll come as I am," I said. I was wearing a tweedy outfit I'd bought a couple of days previously on a shopping spree in Oxford Street. If nothing else, it would keep me warm.

"Actually," said Alexandra, as if she'd been following a totally different conversation in her head, "actually I think Nick—Nicholas Weston—is your type, for sure. I'll tell Jenkins to seat you next to him." In a couple of quick strides she was at the door, opening it. "See you later."

Before I could say anything, she was gone. Girls like her, I thought to myself, make me feel too old.

The mellow sound of a dinner gong from downstairs echoed through the mansion at precisely seven o'clock. I walked down the hallway just in time to see a middle-aged man in a loud checked suit stepping out of another of the guest rooms ahead of me.

"Mr. Masterson?" I called out, on impulse.

He turned to look my way and frowned.

"I'm Christina Van Bell," I said, putting out my hand. "A girl named Alexandra told me a Mr. Masterson was staying here, and I just guessed you might be him."

"Well, you guessed right, young lady." He shook my hand warmly but with dignity. He had Southern Gentleman written all over him. A slow-moving, kindly man, silver-haired, with long sideburns. I liked him immediately, and from the way he looked me up and down, I think he liked the look of me, too. "I'll be pleased to escort you to the dining room, ah, Miss Van Bell."

"Why, thank you, sir."

"My pleasure, ma'am." We started down the hallway. "You just arrived today?"

"Only a couple of hours ago. I'm still trying to find out exactly what happens here."

"Ah." He chuckled. "Best if Mr. Zenya gives the explanations, if it's all the same to you." So I wasn't going to get any information out of Masterson, either. This was like knocking on the door of a secret society.

He escorted me down the stairs, through a couple of big, bare, almost empty rooms, and then into the dining room.

The walls were of unfinished gray stone. The space was lit by dozens of candles set in brackets between the ubiquitous oil paintings. A huge log fire burned in the biggest fireplace I had ever seen—big enough to roast a couple of pigs in. The whole room smelled of wood smoke and was alive with soft, flickering candlelight.

Jenkins, dressed in a formal black jacket now, directed me to my place at a table that was long enough to have accommodated a couple of dozen guests. Only six place settings were laid, however, close to one another at one end of the table.

I sat down and admired the antique silverware, polished to a mirror finish. "Seems we're the first down here tonight," said Masterson, stating the obvious, as he made himself comfortable opposite me and unfolded a napkin that was as spotlessly white as the cloth on the table. "Ah, now, here are the others."

I saw a man in his early thirties walk in, looking well scrubbed and neat. His black hair was cropped short and his black shoes were scrupulously clean and shiny. He was wearing a gray suit. Undoubtedly this was the Nicholas Weston that Alexandra had mentioned. She walked in right behind him and winked at me.

Weston sat down beside me. "You must be Miss Van Bell," he said. "Awfully pleased to meet you."

Awfully, indeed. He was that type of Englishman: *awfully* polite, and *quite* upper-class. At the same time, I instinctively liked him. He had a sharp, intelligent face, and when he looked at me it was with a kind of frank appreciation. I guessed he wholeheartedly liked women and enjoyed them.

"Pleased to meet *you,*" I said, going through my half of the ritual.

"Understand you just got here this evening," he said. "Terrible weather, isn't it? You must have had a difficult drive. Was there much snow?"

It went on like that for a couple more minutes, talking with apparent enthusiasm about the weather. Meanwhile, out of the corner of my eye I saw Alexandra murmur something to Masterson, beside her. And the remaining two chairs stood empty.

Finally Zenya entered. All conversation ceased. He paused at the doorway, surveying the people at the table. Then he clasped his hands briefly, bowed very slightly toward us, and took the seat at the head of the table, still dressed in the gold robe he had worn earlier.

The girl who sat down at his right was, I guessed, the Stella that Alexandra had mentioned. She was dressed in a white sweater and white pants. She was only around twenty-one, I guessed. She had very pale blond hair and wore slightly too much makeup. Her figure was well rounded under the sweater, and she flashed me a sudden quick look that seemed anything but friendly. I immediately got the message: she was Zenya's little girl, and possessive as hell. If I tried to get my hands on the Great Man, I'd find myself faced with a little jealous bundle of pure fury.

Interesting, I thought to myself. There were all kinds of other little eye messages and tensions in the group, too; Alexandra didn't look at Nick Weston, and Weston didn't look at her; Weston and Zenya exchanged a cordial hello, with something else behind it; Alexandra seemed more than a little friendly with Masterson, who must be close to double her age.

Zenya clapped his hands twice, and immediately a

pair of waitresses entered carrying silver platters. The women were middle-aged and reminded me of some of the staff at the Ritz—indestructible old creatures who seemed to have been in service all their lives. They gave us generous portions of what turned out to be a fine fresh crab cocktail.

"My guests, my Circle, let us enjoy our meal," Zenya said. "And afterward we will turn to serious matters."

We took the hint and concentrated mainly on the food, with only trivial conversation, during which I gave them my brief biography, and the other guests told me theirs.

Alexandra seemed to be the kind of girl who survived by her wits, with no special career or vocation in life. She said she'd been at Smith College but had had to drop out in her second year, when her father had lost his fortune as a result of some real-estate con men. Her father was now dead.

Masterson had retired at age fifty and seemed happy to travel around slowly using up his millions. He had a wife back in Texas but didn't seem to care much for her. He had a daughter who was a nurse in Houston, and a son who had been lost, missing in action, in Vietnam.

Weston was a successful member of Parliament who had recently been elected to the House of Commons by his constituency somewhere in the south of England. He was the kind of bright young man who might be a cabinet minister within ten more years. But he seemed troubled by the recent death of his father.

It seemed clear enough. All of the guests had dead relatives. Of course, that could have been merely a coincidence. . . .

We finished the meal, which was delicious. But throughout, there was nothing stronger than water for us to drink. I questioned Zenya tentatively. "Alcohol blurs the perceptions," he said softly, staring at me with his dark, intense eyes. I noticed that all other conversation at the table stopped whenever he spoke. "There is nothing wrong with that, of course. It is pleasurable. But it is not helpful for us when we work as a Circle."

There was no doubt about it. That word "Circle" began with a capital letter.

"A Circle?" I questioned him, all wide-eyed and innocent.

"You have very little longer to wait now," he said obscurely.

Idle conversation eventually picked up again, to fill the silence, but I sensed no one's mind was on it. There was a tension growing slowly among the people at the table. Whatever was going to happen, it was going to happen very soon. I found myself picking up the sense of nervous anticipation, as the flickering candles burned lower and the waitresses cleared the last of the meal.

Finally Zenya stood up. "We are ready now," he said, and I couldn't tell whether he was just speaking for himself, or all of us.

Immediately everyone else stood up and followed him as he walked out of the dining room and up the stairs. He paused, opened the white-painted door with a heavy brass key, and ushered us in.

There was an air of electric expectancy now. I followed the other guests through the door in single file. I was the last in line; Zenya touched my arm. His touch startled me, just as it had when he had touched me earlier. "You will sit to my right, since you are the neophyte here," he said quietly, ushering me into the first room off a long corridor that stretched away down the whole length of the east wing of the castle.

The others were already seated in chairs around a small round table. It was of bare wood, stained so dark that it was like ebony. And the rest of the room—

every detail in it—was black, also. The walls had been stripped down to the stone, and painted black. If there was a window—I couldn't tell, for sure—it had been bricked up and painted over black. The floor was of polished black stone. The simple wooden chairs that we sat on were black. The only light was from a single large black candle in a tall black candlestick in the center of the table.

As soon as I walked into the room it closed around me. I felt suddenly as if I were inside someone's mind —my own mind. I felt as if I were suffocating.

Zenya entered behind me, shut the door firmly, and locked it. Evidently he sensed my discomfort. He guided me gently to my chair. "Soon we will put out the candle, and you will not notice the closeness of this room," he said.

Put out the candle? That was the last thing I wanted him to do. Stuck here in this room with no window and a locked door and a mystic man and his tribe of Believers—all of them just a little bit screwball, if I wasn't mistaken.

"I'm not sure I'm cut out for this kind of entertainment," I said, glancing quickly at the other people.

Their faces flickered in the candlelight. Masterson, on my right, patted me on the arm. "I know how it feels, my dear," he said. "I was a trifle, ah, ill-at-ease, my first time around. But you know, there's nothing to be scared of."

Zenya seated himself on my left. I saw Stella, his girl, sitting just the other side of him; again she shot me the warning glance that said: Keep your hands off my man.

I looked from her to Nick Weston, sitting on her left; then Alexandra, then Masterson again. I noticed that male and female alternated around the circle. The skin of each person's face looked yellow in the flickering light. The black walls and ceiling seemed both a million miles away, lost in the shadows, and yet at the same time closing in on me.

"It is not an entertainment here, Christina," Zenya said. His voice seemed to bounce back off all the walls, so that it sounded close around my head, almost *inside* my head, low-pitched, hypnotic. "It is an exploration. One of the most important explorations in your life. But safe, quite safe. The room, here, is black only because we wish to eliminate any external stimuli from the so-called real world. The room is bare so that no one may suspect any trickery. None of the wall hangings and tablecloths that the old mediums used to use to hide their special effects. Plain, bare stone, blocking off everything but . . . the world beyond."

My skin prickled. I didn't like this. I didn't know anything about spiritualism, because I'd never believed in it. But there was a casual certainty about Zenya's voice, and my lack of knowledge of spiritualism suddenly made it seem unknown and terrifying. This man *knew*—knew things I had never guessed existed. And he used them. He was in control. There wasn't a moment's doubt. And the other people in the Circle, they knew, too. I realized why no one had wanted to tell me anything in advance: you had to be there and experience it for it to make any sense at all.

"We will begin," Zenya said, before I could object further. "Each person will cover the hand of the person to the right."

I laid my hand hesitantly over Masterson's. "Like that?" I whispered, wondering if there was some special way of doing it.

"Yes. So." Zenya laid his right hand over my left. For a moment our eyes met. I had to look away quickly. I felt I was spinning. I felt he could have put me in some kind of trance right then, inside of a few seconds.

"We are joined," he said then, as each person in the group laid his or her right hand over the left hand of the person to the right. "We are a Circle. We contain the energies of the mind, among us. May they unite and grow. The orgone energies, the psychic energies, the energies of the soul, united. We can feel them growing."

I couldn't feel anything. I was so jittery, half of me was in a panic and expecting the devil to appear. The other half of me was stupidly worrying that my right palm was sweating and must feel unpleasant laid over Masterson's hand. And anyway, I didn't *want* to feel anything. I wanted the whole thing to be a washout.

"There will be a sign," said Zenya.

And right then the candle went out. I screamed, and my scream was incredibly loud in the little room. I tried to pull back, but my muscles wouldn't work. My hands seemed trapped, just by contact with Zenya on my left and Masterson on my right.

"We have nothing to fear," Zenya said softly, somewhere in the darkness. "We are using the natural forces, the forces of life itself."

I didn't disbelieve him for a moment. *Something* had blown that candle out—in this windowless, draftless room. *Something* was holding my hands on the table, in the Circle. And it was scaring me rigid, no matter what he said about it being a "natural force."

"The chant will begin," Zenya said; and then they all started repeating one word, over and over. It sounds insane, but I can no longer remember what that word was. In all the times I said it, then and later, I could never recall it outside of the Circle. No one else could, either. Zenya began the chant; everyone else took it up from him. It was a meaningless word, maybe an Arabic word. But inside of five minutes, repeating it over and over in the tiny black room, in total darkness, that word took on a significance. It became the totality, the universe. It described everything that existed.

And then, above the sound of our slow chanting, came the sound of other voices. Above us and around us I heard what sounded like a vast crowd chanting with us. Unseen multitudes, on all sides, even *below* us, as if we were suspended in space.

Zenya stopped the chant. The rest of us stopped too. But the unseen multitudes kept it up, so that it surged around us now with a life of its own, like the wind or the ocean.

"We seek friends among you," Zenya said suddenly, very loudly. "We, the Circle, seek those we know."

The chanting went on, rising and falling. Other voices started, gabbling in languages I did not understand. Then a high-pitched woman's voice, shouting out manic laughter. Then a man's voice, again in some foreign tongue.

"May those we know come to the Circle!" Zenya intoned boldly and loudly, as if he were commanding the whole universe.

And then a new voice surfaced above all the rest, a man's voice, saying, "I hear, I hear, I hear."

"Who comes to the Circle?" Zenya demanded.

The voice said something, loud but indistinct, almost like the speech of an autistic person. It sounded like "Lessing."

"Repeat!" said Zenya.

This time it was clear. "John Weston. I hear. Who summons . . . where . . ." The gabble of other voices rose up again, engulfing John Weston.

"There is one among us here who would speak to you," said Zenya.

"Tired . . . so very tired . . . the time . . . my son . . ."

It was all confused, rising and falling. I imagined poor Nicholas Weston sitting across the table from me in the darkness, straining to hear the words of the spirit of his dead father. Suddenly I felt guilty—perhaps it was my fault, I was the weak link, the flaw in the Circle. I willed myself to share these energies that Zenya had talked about. I wanted desperately to bring it all to life.

"Do not leave us." Zenya's command was firm. But I think he could feel the voice slipping away.

"Another time . . ." The voice that was John Weston spoke.

And then he was gone, back into the murmurings of the multitude.

"We summon another. Another whom we know."

That was when it happened. Suddenly—without any warning—so loud it sounded like a person shouting in my ear. "Christina! Christina, you've come!"

There wasn't a moment's doubt. I knew. It was my dead sister.

I think I screamed again. I don't know for sure. All that's certain is that, there and then, I fainted.

CHAPTER FIVE

Later—I'll never know exactly how much later—I regained consciousness and found myself lying on the four-poster bed in my room. It wasn't easy, coming out of my faint; it felt as if I were struggling slowly, slowly up out of a deep, dark cavern. And in the cavern I could hear my own heart, echoing, beating so slowly it sounded as if it might stop altogether.

But someone had some smelling salts under my nose, and someone else was slapping my cheeks, and someone else was rubbing my hands and feet, and finally I opened my eyes.

"Fran," I said, not yet realizing where I was.

"Your sister is gone now," said Masterson gently, standing beside me. "But you can find her again, Christina. There will be many more times."

I made out my surroundings. I saw Alexandra, next to Masterson; and Nick Weston. They were all watching me with friendly concern. And then I noticed Stella, not standing as close to the bed as the rest of them. No friendly concern on her face. Just a morbid curiosity to see whether I would wake up or not.

The only person missing was Zenya. "Where's—?" I began.

"He always rests after a meeting of the Circle," said Alexandra. "He finds it exhausting."

"I can believe that." I struggled to sit up on the bed. I was still dizzy. I could still hear the multitude of voices shouting incoherently in my head, and the memory of my sister's voice was so vivid it seemed a presence I could almost touch. "I'm sorry I messed up the event," I said, "passing out like that."

"You didn't mess up anything," said Stella. Her voice sounded pitying and scornful.

"It was not until the end of the meeting that we even realized you had fainted," Nick Weston explained. "Hard to tell what's really going on in there, you know."

"Your energies remained part of the Circle even though you were unconscious," Alexandra added.

"Did I miss anything more that Fran . . . my sister . . . ?"

"She called to you, my dear," said Masterson, "but soon left. And then we spoke to others. Some familiar, some strangers."

I looked up at him. "Your son?"

He looked weary. "As yet, my dear, we, ah, haven't contacted my son. But you see, that could be because he's still alive somewhere. I just don't know. The Circle can only touch upon the energies of the dead."

I shook my head. "This is all too heavy for me right now."

Stella laughed, and then turned and walked out of the room. I think she'd decided in her own mind that anyone as psychically naive as I was couldn't possibly be a threat to her with Zenya. I immediately had an evil notion to prove her wrong about that. I don't like being upstaged by cheap little tarts—which is how I thought of her. And I was willing to bet that being Zenya's lover could be an extremely . . . unique . . . experience. Something that a little brat like Stella wouldn't have the wits to appreciate.

But that was more than I could think about right then. All I knew was that I had been inducted, I was one of the Circle now, no longer a skeptic. It was frightening; it sounded so irrational, but so powerful.

"We were, er, thinking," Weston began. "That is, ah, Alexandra, here, suggested something that sounded pretty sensible."

"You might like to go out for a little drive," said Alexandra. "The castle can get to you, at least I know it got to me, when I was first here. It can clear your head to go outside for just a little while. It makes the voices go away."

It was true, the voices were still in my mind, though I could no longer hear what they were saying. I almost asked the people standing around me if I were going crazy; then I realized they were the wrong people to ask. If I were crazy, they were crazy too, in the same way.

"I don't feel like going out alone," I said.

"I'll take you," said Nick Weston very quickly. "That is, ah, if you're game for it. I mean, you know, if you like."

I thought it over. "Sure. Why not? You people know more about all of this than I do."

A little later I was sitting with him in his Jaguar XJ, running the engine till the heater warmed up. He turned on the demister, then used the windshield wipers to clear most of the loose snow off the outside of the glass. He switched on the headlights and drove away from the castle, down the drive, out between the gateposts.

"It's a queer business, all this mystical stuff, isn't it?" he said, following the narrow road that ascended gradually, up to the hillcrest from where I had first seen Downton Castle. "Not the kind of thing I've ever taken seriously in the past, you know."

"Me neither." I glanced back at the castle. A few windows glowed yellow in the stormy night. Alexandra had been right; I felt relieved to be outside those stone walls. I needed the breathing space. And yet, equally, I knew I would have to return again, to experience once more the incredible things that had happened in the black room.

"First I knew about it was a phone call from Zenya just a couple of days after my father died," Nick went on. "Very mysterious, he wouldn't say much, but he obviously knew some things that I didn't think anyone could know, so my curiosity got the better of me. That's how he deals with it, you know. He gets information from one of the voices, in the meetings of the Circle, then makes a phone call, just delivers the message, and leaves it at that. I expect that's what he did with you, too."

"Absolutely right," I said.

"Yes. Quite. He says that's all he's interested in, passing on information. He says it's up to the person who gets the information how they use it, whether they bother to follow it up and come out here. Zenya reckons that the people who don't bother to come here aren't worth having in the Circle anyway. Queer business, isn't it?"

"It must cost him a fortune. Psychically and financially."

"Well, he thinks it's important enough to be worth it, I suppose. Can't say I disagree with that, either."

"Amen." I saw that Nick was stopping the car in a spot overlooking the castle and the rest of the valley. He pulled on the handbrake and switched off the lights. He left the engine running and the heater blowing softly over my feet and legs. It felt very comfortable in that car, with the smell of the leather upholstery, and the closeness of this Englishman who no longer sounded quite so awkward and funny but began to seem reassuring in his matter-of-fact outlook.

"I say, would you fancy a drop to drink?" he said

with an engaging smile. "The castle doesn't have so much as a bottle of wine in it, but I happen to have some Martell in the glove compartment. For emergencies, you know."

"Then this is an emergency," I said.

"Rather thought it might be." He took out the bottle and a couple of small picnic-style plastic cups. He poured me an ample shot. "Here's to the spirit world!" he said, and we clunked our cups together.

The brandy spread down through me, and I suddenly felt very mellow.

"Of course, shouldn't really joke about it, I suppose," he was saying. "There's still things about the way my father died . . ."

I laid my hand on his arm. "Please, Nick. No more heavy stuff. I can't deal with it."

"Oh. Yes. Of course. Inconsiderate of me." He stared into his drink. Then he glanced at me, looking embarrassed. Then he looked out of the window. "You know, Christina . . ."

I waited.

"You know, I think you're frightfully attractive."

At last! I thought to myself.

"I hope you don't mind my saying that," he added quickly, looking straight into my eyes.

"That's the kind of comment I never mind hearing," I said quietly, enjoying being very offhand and cool in response to his self-conscious little routine—which, secretly, I was getting off on.

"I expect you'll think I'm being terribly forward," he said. He put his cup of brandy down. Then he picked it up, drained it in a gulp, and put it down again. He turned back to me. "I just find you quite irresistible."

He didn't give me a chance to answer that one. Before I knew what was happening, he was all over me. His mouth was on mine, his left hand was feeling inside my coat and grabbing my breast, his right hand was on my knee and moving up the inside of my thigh.

I managed to pull free. "Hey," I said, "hold it a minute."

"Oh. I mean, I'm terribly sorry."

"Nothing to be sorry about." I took off my coat slowly, methodically, arching my back so that my breasts stood out provocatively. I threw the coat in the backseat. I shook my hair out of my face. "But we can take our time over it, all right?" I smiled at him.

"Oh. Ah, I see. Well, I mean, of course."

I leaned forward and kissed him, at my own pace this time, slowly and thoroughly. His self-consciousness dissolved away; within moments he was holding me to him, firmly but gently, kissing me with tenderness and feeling.

I reached up and started undoing his necktie, but I had trouble with the knot.

"Ah, let me," he said. "It's a double-Windsor, you have to get the knack of it, to get it undone without stretching the cloth."

I giggled. The brandy was getting to me. "You're fun," I said.

He laughed. "Really? That's nice." He got his tie off. It was quite an operation. I leaned over him then, tantalizing him with the closeness of my body as I undid the buttons on his shirt. I slipped my hands inside and ran my fingers over his chest. He was skinny, like many Englishmen, but muscular, too. I reached down and undid his fly and pulled his cock out. He had pale skin that was incredibly soft to the touch. But his cock was hard enough.

He started breathing heavily. His hands fumbled with my dress, unbuttoning it and touching me, my neck, my shoulders, my breasts, my nipples. "Christina," he murmured. "I say, Christina, you really are . . . quite exceptional. I mean . . ." He trailed off. "Ah, let's get in the back, shall we? We can tilt the front seats forward, you see, and that way there's a lot more room."

I laughed. "You've done this before, a few times, in this car."

"Oh! Well, you know, I suppose I have. Meet a lot of women as an MP, you know, and once in a while, you know, ha ha." At the same time he was talking he was making the arrangements, helping me into the back, stretching me out on the leather upholstery and shifting the front seats out of our way. "Now, Christina," he said, and he fell upon me then with a kind of eager, youthful passion.

For a moment I thought of Mel, who'd been sleeping with me less than twenty-four hours ago. A pang went through me. I really liked Mel, really cared for him. But Mel was a long way away now, and I was alone in this incredibly strange place, under such strange circumstances. I really needed the simple physical bond that sex with Nick would provide. I needed the sense of identity it would give me. I thought Mel would have understood that.

And then I forgot about Mel. Nick had opened my clothes and was eagerly caressing my body. He cupped my left breast between his two hands and started kissing and tonguing the nipple, drawing it into his mouth, letting me feel just the touch of his teeth, then flicking his tongue to and fro, till I felt a warm glow and a tingling in my skin. He did the same thing to my other breast then, and kissed all around, giving little nibbles and nips with his teeth. He kissed my belly, then wriggled lower and nuzzled down into the bush of my pubic hair.

I sighed and made myself more comfortable, lying on my back across the rear seat of the Jaguar. I spread my thighs wide and pushed my hips up. He buried his face between my legs and started sucking on my clitoris, making little "Mmmm, mmmm" noises as if it turned him on as much as it did me. His tongue lapped across the swelling, sensitive skin, then probed between my labia, and I felt the juices start to run inside me as his lips massaged all around my cunt and he kept sucking, licking, nibbling me with amazing devotion and energy.

He kept it up as if he could have done it all night, and I wasn't going to stop him—not yet, anyway. The wind howled around the car and a fresh shower of fine snow and frozen rain sprayed across the windshield, and I imagined the icy, gloomy, storm-torn landscape outside. But inside it was warm and snug and totally private, with just the dim glow from the instrument panel and the map-reading light.

I linked my hands behind Nick's head and pulled him harder up between my thighs, urging him to press harder with his lips and tongue. He did, and the sensations multiplied, radiating from my groin in warm waves. I let it all wash over me, let the sensations take over completely, and wriggled and writhed and gasped with delight as he went on and on sucking and licking at me, his hands reaching up to my breasts and caressing them almost as if he were worshiping them, touching tentatively, lightly, as if to say: May I? May I touch your beautiful body?

I felt myself getting very near orgasm. I started moving my hips up and down, up and down against his face, and he picked up the rhythm with his tongue, fast and insistent. I put my hands over his and pressed them hard onto my breasts. He curled his fingers and clung to me. "Just a little more," I said, "a little more, a little more . . ."

His licking and sucking reached a frenzied pitch. His tongue probed and worried at my clitoris. I felt as if I were getting hotter, and fuller, and higher, to the point where I would burst. I gasped and cried out, and then I climaxed, quivering and shivering with pleasure.

Lost in that ultimate moment, I think I made a lot of noise. As I came out of it I opened my eyes and saw Nick looking at me, breathing hard from his own exertions, and smiling. His mouth was wet from my juices. I pulled him to me and kissed him hard, tasting a marvelous mixture of myself and Martell cognac.

"Was that nice?" he said.

I laughed. "Good God, couldn't you tell?"

"Well, I suppose actually you did seem to rather enjoy it."

"And actually, so did you, rather," I said, mimicking his accent.

He turned slightly pink. "Yes, well, that's true," he said. "I've always had a liking for that kind of thing."

"Going down on a woman, you mean?"

"Ah, yes." He looked self-conscious.

I shifted so I was closer to him. I kissed him on the cheek, then on his neck, then I tickled his ear with my tongue. "What else do you have a liking for?" I whispered.

He hesitated. "Oh, well, you know, the usual kind of thing."

I kissed his forehead, his mouth, his chest. I reached down and touched his cock, which was bigger than before and standing up hard and ready. "Don't be shy," I murmured. "I'm a liberated American woman. Tell me what you really like."

He hesitated again. I could tell he had some kind of secret thing that he thought was shamefully kinky.

"Tell me!" I insisted, running my fingers lightly up and down his penis, then dabbing my finger in the tiny drop of lubricant that had exuded from its head and rubbing it around in little circles.

"Well," he said, watching my fingers at work on

him. "Well, I sometimes enjoy a kind of a passive role. I mean, sometimes, if a woman takes command, I find that rather, ah, interesting. I mean, she can tell me what to do for her, or she can do things to me herself."

"I understand," I told him quietly. "And, you know, that's not so unusual. I've known a number of men who exert power in their jobs and everyday life and like to be just the opposite—powerless—during sex with a woman."

"Really?" He still sounded uneasy about it.

"Some of them," I said, still touching his cock while I watched his face, "even like to be tied up while a woman makes love to them. Then they *can't* fight back." And my fingers closed around his cock, gently but very firmly holding it.

He took a deep breath, then let it out in a gasp. "I don't know," he said, "it all sounds . . . I mean, I'm not used to talking about this kind of thing."

How very British, I thought to myself. "All right," I said, kneeling on the car seat so that I could look down at him from a more commanding position, "there's no need for any more talking. Just lie down on your back." And while I spoke, I still kept a firm hold of his cock.

He understood immediately. "Like this, Christina?" He stretched out.

I surveyed him. Though he must have been a year or two older than I, his boyish looks and his shyness made me feel as if he were a schoolboy and I were his teacher. His lean body, in the soft lighting, looked young and defenseless. And against the slimness of his hips his cock seemed enormous. I found myself getting turned on already, and judging from his expression, the scene was arousing him, too.

"That's fine," I said, running the fingers of my free hand up and down his chest. "Your skin is so soft, very delicate . . ." I touched his face. "And you're such an attractive young man. Do you think I'm beautiful?"

He looked up at me, and my heavy breasts hanging above his face. "Oh, yes," he said. "You're quite lovely." He reached up to touch me.

I quickly held his wrist and put his arm back down on the seat. "I didn't say you could do that," I told him. "You're not to do anything unless I tell you to. In fact, I want you to put both your arms behind your back now, so you're lying on them. Go on, now."

He obeyed me, still staring up at me, his eyes wide.

"And you just keep your hands and arms behind you until I tell you different," I said. I started masturbating him then, pausing to moisten my hand with my tongue, then rub it up and down the shaft of his cock. "I expect you like that," I said.

"Yes. Yes, it feels marvelous."

I shifted around so that I was straddling him, with one knee on either side of his hips, and the head of his cock just a couple of inches below my vagina. "It'd feel even nicer inside me, wouldn't it?"

He nodded, speechless.

I smiled and leaned forward and low, till my nipples barely brushed the skin of his chest. I wriggled my shoulders and trailed my full breasts to and fro. And still in one hand I kept hold of his straining cock. "I don't know that I'm ready to let you come inside me yet," I told him mischievously.

"Please, Christina!"

I let more of my weight fall forward, till my breasts were squashed against his chest. The feel of flesh on flesh was seductive, incredibly arousing. I kissed him very, very lightly and with the tip of my tongue traced little paths across his lips.

"Oh, please, Christina!" he said again and squirmed on the seat.

I drew back. "I won't let you have me at all, if you don't do what I tell you," I said, noticing that one of his hands had started edging out from behind him, as if to grab my breast.

He quickly pushed the hand back behind him. "I'll do whatever you say, Christina."

"That's good." I lowered my hips then, till the head of his cock nudged just between my labia. I wiggled and wriggled, tantalizing him till he groaned and gasped. "I want you to suck my nipples first," I told him. "Then you can have me." I pulled his head up to my breast, I guided my nipple to his lips. His mouth opened wide and he sucked and tongued the flesh with an urgent desperation. It felt wonderful; my nipple tightened and stuck out pink and hard. I made him do the same to the other. Only then did I let him fall back on the seat, gasping for breath.

"Now, then," I whispered and at last guided his cock between my legs and slowly sat down on it.

He cried out—"Oh!"—and made little pushing motions with his hips. I started rocking up and down on him, slowly but persistently. His eyes were fixed on me. I ran my hands up my own body, displaying myself to him, turning first one way and then another. I cupped my breasts, rolled the nipples between fingers and thumb, parted my lips and ran my tongue over them, shook my long hair to and fro, and kept on moving on his cock, while he lay immobile, staring at me as if he could hardly believe it.

From the speed of his breathing and the tension in his body I knew I'd worked him up so much that he was close to coming. I slowly lowered my body onto him, and then I kissed him on the mouth, very deep and long, pushing my tongue between his lips, while my hips increased their tempo. "It's nice," I whispered to him. "It's so nice. You can help now." I raised my hips till his cock almost came out of me and held myself motionless. "Fuck me from underneath now. You can do it, if you want it."

He braced his legs and brought his hips up from under me as I had told him to. His cock jammed deep into me.

"Faster," I told him. "Come on, now." I wriggled my body, rubbing my breasts across his chest.

His cock started plunging in and out, in and out. His naked body made sticky rubbing noises on the leather upholstery. Perspiration broke out on his forehead. His breathing was fast and shallow. His lean body tensed and quivered under me. Again and again he brought his hips up, plunging his cock in.

"Now," I whispered, feeling very aroused myself and only just managing to keep control of the situation. "Now, do you want me to let you bring your hands out and touch me?"

"Yes!" he gasped.

I rubbed my breasts across his chest again. "Are you sure?"

"Yes!"

I tried to look as if I were weighing up the situation. "Just your . . . left hand, then," I told him.

Immediately he was touching me, my face, my lips, my neck, and then my breast, the fingers digging into the softness, the thumb pressing down onto the nipple. His movements became erratic and desperate. He freed his right hand, too, and held on to me with a kind of helpless passion. It got to the point where I could no longer hold myself back. I started moving just as frantically as he was, slamming my hips down to meet every upthrust of his. Our bodies slapped against each other. Our breathing sounded harsh and loud in the car. My fingernails dug into his shoulders.

The pressure of the fingernails seemed to set him off.

His eyes widened, his back arched, and he moaned. I felt his cock strain and I dug my nails in harder and then harder still. He cried out and came, twisting and jerking under me.

Seeing him come was the stimulus I needed myself. I bore down on him so that my clitoris was pressed firmly against the shaft of his spasming cock. It sent a wave of pure pleasure through me and I climaxed, drowning his cries with my own.

Then I relaxed, stretching out over him, covering his body with mine. His cock, still held inside me, gradually started shrinking. Together we enjoyed the afterglow of our lovemaking.

Eventually we separated our bodies and wriggled around so that we were sitting side by side. His face was flushed and he looked a bit self-conscious. "That was quite delicious," I told him, thinking he might need that kind of morale boost.

"I don't normally confess that kind of thing about myself to a woman I've only just met," he said.

"You mean enjoying a passive role?"

"That's right," he replied, avoiding my eyes.

I kissed him on the cheek. "It's nothing to be embarrassed about. Some people like it one way, some people like it another. Me, I can get off on all kinds of things."

"You're not just humoring me, I hope, Christina."

"Of course not! Hell, I could have gone a lot further. I mean, it's lucky you didn't have any rope in the car. I'd have really taken advantage of you then!"

He retrieved his shirt and started putting it on. He gave me a cautious glance. Then he seemed to relax a little. "Well, I must say, you're a remarkable woman. Remarkable."

"So I'm told."

He finished buttoning his shirt. Already he was looking more like a young English gentleman again, self-possessed and in control. He reached out, touched my naked breasts, then leaned close and kissed me briefly on the lips. "I do want to be sure, my dear, that you realize it's only in moments of passion that I adopt that kind of defenseless persona. I'm really not like that at all, at other times."

"Of course. And I'm not the kind of woman who normally orders men around, either. It's just sexual role-playing."

He laughed shortly. "Well, you Americans have a label for everything. Remarkable. Can you reach my trousers for me, Christina?"

I found them for him, then located my own clothes, and we both got dressed. The windows of the car had become completely misted over on the insides, enclosing us in our little private world of brown leather seats and walnut trim, thick carpeting and dim lighting. We climbed back into the front of the car, and I gave Nick a tight hug. "Back to the castle now?" I said. "It must be late."

He checked the dashboard clock. "Almost midnight." He used a cloth to wipe the condensation off the windows. Then he leaned forward, peering out. "My God, look down there."

Somcthing in his voice went right through me. Suddenly I no longer felt the warm, relaxed afterglow of our lovemaking. The tensions I had felt at the castle came back to me full force.

"What is it?" I asked.

He turned out all the lighting inside the car, so that it was easier to look at the landscape outside. "There. Above the castle."

I stared out. My eyes gradually became accustomed to the darkness. Then I saw what he had seen.

Above the castle was a faint luminescence, like a swirling cloud of pale blue-green gas, glowing softly in the stormy darkness. As we watched, it pulsed and writhed and extended itself like a vaporous column linking the castle to the storm clouds hanging above it. The glow was faint but definitely not an illusion; now and then, at its brightest, it reflected on the battlements of the castle.

I found myself clutching Nick, and I realized he was clutching me, too.

"It's over the east wing, you realize," he said. "And I happen to know that Zenya sometimes goes into a period of meditation—he calls it spiritual communion—on his own in there, about this time at night."

"Jesus Christ," I whispered. Then: "Do you think he knows what he's doing?"

"How can he?"

"I'm scared, Nick."

His arm tightened around my shoulders. "Naturally. Still, it's not the kind of mystery you can just turn your back on and walk away from, is it?"

I saw what he meant. If I ran from the castle now, I'd be passing up a unique—and unrepeatable—experience.

We watched that glowing gaseous form for another few minutes. The wind hissed and moaned around the car. Occasionally a dim trace of moonlight showed between storm clouds in the south.

And then suddenly, without warning, the phosphorescence vanished. One moment it was there; the next it was gone.

"But it *was* there," I murmured. "We both saw it."

"Indeed we did." He started the car. "Evidently Zenya finished his spiritual communion and has gone to bed. Maybe we should follow suit." He turned on the headlights, backed the car with difficulty, turned, and headed for the castle.

"Stay with me tonight, Christina," he said.

"I was just going to ask if I could," I told him. "This isn't the time or place to sleep alone."

CHAPTER SIX

In Nick Weston's bed that night, I managed to sleep soundly, reassured by his presence beside me, and sedated by a couple of Valiums that I happened to have with me.

I slept late, and when I finally awoke I felt a sense of well-being and relaxation. As I opened my eyes I realized that the bed now only had me in it—which made sense, because I imagined Nick was the kind who would be an early riser. But at the same time, I had the strangest feeling that someone was watching me.

Daylight was streaming into the room—an antique-style guest room very similar to my own. I blinked, rolled over, and found I was right—there *was* someone watching me.

Zenya was standing at the foot of the bed, his hands clasped in front of him. As usual, he was wearing his embroidered gold robe. His dark eyes regarded me steadily, studiously.

"My God, you have a way of just *appearing* places," I said, feeling groggy and sleepy, and self-conscious, too—I had no idea what I must have looked like, with my hair all tousled, and no makeup on my face. "I mean, you could at least knock or something."

He went on studying my face and didn't answer, as if my conversation was too trivial to be bothered with. Then, deliberately, he walked around the bed, closer to me. Gently he placed his hand on my forehead and stroked it. "You are well today," he said.

I cursed myself for feeling so awkward, so self-conscious in his presence. I didn't know what it was that enabled him somehow to take control of the situation every time we were face-to-face. "Sure, I feel fine," I said.

"I was concerned for you last night," he went on. "When you were overcome, in our Circle."

The word "Circle" brought back a sudden rush of images—the little black room, the flood of voices, my own fear of the darkness and the unknown. "I just fainted," I said. "It's not like me to pull that kind of stunt. I mean, I don't want you to think I'm the kind of fragile creature that often goes around fainting all over the place."

Slowly he sat down on the bed, facing me. His dark skin and dark eyes were a compelling combination. When he smiled, behind his neatly trimmed mustache, he seemed very kind and benevolent. When his expression became more serious, he was so intense it was frightening.

"You are no fragile creature, Christina," he said. "Just the opposite: you are very strong. I could feel it in the Circle last night. Your energy was there."

"You mean it?"

"Of course."

"I was afraid I wasn't contributing much." While I said the words, part of me saw how mystical the conversation sounded. Yet it was a description of something that had actually happened to me, something I had lived through. Mystical or not, it was the truth.

"You have a lot to contribute," he said. "It is good that you came here. I have a talent—a sensitivity. But I need the help of others to explore it. The Circle gives me my strength. Did you not feel it yourself?"

I laughed uneasily. "Sure. It gripped me like . . . like

a pair of handcuffs. I tried to pull out at the beginning, but I couldn't even take my hands off the table."

He nodded. "It confirms what I just said. You have much spirit." Casually, then, before I realized what he was doing, he pulled the bedcovers down and put his hand over one of my naked breasts. His touch was firm and deliberate. His hand was warm and soft. His grip was hard. He leaned forward, held my shoulder with his other hand, and pressed me back into the pillows. His robe rustled as he shifted his weight over me. My mouth opened in surprise. His face came closer to mine, very close, till his eyes filled my field of view. He kissed me then, forcefully but with a kind of yearning, romantic spirit. Surprised as I was, at the same time I felt a flood of sudden responses. He had such magnetism, such power. I don't think I could have resisted him if I'd wanted to—and suddenly I knew I didn't want to. All my muscles went limp and I opened myself to him. My breathing speeded up. My skin tingled.

He drew back then and smiled at me like an indulgent father. His grip on my breast relaxed, and his fingers trailed lightly over the skin. "And that is just one aspect of your spirit, Christina," he said softly. "You are a passionate woman."

I wanted him to stop talking. I wanted him to get in bed with me. I didn't know what to say.

"There are all kinds of energies in the mind," he was going on. "Sexual energies are much a part of the spirit. We tap the libido when we tap the soul, whether we know it or not. The sexual impulse is a life impulse. The most fundamental of all. Have you read Reich?"

"Huh?" I was still in a sensual daze.

"Wilhelm Reich. A disciple of Freud who developed his own philosophy. You will find his books in my library downstairs. Please read them. It is important."

He stood up, as if the encounter was over as far as he was concerned.

I touched my breast where he had touched it. I rubbed my hand slowly over the skin. "Where are you going?" I said, looking up at him. "Wouldn't you rather stay here with me?"

He studied me for a minute. "Now is not the time," he said softly.

I've never been a woman who accepts rejection easily. I felt slapped by his toying with me and now leaving. I pulled the covers quickly up over myself. "Okay," I said, trying to sound uninterested.

"But perhaps you should sleep in your own room tonight," he went on. "Alone, in your bed."

And then he turned and walked to the door. "Remember to read the books," he said over his shoulder as he walked out.

I lay in bed digesting this new twist of events. On one level I wanted to know more about the supernatural experience I had been in the previous evening—so naturally I would listen to anything Zenya had to tell me. On another level I just wanted *him* . . . wanted him to shut up and make love to me. The two things were hopelessly tangled up.

But in a way, wasn't that what he'd been saying? That the sexual drive was all part of the spiritual effects? And hadn't he just implied that I could expect a nighttime visit from him if I waited for him alone in my room tonight?

I decided I didn't have anything to complain about. I was just too impatient, that was all.

I showered, dressed, and then went downstairs to the dining room. The morning was bright, and sunlight struck through intermittently between a sky of puffy white clouds. The landscape outside was still bleak and snow-covered, but it shone brilliant white. Birds were singing.

In the dining room I found Nick Weston sitting with his elbows on the table, reading a newspaper. He stood up as soon as I walked in, and I went over to him and kissed him on the cheek, feeling slightly guilty about my recent sexual desires for Zenya. "Hi, Nick," I said cheerfully. "You were up early."

"Always go for a walk before breakfast," he said. "And today's the one day a week when Jenkins goes to Hereford for supplies. He came back with some newspapers. I like to keep up with the political news, such as it is. God knows how long I can hide out here instead of being in the House, voting on one bill or another. Anyway, want some fried eggs? They'll cook you some right away, and toast, porridge, whatever you like."

"Kippers?" I had a vague idea any true Englishman ate kippers for breakfast.

"Certainly, certainly." He went and got one of the middle-aged waitresses, and, sure enough, I was shortly eating a classic English breakfast.

Afterward I went and found Jenkins, who was supervising a young assistant in the laying of logs for a new fire in the reception room.

"Mr. Jenkins," I said, "is there any possibility of my telephoning America from here?"

He turned his rheumy eyes toward me. "Certainly, madam. There's a guests' phone in the small room just across the hall."

"Thanks," I said. "I have a telephone credit card, so there won't be any charges."

"Miss Van Bell," he called after me. "Just one moment."

"What is it?"

"You do realize the five-hour time difference? Although it is half-past eleven here, it will be much earlier there. About six-thirty."

"Yes, of course. Thank you."

He shrugged and turned back to his task of building the fire. I shook my head in puzzlement. There was something off-key about that little old man knowing the facts of international time zones.

I managed to get through to the operator, who connected me to the international operator, who took my credit-card number and checked it, and then put my call through. All of this took a long time; by the time I heard the far-off ringing tone, it was almost midday. Fine, I thought, that's seven o'clock in the morning in New York. Mel will just be waking up anyway, to go to work.

Sure enough, he answered on the third ring, sounding still a little sleepy.

"Mel," I said, "it's Christina."

The line was terrible—a mess of cracklings and hissing noises. I remembered how it had sounded when Zenya had called me from the castle, while I was at the Ritz. This was not much better.

"Christina?" he said, obviously waking up in a hurry. "Where are you?"

"Downton Castle," I told him. "Where did you expect?"

He laughed. "I should have known you'd go through with it. So what's the story?"

I knew right away I couldn't begin to explain. He'd think I'd gone crazy. "There's a simple explanation for everything, but I can't talk long," I said. "Look, I want you, if you can, to do some checking for me. About that man Schmidt who handled my sister's affairs. I want to know where he is now and if there's ever been any suspicion of him acting unethically. I've got good reason to think that there actually was something wrong with the way he handled our inheritance."

There was a long pause. "You serious?"

"Of course! Look, I know you've got a hell of a lot of other things to do, but this is so important."

Another pause. "You sound strange, Christina." And now there was worry in his voice.

"No, I'm fine." I tried to make it sound casual, but I could hear myself, and it sounded wrong. "Mel, please, just help me out. I'll give you the number here." I read it to him off the phone dial.

"You're staying there for a while?"

"I . . . suppose I am, yes."

"Christina, are you all right?" Now he sounded really nervous. "You're not . . . is someone else there? Are you being compelled to make this call? Look, if you are, and you can't talk to me freely, just say to me now, say, 'I've got to go.' If you say that I'll know you're in trouble and I'll call the police, or come right over myself."

"Mel, stop it! You're crazy! Darling, you're lovable, but you've got criminals on the brain. I'm in no trouble at all, I'm having a fine time. I just want to follow up on this thing about my sister, Fran, that's all."

A long, suspicious silence. "Okay," he said, obviously wondering now if other people were listening in on the line. "I'll get back to you as soon as I have any information. When are you coming home?"

"In just a few days," I told him, though the whole idea of *coming home* had already begun to seem meaningless. "Must hang up now. See you soon."

And when I put the phone down I felt relieved. It was not that I'd had to lie to Mel; just that he couldn't possibly understand what had happened to me. He was like a stranger now. And I knew that he was the kind of sensitive guy who would hear that in my voice and wonder what was happening.

I tried not to feel guilty. I found my way to the library that Zenya had mentioned, and there, surrounded by leather-bound volumes in antique glass-fronted bookcases, I sat down to read Wilhelm Reich.

I didn't get very far. There was a lot of stuff about orgone energy and sexual forces that didn't altogether make sense to me, and it was kind of crazy-mystical, and my mind kept wandering back to Zenya. No matter how I tried to be rational and reasonable, I was pissed at him for having tempted me up in my room and then having left without following through. The more I thought about it, the more frustrated I began to feel.

And then the door of the library opened and Nick walked in. He said hello to me and walked to one of the bookcases.

I put down Wilhelm Reich, stood up, and went over to Nick. I came up quietly behind him and placed my hands on his tweed-jacketed shoulders. I let the front of my body press gently against his back. "What are you looking for?" I said in his ear.

"Oh, I, ah, just wanted to check on something." He turned around, which brought him face-to-face with me. He looked embarrassed to find himself suddenly so close to me. "What were you doing in here, Christina?" he said.

"Just hanging out," I said. "And feeling kind of frustrated, if you must know."

He tried to disengage himself from me, but the bookcase was right behind him, so he didn't have much room to maneuver. "Frustrated? How do you mean?" he asked.

I stroked the side of his neck. Then I ran my fingers through his carefully combed hair. It was a pleasure to dishevel it. And then I kissed him hard on the mouth. "I think that answers your question," I told him.

He had turned quite pink. He was so wonderfully inhibited; it made me feel powerful over him, which was what I needed, after having been left hanging by Zenya.

Nick glanced at the open library door. "Really, Christina, this is rather indiscreet."

"All right." I went over to the door and closed it. Then I walked back to him and kissed him again. This time he responded a bit more, and I thought I could feel his cock swelling up a little, pressing against me. But still he was embarrassed and edgy. "Christina, just anyone could walk in on us here," he protested.

I gave him a hard look. I was sure as hell not going to let *him* leave me hanging, with some feeble excuse about it not being the right time and place.

I walked quickly to where I had been reading the Reich book. I picked it up, went to the library door, stooped down and managed to jam the book into the gap between the door and the floor. I gave it a couple of good kicks and wedged it in tight. "Now *nobody* can walk right in on us," I told him.

"But, my God, Christina, you shouldn't do that! I mean, you simply don't use a leather-bound book to wedge a door! Most of these volumes are first editions. Didn't anyone ever tell you how to treat literature?" He looked quite shocked.

"Didn't anyone ever tell you how to treat a lady?" I said, closing in on him.

"What do you mean?"

"You don't say no to a lady." I kissed him again, very passionately this time. And at last I felt him really responding. I savored it, feeling my influence on him. "Let's go sit down on the hearth rug in front of the fire," I told him.

I took him by the hand and led him after me. A

couple of logs were burning in a big marble fireplace. The wood hissed; the flames flickered. On the floor was a fine Indian rug. Ranged around the hearth were big, comfortable, high-backed, leather-upholstered chairs. It was the perfect spot for a leisurely midmorning seduction.

I took Nick by his shoulders and pushed him down onto the floor. He looked uncomfortable, probably afraid he would get his clothes creased. Well, there was a simple answer to that. I started undressing him.

"Christina, I really don't think this is wise," he was saying. But at the same time I could see he was breathing faster now, and his eyes kept coming back to my body.

I pulled off his pants and tossed them on one of the chairs. Then I pulled his underwear off. His cock was already large and hard. I looked at it, and then looked up at his face. "Your genitals have the right idea," I told him. I reached out and held his penis and masturbated him lightly. "Stop protesting, and enjoy it." I made it sound like an order, knowing his weakness for women taking the dominant role.

"Oh, Christina . . ." His voice stopped suddenly, and he gasped, as I fell down onto him and quickly took his cock into my mouth. I sucked on just the end of it, very hard, and felt it swell between my lips. Then slowly I took more of the length of it into my mouth. I ran my fingertips through his pubic hair and then cupped his balls in my hand, playing with them very gently, teasingly.

He slumped back onto the rug. He was breathing fast and his eyes were open wide, as if he couldn't believe what I was doing to him. My head bobbed up and down, up and down. I raked my fingernails along the insides of his thighs. Then I started massaging, insistently, behind his balls, where his prostate lay just under the skin. I knew the pressure on that spot would increase his need for fulfillment. I kept doing that, and kept sucking on him, and felt all his muscles gradually become more and more tense. His hips shifted. His balls contracted. He was very nearly coming. I could hear him gasping for breath.

Then, when he was right on the edge of orgasm, I took my mouth and hands off him and sat back on the rug, watching him. I was breathing fast myself, partly because it had been hard work, but partly because it had turned me on, feeling his arousal completely under my control. I looked at him stretched out on his back, with his cock straining hot and hard and wet. He was still fully dressed from the waist up; I liked the contrast between his naked legs and his respectable jacket-and-tie outfit.

I touched his cock fleetingly with my fingers. "You want more," I said, and it wasn't a question, it was a statement of obvious fact.

He nodded dumbly. He started to sit up, and he reached for me.

I pushed him gently back down. "You'll have to be patient," I told him. "You just lie there."

I stood up slowly and brushed my long blond hair out of my face. I surveyed him, lying beneath me. He stared up with a kind of helpless yearning look on his face. I liked that.

"Just lie there and watch me," I told him. "Until I tell you you can do anything else." And then, slowly, I started pulling my skirt up, revealing my legs to him. I ran my hands over my thighs and pulled the skirt higher, very gradually. I was wearing stockings but no panties. My pale pubic hair came into view.

I stood with my legs apart, one foot on either side of Nick so that I was literally standing over him. I wriggled my hips and reached down between my legs and pushed one finger into my vagina. There was a faint wet noise. I started working my finger in and out and all around my clitoris. I sighed happily.

"It feels good," I told him. "Maybe it would feel even better if your tongue was here instead of my finger." I looked down at him. He realized what I wanted and quickly sat up. I moved forward a little so that his head was between my thighs. I put one hand behind his neck and urged him closer to me.

I loved it, standing there, with him sitting on the floor between my legs and straining to lick my clitoris. My thighs were pressed right up against his face, almost suffocating him, but I didn't care. I pulled his head harder against my groin, forcing him to satisfy me. His tongue wriggled to and fro across my labia and probed into my cunt. He sucked on me and worked his lips around my clitoris, all wet and warm and slippery and delicious.

I stood there savoring it. The fire crackled in the hearth. Faint sunlight filtered through the diamond-paned windows. The room smelled of leather and old book paper and wood smoke. I sighed happily as Nick's busy tongue and mouth sent tingles of pleasure spreading from my vagina all through my body.

"All right," I said after a little while. "That's enough." I released him and allowed him to lie back down on the floor. He looked dazed. He was out of breath and his hair was all mussed up. His jacket was rumpled and his tie was askew. His face was bright red and his mouth was all wet. I glanced down at his cock and found it standing up even bigger and harder than before.

I reached behind me and unzipped my skirt. I kicked it off and then removed my blouse. I took my time, undoing each button carefully, while he lay watching me with a desperate yearning look on his face. Slowly I revealed my breasts; I cast the blouse aside and started stroking my fingers up and down my body. I turned first one way and then the other so that he could admire me. I cupped my breasts and held them up high on my chest. I rubbed the nipples between finger and thumb. It was like an aphrodisiac to me, showing off my body to him.

I bent my head down and held my breast up high so that I could just reach its nipple with the tip of my tongue. I licked it, then rubbed my fingertip in little circles around the nipple, in the moisture. I did the same with my other breast. It all felt so good.

"You can touch yourself," I said to Nick then. "In fact, I want you to. Go on, touch your cock while I watch you." I smiled wickedly. "But I warn you, if you make yourself come, I'll be very angry."

Slowly, shyly, he started moving his hand up and down his cock.

"Do it a little faster," I told him, still standing over him, with my hands massaging my own breasts.

Dumbly he obeyed me. I realized I had worked some kind of spell on him; he seemed totally under my control.

I let one of my hands drop back between my legs and started touching myself while I watched him. And at the same time, he was watching me, staring up with wide eyes.

"I expect you'd like to be able to put your cock where my fingers are now," I said softly, working my fingers in and out of myself. I squirmed and jerked my hips, enjoying being naked and desirable and unattainable. "Would you like that?"

"Yes," he gasped. I could see he was still masturbating himself, and once again he was close to orgasm.

"Well, maybe I'll let you," I told him. "Maybe I'll allow you to fuck me." As I spoke, I knelt down slowly, astride him, just above his hips.

He reached for me immediately. I caught his wrists and pushed them away from my nakedness.

"No, you're not allowed to touch," I told him. "Not yet, anyway. And I didn't tell you that you could stop masturbating." I directed one of his hands back to his cock.

He groaned and shifted uneasily under me, stretched out on the floor. "Christina . . ."

"Shhh." I placed my finger across his lips. "If you want to have me, you'll have to do exactly what I say."

He closed his eyes. He seemed in a wonderful agony of need for me. I wanted to prolong it and prolong it. I wanted to have him absolutely craving me.

I leaned forward and touched my mouth very, very gently to his. His lips opened and he tried to kiss me hard; I pulled back immediately and held him down, out of reach of me. Then I did it to him again. He made a desperate moaning sound.

Finally I relented a little. I kissed him, and for just a few seconds I pressed the whole of my naked body onto him and forced my tongue into his mouth. I writhed over him. And then, quickly, I pulled back.

"Soon, now," I told him. "Soon you can have me."

"Don't make me wait any longer," he gasped.

"What's the matter?" I asked playfully. "Don't you like being tantalized?" I reached behind me and ran my fingertips lightly up and down his straining cock.

He groaned and clenched his fists.

"All right, Nick," I murmured. I was very aroused myself now, and there was a limit to my own self-control. I edged down till my ass was over his hips. I lowered myself very slowly, till the head of his cock fleetingly touched the mouth of my vagina. "Don't move now," I cautioned him. "You have to lie there without moving."

He groaned again. But he did as I told him.

Slowly, inch by inch, I let myself down onto him, till I was sitting on him, with the entire length of his cock embedded in my vagina. I wriggled my hips from side to side. My breasts jiggled as I did so, and I saw him watching me, flat on his back, still with that desperate look in his eyes.

"All right now," I told him. "You can sit up."

He gasped and struggled and levered himself up. His hands grabbed my breasts with a kind of eager desperation. His mouth closed on mine. I clutched him against me and kissed him back, just as hard as he was kissing me. Suddenly all the pent-up passion was being allowed out.

His jacket was rough and unpleasant against my naked skin. I managed to pull the garment off him. And then his shirt. I didn't care whether I ripped it or not; several buttons were torn off. He didn't even seem to notice. His tie—I couldn't unknot his tie, there wasn't time, it didn't matter. So there on the library floor, in front of the fire, we had sudden violent passionate sex together, me completely naked and him with all his clothes ripped off except for his socks and his tie! I mean, if you're going to have sex with a member of Parliament, what better way is there?

I bounced up and down on his cock and wiggled my hips in a little frenzy of excitement. I clutched him up against me and we kissed and kissed, mouths wide, tongues touching. Warm sun struck through the windows onto my naked back. Gentle heat from the open hearth played onto our bodies. The Indian carpet was like velvet under us. His hands were all over me, grasping and holding and clutching at me. His cock seemed enormous.

Finally we slumped to one side and lay tangled together, side by side, on the floor. His cock was still jammed into me, and he fucked me in a burst of urgent thrusts of his hips. I closed my eyes and let my head fall back as I savored the waves of erotic feeling.

I heard him gasping and felt his movements becoming erratic. I let go of the last vestiges of my own self-control. The orgasm hit me in a succession of powerful shuddering bursts of fulfillment. And I sensed him coming, too.

I reached for him, found him, hugged him, kissed him, and lay there with him on the floor. We were both dizzy and out of breath. The excitement gradually dissipated, fading into a mellow glow, like the logs in the fire, subsiding into a bed of red embers. Gradually his cock shrank, and finally it went out of me.

As Nick came back to reality, I saw his blissed-out expression change to a look of guilty confusion. He became aware of where he was and he self-consciously pulled back from me a little. He realized he was still wearing his tie, and he turned pink, and then couldn't help laughing. "My God, Christina," he said. "I mean, really, you're . . . you're a disgrace."

"*I* am?" I said, raising my eyebrows.

He sat up. He looked at my naked body, stretched out languorously. He looked away. Then he couldn't resist looking back again. "You're a corrupting influence," he said. "I mean, a man of my position . . ."

"Didn't you enjoy your position just now?" I asked innocently.

He groped for words. He gestured helplessly. "Well, of course I enjoyed it!"

I kissed him on the cheek. "You're a dear."

"But really, you know, I mean, it wouldn't do for this kind of thing to happen too often. I mean, if Zenya found us, I'm sure he wouldn't approve."

True, I thought to myself. On the other hand, it was Zenya's fault for having gotten me all turned on in the first place.

"Well, what do you English say? Let's not cry over spilt . . . spilt semen," I finished, noticing a little stain on the oriental rug. "Oh, hell. Still, I don't suppose anyone will notice."

"My shirt has had half its buttons ripped off," he said, ignoring me. He held up the garment. "Christina, really! This is a Moss Bros. shirt, and it cost me a fortune!"

"Worth it," I told him. "Worth every minute of it."

"I can see it's liable to be expensive, knowing you. I'll have to sneak upstairs and change into clean clothes before lunch. Look at this jacket! It needs to be pressed now. I notice none of *your* clothes suffered in our romantic interlude."

He had a point there. "That's because *I* seduced *you,*" I told him. "If you hadn't been so uptight about it, I wouldn't have had to take control like that." I started getting dressed.

He pulled his underwear and pants on, and tied his shoes. "Hm. Well, let's say no more about it."

Obviously it was embarrassing to him to remember how I had dominated him playfully through our love-making, and how he had enjoyed it.

I ran my fingers through my hair, trying to get rid of some of the tangles. Then I walked to the door, reached down, and pulled out the book I had used to wedge it shut.

As I did so, there was a mellow sound from outside the door, echoing through the hallway.

"They're ringing the gong for lunch," said Nick. "Oh, hell. Christina, you'll be the end of me."

"Are you complaining?" I said, catching him by the arm and pulling him close to me.

He looked into my face. He showed conflicting emotions. Suddenly he kissed me. "Of course I'm not complaining," he muttered. And then: "Wait for me in the dining room while I run up and put on a decent shirt."

Lunch at the castle was informal. The staff provided sandwiches; the guests helped themselves. Zenya and his girl-in-white, Stella, stayed out of sight upstairs. And Masterson and Alexandra appeared only long enough to grab some food and retreat back to his or her room.

Nick showed up with his hair combed and his clothes once again immaculate. We pretended polite interest in each other. Making conversation, I asked if he'd read any of the Reich books Zenya had told me to read. "Well," he said, "I'm quite prepared to believe there's some truth in Reich. But you know, a lot of great men —and I regard Zenya as a great man, in his way— have been influenced by lesser men. They've taken philosophies that were inadequate, and they've made them work by adding the missing ingredient of their own genius."

I felt I'd just been given a lecture by a school principal, and I said so. He laughed self-consciously. "Sorry," he said. "That's the trouble with us politicians, always making speeches." He finished eating. "Well, back to work."

"Work? What work?"

"I'm on a parliamentary committee, and there's a report to be prepared. Can't get away from that kind of thing altogether."

"Well, let me know if you need some rest and recreation," I said, feeling slightly miffed.

He leaned down and kissed me on the forehead. "Perhaps tonight?" he murmured.

I just smiled at him.

"We're supposed to use the days here to reflect and

meditate and educate our spiritual selves," he went on. "Or didn't you know?"

"I've never been too good at that kind of thing."

"Well, if you can't get into Wilhelm Reich, try J. W. Dunne. And if he doesn't appeal, try—"

I waved him away. "Go write your report."

He laughed and left.

I stood up and paced around the house. The snowy wilderness outside looked uninviting; I didn't feel like taking a walk in it, or going for a drive. In fact, I was simply impatient for evening to arrive, with its promise of another séance, and then, later, maybe a visit to my room from Zenya himself.

Restlessly I walked upstairs and into the west wing. I opened the door to my room . . . at least, I had thought it was my room. As I walked in, I realized it looked slightly different. And then with a shock I saw that it was occupied.

Alexandra was there. She was lying stretched out on her back on the bed, with her shirt unbuttoned and open, exposing her high, firm breasts. From the waist down she was completely naked, her legs spread wide and her knees pulled up. Prostrating himself in front of her pussy was none other than Masterson, fully dressed, his portly figure heaving and squirming as he licked and sucked at her vagina.

Alexandra had heard me come in, and she lay glaring at me. She tried to keep Masterson's head pressed between her legs, but he realized something was going on. Before I had time to creep out and leave them to it, Masterson wriggled free of Alexandra's grasp and sat up, gasping and blinking. His face was all wet; he rubbed his handkerchief quickly across his mouth. He turned bright red.

"I'm sorry," I was saying. "I came in the wrong door, I thought this was my room. I'll forget I saw anything."

Alexandra was still glaring at me. Masterson was muttering something about it being an inexcusable breach of his privacy. I turned and got out of there as quickly as I could and retreated to my room—the right room, this time.

It was no surprise when my door opened a couple of minutes later and Alexandra walked in, now with her shirt buttoned and her pants back on. She looked both aroused—her face was still flushed—and irritated. "Well, you surely screwed up that one," were her first words.

I stood up and walked to her. "Truly, it was a mistake," I said. "If only you'd locked the door or something—"

"There aren't any locks! Haven't you noticed? They've all been removed. Part of some belief of Zenya's or something, dammit." She paced restlessly to the window and back again. Her movements were lithe as a cat's, and all her mannerisms were quick and precise. Like her mind, I thought to myself. She's the sort of girl who knows exactly what she wants. And goes after it. A bit like me, except I was more interested in indulging myself than in going out running around. I was more the type who liked to pay for something to be done. Alexandra was the type who went and did it herself.

"Well, I've said I'm sorry," I finished up. "That's all I can do. What happened, anyway?"

"Oh, he's run off and hidden somewhere. It's a farce. He's guilty about being unfaithful to his wife back in Texas." She threw herself down casually on my bed and squirmed around as if trying to get comfortable. "This is the closest I'd come to seducing him, too."

I laughed. "I shouldn't have thought he was that great a catch, frankly," I said. "I mean, he's a sweet man, but he must be twice your age."

Alexandra just stared at me moodily. Her thoughts were unreadable.

"I should have thought Nick was more—"

"No, I told you yesterday, Nick's your type, not mine. He drives a Jaguar; Masterson has an Eldo."

I tried to figure that one out, but Alexandra started talking again. "Come over here, Christina," she said. "Or does anyone call you Chris? I'd prefer to call you that."

"Whatever you like," I said, suddenly feeling cautious of this young woman. I sat down on the foot of the bed.

Alexandra was still watching me, still thinking hidden things that I couldn't guess at. "The outfit's nice," she said, her eyes looking from my face to my clothes. I was wearing a simple gray dress, belted at the waist. "Must have cost an arm and a leg."

"I got it in Paris," I said. "I have enough money to be able to indulge myself, on clothes."

Alexandra sat up impulsively and leaned closer. She touched the fabric. "Feels nice." Her hand moved up my side. "It fits perfectly. Was it made for you?"

"Yes."

Her hand passed casually over my breast. "It's flattering, you know that? Not that you need it. You're very full breasted."

This time I didn't say anything.

"You're a beautiful woman, Chris. Beautiful and rich." Her hand dropped down to my leg and rested there.

"You're attractive yourself, and you know it," I said carefully.

"Yes, and one day I'll be rich, too. I mean, I have money now, but one day I'll have a *lot* of money." There was a quiet determination in her voice. Then she looked back up at my face. "There's so many things I want, Chris. You know what I want now?"

"What?"

"I want you, Chris." Her eyes were steadily focused on my face.

I laughed. "Oh, come on."

"But it's true. I do. God, you must have had sex with women. You're a sophisticated person."

I just smiled and said nothing.

"Masterson got me all horny and then you came in and then he ran off and I'm just *hanging,* Chris. I mean, Christ, it's your fault, isn't it?" Her hand rubbed my thigh, through my dress. Impulsively she took my shoulder with her other hand and pulled me close to her and started kissing my neck. I smelled her perfume and felt her lithe body, tense and full of energy and impatience. Her mouth moved up my neck, to my ear, then my cheek.

"There're other ways to deal with frustration," I said.

"But masturbating's no fun." Her lips crept around to mine. I turned my head, but she pursued me. She pushed me and I fell backward, losing my balance. She was on me immediately, her slim body pressing all over me, her mouth trying to close over mine, her hands in my hair. "Please, Chris. You said I was attractive. It'll be nice."

"All right, all right!" Actually I was more worried about her creasing my clothes than anything else. "But let's get this straight—are you basically gay, Alexandra?"

"Oh, hell, no. I just find women attractive sometimes as well as men."

"All right," I said carefully, "just so long as this is a one-time thing, not an emotional thing. I got into a heavy relationship once with a gay woman, and it was hell getting out of it."

"Oh, no." She smiled and looked quite childlike. She reached out unexpectedly and caressed the roundness of my breasts. "No, I'm not like that." Her hand rubbed over my breasts in a slow, circular motion. "I just want you now, that's all. Don't you feel like it? Not even a little? Aren't you interested in me at all?"

"Well, I don't know. This is kind of a sudden idea. Everything here has been happening kind of suddenly."

She lay down beside me, pressed close to me, and started kissing the side of my neck again. Her lips were amazingly soft and gentle and gave me little cascades of shivery feelings. "But that's what's so great about this place," she whispered, squirming against me so that the whole length of her body rubbed against mine. "Anything can happen, anything at all." Her lips started toward mine again, and this time I didn't turn my head away. Alexandra *was* an attractive girl, and I knew I'd enjoy it at the same time that it would make her happy, and anyway, what else was there to do this afternoon, with Nick attending to his political homework and Zenya shut away with his mistress in the east wing of the castle doing who knew what?

Alexandra's mouth touched mine lightly, hardly making contact at all. I felt her experience a little shiver of excitement. Then her lips came close again and her tongue crept out and delicately, lightly, licked around the edges of my mouth. And then her mouth closed over mine more firmly, and her tongue probed for mine, and her breasts pressed into mine.

It was a strong, heady, demanding kiss. She caressed my face with her hands while she kissed me; her finger-tips were light and gentle. She shook her head and her hair fell down around us, soft and tickly, sweetly perfumed. She rolled onto me and her groin pressed into mine. She rolled her hips impatiently.

"I want it," she whispered. "God, I'm so hot and

horny, and there hasn't *been* anyone, I've been chasing Masterson ever since I got here, listening to all that shit about how he's never cheated on his wife in thirty years of married life and . . . I *want* it, Chris."

I still wondered why she'd ruled out Nick Weston, but now wasn't the time to pursue that. "How do you want it?" I said.

"Oh, just touch me—your hand—I know you'll feel good." She took my wrist and guided it down between her legs. She pressed my fingers up against the fly of the pants she was still wearing. "Oh, yes—let me get these off." She fumbled impatiently with the zipper, then squirmed out of the pants. She wasn't wearing anything underneath.

I quickly pulled off my dress and threw it onto a nearby chair. Then I held Alexandra away from me long enough to get her shirt off. And then I pulled back the bedcovers and we wriggled down under them, huddling close for mutual warmth. She kissed me several times, quickly, her mouth moving across mine, over my cheeks, to my forehead, back to my mouth again, then to my shoulders, my neck. The touch of her lips was delicate and tantalizing, very feminine, very sweet. I smiled and closed my eyes and she kissed my eyelids. Then our mouths met again and our tongues touched tentatively, exploring, making delicate little movements. She shifted her body and her breasts brushed across mine, and I felt the goosebumps on her skin. "You're cold," I whispered.

She nodded.

I stroked her rich brown hair and moved my hand down around behind her so that I could pull her close to me. She snuggled close and gave a little sigh of pleasure. She took my head in her two hands and kissed me more, quickly and urgently now. I reached down with my other hand and slid my fingers between her thighs, and immediately she opened her legs wide. My fingers slid up into her; she was so wet and hot, so eager.

"You can touch me hard," she said, her lips close to my ear. "I want that, want you to press hard on my clit . . . that's right . . ."

I had found her swollen clitoris and was rubbing it quickly with my forefinger. Her breathing quickened straightaway and her hands started roving over my body, behind me to my buttocks, then to my waist, finally to my breasts. She felt me tentatively, as if she were discovering a woman's body for the first time. She made little passionate noises. She was like a teenager.

I plunged my fingers deep inside her, where all the thick, slick wetness was, then rubbed her clitoris more, as fast as I could. She wriggled her shoulders and rolled onto her back. She turned her head from side to side, hiding her face under a tangle of hair. I got up on one elbow, still touching her insistently, and I leaned over her and kissed her long and deep. She reached down and grabbed my wrist and suddenly jerked my hand up against her clitoris so hard that I thought it must hurt her. At the same time she pulled my head down and kissed me with her mouth wide open, her tongue thrusting urgently. Her whole body quivered. The bed squeaked under us. She broke our kiss, tilted her head back, and moaned, and then she came, her eyes closed and her teeth clenched. She looked beautiful, and I enjoyed simply watching her.

As her climax subsided, I relaxed the pressure of my fingers on her clitoris but left my hand down there gently between her legs, my palm covering her pubic mound. "Better now?" I asked softly.

"Mmmm, yes." Her eyes were still closed. She was savoring the last of the good warm feelings. "Oh, Chris, I could lie here and soak up sex all afternoon." She opened her eyes then, looked at me, and kissed me on the mouth. "That was lovely. How about you? Are you feeling turned on?"

"I guess I am," I said slowly, trying to decide exactly what I did feel. "It's almost as if sex is in the air here, in this place. At dinner last night I could feel it, a kind of sexual tension."

"Oh, for sure." She nodded, absolutely seriously. "I've been horny ever since I first walked in the front door, whenever it was. I would never have gotten anywhere with my Mr. Masterson, either, if it wasn't for that feeling in this place, I'm sure of that. I mean, it takes a lot to make a nice old guy like him cheat on his wife for the first time in thirty years. Well, of course, he hasn't quite gone through with it yet . . ." She gave me an ironic smile. "But he will, all right."

"I still don't know what you're so hung up on, about him."

She shrugged. "It doesn't matter." Which meant she simply wasn't going to tell me. "Anyway, you're right, sex is in the air. Zenya's got his own ideas about that, you know."

"The creative force, the primal energy of the spirit?"

"Ah, he's told you already. Mmmm. You think *he's* sexy?" Her bright eyes moved quickly and met mine. Her alert face seemed ready to register the smallest detail of anything I might say.

I decided to be straight with her. "He's got the most amazing presence of any man I've ever met," I said.

"Absolutely. I wish he'd spread it around some." She smiled mischievously.

I wanted to boast, then, and tell Alexandra that Zenya had already made an advance to *me*, even if he hadn't approached her. But something made me hold back and say nothing. I'd been in the castle for less than twenty-four hours, and already I'd gotten involved in what seemed to be shaping up into some complicated intrigues; and at the same time, I suspected I had only just scratched the surface. "Everyone seems to be screwing everyone else, or wanting to," I murmured.

"You don't know the half of it," said Alexandra. Then she, too, seemed to decide she didn't want to say any more. She yawned and stretched and sighed cheerfully. "Want me to go down on you?" she said.

I laughed. "No, not now. You're very sweet, Alexandra, and we can do this again sometime, but right now I think maybe I need a little while to myself." In reality I wanted to compose myself for the activities of the evening, whatever they might turn out to be. I needed to shower, and dress, and feel rested and ready.

"Okay," she said. She raised to a kneeling position, exposing her body. "You really think I'm attractive?"

I looked at her. Her shoulders were a little broad, but there was no surplus weight on her anywhere. Her skin was smooth and very slightly colored by what must have been last summer's tan. Her breasts were ample without being overlarge, and they were very tightly rounded, high on her chest. Her face, with its oval shape and fine features, was simply cute; there was no other word. She was so youthful and so lively, I hated her for it.

"If *you* can't seduce Masterson, I don't know who can," I said. Although actually I thought I'd have a better idea of strategy than she did—God knows what she had been up to, getting him to go down on her as a preliminary to her seducing him. The way I would do it . . . But no, I cut off that line of thought. I would leave Masterson for Alexandra. Things were complicated enough already. "Well, it's too bad you can't get him drunk, with there being no liquor here," I ended up. "But I'm sure you'll manage anyway."

She got out of bed quickly, grabbed her clothes, and

pulled them on. "Thanks, Chris," she said. She strode quickly to the door, turned and blew me a kiss, and then she was gone.

As she left, I felt oddly as if she had just taken advantage of me and used me somehow. And yet I couldn't figure how. Certainly I didn't resent our little interlude. It had been interesting, and fun. But there was something behind Alexandra's careless manner and flippant style. Something calculating.

In the end I had to give up trying to figure it out. For the time being it would remain a mystery, like so many other aspects of life in the castle.

CHAPTER SEVEN

That night there was the same tense air of expectancy at dinner that I had noticed the previous night. But this time I knew why. And I knew, too, why Masterson avoided my eyes, and why he seemed embarrassed when Alexandra, sitting beside him, occasionally whispered something in his ear. I still didn't understand the strange kind of wariness that seemed to exist between Zenya and Nick Weston. But already I was feeling more like an insider and less of a stranger in the group. It was a seductive feeling; I was being drawn into a hotbed of secrets and desires and mystic obsessions. And though it had overtones of craziness, I wanted to be right there in the middle of it.

We ate and pretended to be interested in idle small talk, while the servants moved discreetly around us and the fire crackled in the hearth, and the flickering candles cast their mellow radiance.

Then, when we had finished dessert and the last of the dishes were cleared away, Zenya made an announcement. He stood up, clad again in the robe I had first seen him in, and he looked at each one of us slowly and carefully. We all became silent; there was absolutely no doubt of the magnetism he had over this little gathering. For, after all, he had demonstrated his powers—powers that most of us had never actually believed in before. This Middle Eastern man had something unique, and he knew it, and he knew we knew it.

"Tonight our Circle will be a little different," he said.

His voice was soft, but the low tones were vibrant and they seemed to resound in the large room. "Tonight we are ready to tap the energies more directly, more intensely than before. I know there have been romantic liaisons between some of you in this group." At this point everyone was careful not to look at anyone else. "This is a dissipation of the energies, a playful, harmless, but wasteful use. These sexual feelings are a manifestation of the core of our spiritual powers. Tonight we will touch for the first time on the reservoir of these powers, by means of a group experience involving sexual contact." He paused. "If there is anyone who does not feel free to participate, now is the time to say so. Of course, it will mean that that person can no longer join the Circle for future sharing of spirit and exploration of the other levels of existence."

Get naked or leave the group, I realized, was the message. In a way it shocked me, because it sounded crass. If I hadn't known that Zenya could have had any one of the women present, anytime, simply by asking—rather, *demanding*—sex from them, I'd have suspected some kind of cynical spiel to justify his having an orgy. But he didn't need the spiel. And it wasn't a spiel; it was what the man believed. Whether he was right or not, I couldn't tell, but what he said certainly fitted in with what I'd mentioned to Alexandra about the castle reeking of sexual tension. There was all that energy in the air, all right. And now Zenya was planning to tap it and channel it some way. The more I thought about it, the more plausible it sounded. And the more plausible it sounded, the more it scared me. Last night's session had been intense enough. I couldn't imagine making it even more powerful, adding sexuality to the equation.

I looked at Masterson. I thought he was probably the only one who'd have moral qualms. Sure enough, he seemed uneasy. "Just, ah, what exactly are you suggesting?" he said to Zenya.

Zenya laid his hands palms-down on the table. "Mr. Masterson, I have told you my philosophy about the sexuality of the human spirit. Our biology, our nervous systems, are dedicated toward reproduction. It is the most powerful drive. We choose to make that drive seem 'civilized' by embodying it in conventions . . . such as marriage, for example. But these conventions are a convenience, nothing more. The power of the spirit cannot be trapped in such rigid social customs, if it is to be used for our awakening. The spirit must be released. To accomplish this, it is necessary for us to come together as naked sexual, biological entities, touching, acknowledging, pooling the sexual forces."

Masterson didn't look too happy. He glanced around the rest of the group, as if hoping for someone else to raise objections. But no one did. "I guess I'll try to go along with it," he mumbled at length. "If it's the only way."

"It is the way," said Zenya, with that tone of absolute conviction that not only made it clear this was the best path to take but said that no other path even existed.

He's a fanatic, I thought, with another twist of fright. But he has every right to be. After all, he *knows*.

"I have prepared the room differently for the Circle tonight," he said. "It will be more comfortable. We will go there now."

He walked calmly out of the dining room, and we quickly got to our feet and hurried after him—like disciples hungry for a revelation, or like lambs being led to slaughter. I didn't know which was the case, but the seductiveness of the event was irresistible.

* * *

Upstairs, the little black room had had its table removed. The wooden chairs were gone, too; instead, there were six large black cushions in a circle on the black stone floor. The black candle in its candlestick stood in the center of the floor, burning steadily. As we walked in. I stared at the candle, remembering the way in which it had been extinguished by an invisible hand the previous night. Then I looked around me at the matt-black-painted stone walls and the featureless black ceiling. I could see nothing to contradict what Zenya had said- -that the room was completely bare, allowing not the slightest chance of any tricks or fakery. Solid stone walls and a locked door of inch-thick oak planks.

"Join us, Christina," Zenya said, interrupting my thoughts. I realized that everyone else was already making themselves comfortable on the cushions; the door had been secured. and I was the last person still standing. I felt embarrassed—guilty, even—to have been wondering if last night's experience could have been faked in some way, when it was so obvious that this man was totally sincere in his beliefs, and the events that I had lived through were so beyond being created artificially.

As I sat down I realized that the only reason I had for wanting to discover fakery was that it still scared me to believe that this was the real thing. I was like a patient in therapy, wanting the therapy not to work, to save me coming face-to-face with any hidden truths.

And yet, frightened as I felt, I couldn't turn away from those truths. I wanted to know, wanted to feel everything.

So I made myself comfortable on that black cushion, on Zenya's right, where I had sat the previous night. It was deadly quiet in the room; I could hear the others breathing. I think everyone was nervous; everyone but Zenya. As always, he seemed serenely in control.

He looked slowly around the Circle, starting with Stella, to his left, and finishing with me. In each case he made eye contact, and the effect was like a sedative. Everyone's attention turned more to him, and each person thought less about his or her own anxiety. Finally, when more of a state of calm prevailed, Zenya opened a tiny gold case that he had taken from a pocket in his robe. In the case was fine powder. He pinched some between finger and thumb, leaned forward, and sprinkled the powder into the candle flame. It was consumed immediately, sparkling and hissing, and a stinging-sweet smell filled the space.

"It is nothing mystical," he said quietly. "Merely a dried spice that is common in my homeland. It has the effect of sharpening one's senses—a very mild stimulant. As we visit the world beyond more often, and gain confidence, we are able to open ourselves to it more, without fear."

I don't know if it was my imagination, but already it seemed that the candle burned slightly brighter, and the faces of the other people seemed more vivid.

"Now," he said, "we begin." And casually, as if it were the most natural action in the world, he loosened the belt of his robe, pulled it open, and threw it aside.

He had a beautiful body, golden brown and totally hairless except for a dense bush of shiny black pubic hair around his phallus. He settled himself serenely on his cushion once more and again looked from one person to the next, around the Circle, as if challenging them to tell him that there was anything unusual or shocking in his sudden nakedness. And he had such a sense of will, of rightness, that indeed it seemed that being naked, then, was more normal than being clothed.

His eyes came to focus on me last of all. I stared

back at him, marveling at his mastery of the situation—I had assumed that if we were to become naked, it would be after the candle was out. But no, that would not have been his way.

He stared at me and went on staring at me. "Christina?" he said, as if waiting.

I didn't hesitate. I quickly slipped my belt out of its buckle, pulled down the zipper at the back of my dress, and hauled it up and over my head. I tossed it aside, then shed my undergarments and shoes. All the time, he watched me. All the time, I tried to look straight back at him, as if to say: Yes, I can do this just as easily as you can. Of course, I wasn't self-conscious about my body anyway—I'd bathed on nudist beaches, I'd been in group-sex scenes. But this was a little different, in a circle of virtual strangers, about to indulge in a rite whose details I didn't know and whose possible effects were quite scary.

I sat totally naked. I don't know if the others were ogling me. I doubt it. Everyone was too much on edge to be thinking along purely voyeuristic lines. I did notice, out of the corner of my eye, that Stella was looking at my body with some kind of resentment—perhaps because I was the first person Zenya had, in effect, told to undress.

Zenya turned to Masterson next. He was sitting beside me, as he had the previous night. Zenya stared at Masterson. His eyes were compelling, commanding. Masterson shifted in embarrassment, then started untying his shoelaces.

Zenya nodded. He turned to Alexandra, seated next around the Circle. Already she was unbuttoning her shirt.

Zenya looked at Nick. He was taking off his jacket.

Lastly he turned to Stella. Reluctantly, I thought, she pulled off her sweater, then took off her bra, exposing ample but soft-looking breasts. And her skin had an unhealthy pallor, I thought to myself; not wanting to be catty, but at the same time pleased to see defects in the girl whom I regarded as my competition.

Within minutes we were all naked. And once everyone had undressed, it seemed completely natural. Even Masterson showed very little self-consciousness, despite his middle-age spread and the excess fat around his arms and thighs. And the candlelight, gently flickering, made it easier.

"We begin," Zenya said. "We clasp hands." He reached out to Stella with his left hand, and myself with his right. He held my hand lightly, without a tremor, with the same kind of self-assurance that he showed in his speech and his movements. I imagined a feel of vitality, of life-force, in his touch. Within moments the point of contact between our palms seemed strangely hot. At the same time, I felt slightly dizzy, off balance, as if I were not sitting quite straight. I shifted, but it made no difference. Whichever way I moved, I felt as if I were about to fall.

I took hold of Masterson's hand, hardly aware of him. I stared at the candle flame as a point of reference. That made it easier. I took a couple of deep breaths.

"We are joined," I heard Zenya say, as each person became linked, hand to hand, in the Circle. I felt his grip tighten, and in turn I held Masterson's hand more tightly. There was already a feeling of power in the room, of a presence that was growing from all of us. I remembered not being able to pull away from the group the previous night; it was the same now, but more intense. My hands felt welded into permanent contact with the hands I held. Part of me panicked, feeling trapped, knowing there was no turning back now. My breathing speeded up.

"We are a Circle," Zenya was intoning. "We unite the energies of the mind. We share the orgone energies, the psychic energies, the energies of the soul. Tonight, more potently than ever before. Naked before the world beyond, we pool our life-forces. We can feel them growing."

I was trembling a little, still staring up at the candle flame. I seemed to be falling toward it, an endless free fall away from the world as I knew it.

"There will be a sign," said Zenya. And the candle went out, just as it had the previous night. This time I didn't scream, but I let out a little cry, like the cry of a bird on the wind being buffeted and blown away, away, into total emptiness of eternal night.

"The chant will begin," Zenya said, his voice coming from everywhere at once around me. And then I found myself speaking the Word in unison with him and the others in the group. My last fragment of consciousness was saying: This man is more dangerous, more powerful, than any mortal man could be! This man is more than a man, he's a god, a devil, he's evil, he has too much power! But all of that was just a frail, feeble protest against the wall of sound, the cacophony of our chant. And already I was hearing the other voices, the multitude joining us, all around us, taking up the Word that seemed to encompass all of reality and the universe.

At Zenya's command we stopped chanting, but the voices of the unseen crowds went on, as they had last night. The sound seemed to grow louder, till I was totally enclosed by it, as if I had floated up into space and the souls of every person who had ever died were gathering in a vast invisible throng.

"Tonight we learn more, we travel further." It was Zenya's voice, his rich baritone cutting through the surging chanting noise. "Tonight we tap the primal forces."

I was barely aware of my physical self by this time. My mind was full of abstract images and colors and sounds. I was in an ethereal world. But at the same time, I could still feel the clasp of Zenya's hand on mine. And I felt him drawing me forward, to the center of the Circle. "We move closer; we unite," he intoned.

In reflex I pulled on Masterson's hand, to my right; and somewhere in the little stone-walled room that hardly seemed to exist anymore, we all gathered more closely. As we did, and it was not an illusion, I felt the tension mount higher.

Now we were not just touching hands. Legs and feet and hips were coming into contact. With every touch I seemed to be becoming more absorbed, more a part of the unity of our Circle. There was no way to tell whose flesh was pressed against mine now. We were one.

At the same time, the chanting voices seemed to rise in pitch and intensity, till they became almost deafening. My mind was reeling. In the total darkness I saw sparkling luminous light patterns, very faintly at first, like the ghostly images you see when you rub your eyes, but more beautiful, more perfect. And slowly they grew in intensity.

Somewhere Zenya shifted his grip on my left hand. I found myself touching his leg instead of his palm. There was no break in contact—all six of us were now more cemented together as one physical form than ever before. But there was a shift. And then I found my hand somehow touching his genitals, and I felt him —I think it was him—brushing his fingers across my pubes, then lower, across the mouth of my vagina.

"We release the life energies," he said, and now even his powerful voice was almost drowned by the other noises in my ears, the chanting of the Word, and overlaying it now a kind of ultimate musical tone. It was as if ten thousand choirs were all starting to sing one eternal note, growing and growing.

I think I started touching Masterson; I'm not sure. It doesn't matter. I know that the hand that was touching me grew bolder, and I felt waves of feeling blossoming, in rhythm with the chanting. The feeling was almost painfully intense, like an electric shock. It radiated though my whole body. The colors in my eyes exploded. More and more the steady singing note drowned out the chanted Word. It was all around me, the warm bodies of the Circle were all around me, I was engulfed and being carried ever higher.

"Is there one we know?" Zenya called, his voice bellowing above the million singing voices of the multitude.

The reply was instant and so loud that it seemed harsh to the insides of my ears. "My daughter!" it shouted. "My daughter, I see my daughter."

I heard a cry from somewhere near, yet far away. Fran's voice. "Where are you, Daddy?" She sounded like a little girl of ten.

"My child . . . I'm here . . ."

But already other voices were intruding. "Nicholas? Is that you? The time . . . the time is . . ."

"Dad?" A new disembodied voice interrupted. I heard Masterson cry out, in shock, in surprise to hear his son.

The voice went on. "I hurt, Dad. It happened . . . the night . . . the blood . . ."

The voices were on top of one another, and incoherent, as if there was so much they had been waiting to say, so much that they didn't know how to begin. I felt waves of emotion, and the sex feelings were part of it, and the singing note that still sounded everywhere was part of it, and my fear and hope and excitement were part of it.

And then: "Christina!"

It was her voice, I knew it, and she sounded so close. The other voices were shouting too, but I heard her: "Christina . . . so young . . . too soon . . . and he took it, took it all . . . so much . . . you must revenge . . . Schmidt . . ."

"Where are you?" I was shouting. "Fran, I want you. Where are you?"

But everyone else was shouting too. The room was a pandemonium of sound. I was gasping for breath. The colors in my eyes were so vivid now they were almost blinding, and I seemed to be able to focus on them as a swirling ball of radiance hanging in the center of the black space in front of me.

And the press of bodies was overwhelming. Hands seemed to clutch me everywhere. And in my own arms I embraced, I held, I touched. I think we were all pressed together, writhing, reaching, and holding. And the voices went on shouting to us, and we shouted back, and the singing noise started rising up in pitch, so high it sounded inhuman. I was sobbing and gasping, feeling as if a vast electric current were surging through me. I trembled. Then I think I had an orgasm—I couldn't even tell—and at the same time the singing noise reached a piercing, screaming crescendo, and the colors flared up like the sun, and the floor itself seemed to tremble, and I was falling. I thought the whole world had exploded. I didn't know which way up I was. There was a roaring and a rumbling and my ears were ringing and there were afterimages floating in my eyes.

Slowly I realized I was prostrate on the cold stone floor, in the darkness. The noises, the voices, had all gone away. I felt horribly alone. "Zenya!" I shouted, and I heard my voice as a pitiful lonely sound. "What . . . ?"

Then I blinked. Zenya was standing in the center of the room. He had relit the candle.

Reality came back to us as a harmless little black room. I gulped and looked around. Everyone was lying stretched out, as if we had all been thrown from the center of the room by some psychic explosion. Our naked bodies seemed fragile and awkward. One by one we sat up, dazed and confused. Even Zenya, standing watching over us, seemed to have less of his self-assurance than before.

"In time we will learn to control that vast power," he said slowly. His eyes seemed unfocused, as if he had seen something awesome and could not yet look back at reality.

I drew my knees up and hugged them to me. I felt suddenly cold.

"Tonight was our first adventure. There will be more. Tonight we were like a child who can only shout and cry. Tomorrow we will learn to speak, to choose, to channel the forces of the world beyond."

No one answered. We were all too stunned. My ears were still full of the sounds; my eyes still flickered with the colors.

Zenya stooped, picked up his robe, and wrapped it around himself. The rest of us followed suit, pulling on our clothes. Still no one spoke. All you could hear in that close space was the sound of breathing and the rustling of cloth and the clink of buckles.

Zenya walked to the door, unlocked it, and opened it. He beckoned to Stella. She stood up quickly and walked to him. He gestured through the door—into the corridor that led to the rest of his rooms in the east wing. She ducked past him and was lost from sight.

"We have traveled far," he said to the rest of us. "Further than I thought possible."

Even he seems shaken, I realized. He's gotten hold of something that's too big for any of us to know how to handle.

"We will share, again, tomorrow. Until then, rest, think, learn." He looked at each person in turn. Finally he looked at me. I looked back up at him, and there was a long silent moment. He seemed to be telling me something with that look. I wasn't sure what it was. Was he telling me I was special in some way? Or was that just my own vanity?

There was nothing I could say with everyone else present. Then Zenya turned and walked out, his shimmering gown of gold rustling and flowing around him.

The rest of us slowly stood up, shakily, and filed out of the black room one by one.

CHAPTER EIGHT

None of us quite knew what to do. We were all shaken by what we had just gone through. Without anyone suggesting it, we found ourselves gathered together in the library downstairs—Alexandra, Nick, Masterson, and myself.

"It was my son," Masterson was muttering, half to himself. "That much is for sure. It was him, no doubt about it."

Each of us agreed we had heard voices of the people closest to us who had died.

"If only it could have lasted longer in there," said Alexandra.

"I don't think I could have stood it much longer," I said.

"Me neither," Nick agreed. He looked pale, and he was avoiding meeting anyone's eyes. "In fact, I must say I'm wondering if this is getting out of control. I no longer believe our . . . our guru knows exactly what he's up to."

"What are you suggesting?" I asked him. "That we should turn our backs on this and go home?"

"I don't know, Christina. All I can say is that it's made me feel pretty shaken. I don't know if I ever want to go back into that room again."

"I think you've got to have more faith," I said. "After all, logically—"

"Logic don't apply in there, no sir," Masterson interrupted me. And of course, he was right.

"Do you think Zenya is . . . evil?" Alexandra spoke slowly, looking from one face to the next, as if expecting to be ridiculed. But no one laughed at her.

"I don't know what evil means anymore," Masterson said at length. "And I've been a churchgoing man all my life."

"I think we're in on the beginnings of what could be something very big," I said. "Think about it. With all the cults and religious movements and leaders that there have been—which of them has ever been able to deliver? To create, on demand, the kind of experience we shared tonight?" I paused. "Personally I can only think of one other man in history who could produce miracles just like that."

"No," said Masterson. "No, that's blasphemy, young lady, and I won't tolerate it."

"You just heard the voice of your own son," I reminded him. "Your son, who you didn't even know, for sure, was dead, until tonight. Isn't that a miracle?"

"I *thought* I heard his voice." Masterson's hands were clenched on the arms of his chair. The cords in his neck stood out with tension.

"What you thought you heard, I thought I heard too," I said. "Shouting to you about the pain, the blood. Isn't that what *you* heard, Nick? And you, Alexandra?"

They both nodded.

Masterson slowly pulled himself up onto his feet. "I don't want to talk anymore," he said. "If you all will excuse me . . ."

Alexandra stood up quickly and went to him. "You shouldn't be alone at a time like this," she told him.

He looked at her almost disapprovingly. And then some of the strength sagged out of him. "Well," he said, "well, all right, thank you, my dear. Your presence would be a comfort."

She escorted him out of the library and I heard them

ascending the old, creaky oak staircase. I listened intently; only one door opened and closed on the floor above. I didn't know whether I thought badly of Alexandra for taking advantage of the man when he was upset by the séance, or whether I simply admired her timing.

I looked at my watch. It was eleven. I wondered again about Zenya and whether he would really come into my room tonight. I didn't want to miss out on that possibility. I stood up and walked over to Nick.

I put my hand on his shoulder. He had been staring out at the night, beyond the diamond panes of the windows, and my touch startled him. He twitched and looked around very quickly, his eyes wide.

"Hey," I said. "It's only me."

"Yes. Yes, of course." He sighed. "Wish I'd been able to actually *talk* to my father up there in that room."

"Maybe tomorrow."

"Yes. Yes, you're right, there's no getting away from it, is there?"

"I'm going to bed," I told him. "I'm tired. I'll sleep in my own room tonight."

"All right." It didn't seem to concern him too much. "I want to stay up and read a little, anyway. Organize my thoughts."

I bent down and kissed him on the cheek, then left the room. I realized that I was the only person in the group whose relative had been dead for many years. So I was less emotionally involved than the others. Of course, I had loved my sister, Fran. But I had had five years in which to reconcile myself to her not being around anymore. Hearing her voice had made me feel a pang, but I wasn't going to kid myself. I knew she wasn't about to come back to life in the everyday sense. Not unless Zenya started resurrecting the dead.

That made me feel uneasy. Zenya had done so many things already that I would have said were impossible. Who was to say what else he could and couldn't do?

I climbed the stairs and paused by the white door into the east wing—the white door that was opened to us only once each night, when we went in for the séance. I would have given a lot to know what the rest of the east wing was like.

Then, as I paused by the door, I heard voices faintly from behind it. I looked quickly around, not wanting to be caught eavesdropping. But everywhere was quiet. No one was watching me. I bent my head to listen at the door panels.

". . . disobey me!" I heard Zenya's voice, raised in anger.

"I didn't mean to." And that was Stella. She was whining, like a little kid who has been caught doing something bad but won't admit it.

"You have exhausted my patience." Zenya again. "Perhaps if you cannot be made to learn, in other ways . . ." His voice trailed off. Then suddenly I heard Stella scream. It sounded more a scream of pain than of fear, and as I heard it I felt chilled inside. God, what was he doing?

"I'm sorry! I said I'm sorry!" she shouted. Though the sounds were barely audible through the heavy door, I could tell her voice was very loud. And then she screamed again.

There was a short silence.

"You ask my forgiveness," Zenya said.

"Forgive me." Stella, sounding shaken.

"You say, 'Forgive me, master.' "

"Forgive me, master."

I couldn't hear any more after that. I think they either stopped talking or moved farther away—perhaps into another room. And I wasn't sure if I *wanted* to hear any more, anyway. I could imagine, all too easily, Zenya using his power, his personality, on that young girl. And I could imagine him showing a sadistic streak. He who manipulated invisible forces could surely manipulate people, too.

In my head I heard Alexandra saying: "Do you think Zenya is . . . evil?"

Quickly I turned and walked into the west wing of the castle, to my own room. I wasn't so sure now whether I wanted Zenya to come to me during the night. The fascination was still there. If anything, I was more fascinated even than before, but at the same time, I was also more repelled. There is a seductiveness about power, regardless of whether it is used for good or evil.

I undressed and showered, then blew my hair dry. I watched myself in the mirror. If I were Zenya, I thought, I'd find a woman like me a hell of a lot more attractive than that little girl he has with him. It was arrogant of me, but facts were facts: I was sophisticated and beautiful, I had poise and style, and Stella couldn't match any of those qualities.

If I were Zenya, I thought, I would dump Stella and turn to Christina and make her my special mistress. If I were Zenya I would lavish gifts upon Christina and share my secrets, my powers, with her.

It was a nice fantasy. To be chosen by the man of magic and elevated to a position of equal power with him. I wanted to believe there was a chance of it happening. At the same time, I knew there was just as much a chance of his using his power over me as there was of his sharing it with me as his equal.

But I was a strong, self-possessed woman. Perhaps even strong enough to cope with a man like him.

I slid into bed. The sheets were clean; the staff of the castle was unobtrusively efficient. I got the impression they'd been here for years, and Zenya had inherited them. Did they know what went on in his rooms? Perhaps they preferred not to know.

I stared up at the canopy of the old four-poster bed. I liked the bed; it made me feel regal, pampered, very special. I imagined I was an English queen of old, and this was my own castle. I imagined that soon the handsome young knight would come to me.

Come to me, I thought, as if my mind could broadcast the message to him. Come to me, O knight.

I turned out the light and lay awake for a while. Then I drifted off to sleep.

I woke instantly at the sound of my doorlatch clicking. Straightaway I pushed myself up on my elbows and peered into the darkness of the room. My pulse was fast. I felt wide-awake. But the door wasn't open; it was shut. Had I imagined the click of the catch? Then I realized: there was someone already in my room. The noise I had heard was of the door closing behind him.

I saw his figure, then, in the faint moonlight filtering through the tall, narrow windows. He was standing, watching me. "Who's there?" I whispered.

He walked to the window, took hold of the heavy drapes, and pulled them wide so that more light from the moon came into the room. I saw then that it was Zenya, naked but for a thin gold chain around his neck. His mane of thick black hair fell to his shoulders in waves. His eyes were hidden in shadow, but I could tell he was looking at me. The muscles in his shoulders and arms were picked out by the moonlight. I looked down, to his waist, and then I saw his cock standing out erect. It looked huge. I drew in my breath; I think he heard my gasp. He walked deliberately over to the bed.

His hand stroked my hair, then touched my face. He didn't say a word. He just stood over me, looking down at me. I could feel his presence, the power of the man. "I knew you'd come," I said, trying to sound offhand, as if there'd been no doubt at all in my mind.

He didn't bother to reply. His silence made me feel foolish for trying to sound self-assured. My self-assurance was pathetic compared to his.

He lifted one knee onto the bed, and then he swung his other leg over me, so he was kneeling astride my body. Still he said nothing. With his weight on his knees on the bedcovers on either side of me, I felt trapped in the bed. It was like being held in a tight-fitting cocoon. His bronze body seemed to tower over me, massive and intimidating. I tried to think of something to say, but there wasn't anything to say.

His strong, smooth hands caressed my forehead, stroking it gently. His touch was warm, and I remembered the heat I had experienced when I had held his hand at the beginning of the séance. It all felt magical. His fingers ran through my hair; I lay there helplessly, my arms still trapped under the covers, while he knelt astride me.

He leaned forward, bending down toward me. His body was a dark silhouette moving to fill my vision, blotting out my view of the rest of the room. His lips touched mine and pressed gently at first, and then more and more insistently. Our mouths opened together. His tongue pushed in. He held my head between his hands and kissed me hard, almost brutally. I felt smothered by him, with his weight upon me. The long, hard shape of his cock was pressing down onto me through the bedcovers.

Finally he paused in his kissing me. But he kept his face very close to mine. His eyes stared at me as if judging me in some way. He ran his fingers across my lips, and his touch made me tingle and shiver. He twined his fingers in my hair, then turned his hand and tugged, harder, till I gave a little cry in response. Then he stroked my cheek thoughtfully.

Finally he moved back from me and shifted his weight so that he was no longer astride me holding me helpless. For a moment I actually thought he was going to get up and go away.

He stood on the floor beside the bed. All the time, he was still watching me. I wanted him to say something —anything. I couldn't remotely guess his thoughts. Then, at last, he took hold of the bedcovers and drew them down and away from me so that my body was revealed to him. Moonlight splashed through the leaded windows, an ethereal glow upon my soft, smooth skin. He stood silhouetted against the light, staring at me. His cock was still standing out hard and big and strong.

"Will you make love to me now?" I said softly, beginning to feel just a little self-conscious under his gaze, though I knew I looked wonderful stretched out naked across the clean linen sheets, my hair a mass of curls on the pillow, my breasts cradled between my arms. Still he watched me and said nothing.

"Why don't you speak?" I said.

"Words mean little." He stooped, took hold of my shoulders, and pulled me up to him. He kissed me hard, then moved his head back just enough so that he could stare into my eyes. At that moment I truly felt that something more than just a man had hold of me. Through him I felt other forces, as if he were some bridge, some channel between reality and other levels, other energies.

He laid me back down on the bed. Then, deliberately, he turned me over so that I was facedown on the bed. Again, I didn't resist; I couldn't resist. It would have been like trying to fight the flow of time and space. I was caught and I had given myself up to these forces.

He lowered himself onto the bed. The mattress sank under his weight, and the old bed creaked. I reached out and grabbed hold of one of the four posts, as if to hold on to something real and solid. The old polished mahogany was hard and cold under my hand.

He lowered his weight over me. His cock pushed between my thighs, from behind me. He took my hips in his hands and raised them, so I was half up on my knees, with the rest of my body still pressed facedown on the bed. He spread my buttocks and I felt the head of his cock pressing insistently, forcing between my labia, reaching the entrance to my vagina, and pushing into me. It went in, and in, and I felt I couldn't take any more of it, but he went on sliding it into me until I gasped. His knees were between my legs; he spread them a little more. Then he bore down on me, keeping his cock embedded in me completely. Under his weight I was pushed down till my belly was once again flat on the bed, and he was stretched out over me, with all his weight resting on my back and my buttocks and my thighs.

He started fucking me then, moving just his hips, while he held my shoulders with his hands. His cock pushed in so deep, so very deep from behind me. I lay sandwiched between him and the bed, his breath hot on the back of my neck. I've never felt so wholly *taken,* almost violated, unable to resist in any way. I let out a little sob and found myself biting the linen of the soft pillow that was under my face. A mass of strange feelings was swirling through my body—excitement, fear, discomfort at being so helpless, and yet the helplessness was turning me on. There was nothing I could do against his will, his forcefulness, the power of him. I felt myself surrendering to the thrusts of his cock, the pressure of his body.

He slid his hands under me, to my breasts, and grabbed them. With his arms circling me that way and my breasts completely enclosed in his grip, I was even more in his power. His thrusts became harder and more purposeful. His hips smacked against my buttocks. With my head turned to one side on the pillow, I couldn't see him, but I could see the window, and through it the night, and the moon. The silver light seemed to swell and grow and fill my consciousness. I felt Zenya behind me, fucking me, forcing his cock so deep inside me. He and the night seemed as one, as if the universe itself were taking me, using me.

Suddenly all the feelings welled up in me and I came to orgasm, before I knew it was going to happen. The feeling was sudden and sharp and intense, and I whimpered and clutched at the bedsheet; it was all so strange. And he barely paused; he went on thrusting into me.

I squirmed under him. He held me down more firmly. I tried to turn, to show him I wanted to roll over, to look at him, to embrace him.

He paused in his lovemaking, and I thought he understood what I wanted. He drew his penis slowly out of my cunt, and I turned to look up at him. But his hand grabbed my shoulder and pressed my body roughly back into the bed again, facedown. And then I felt his cock probing at the opening of my anus.

I pulled my knees up in reflex, so that it wouldn't hurt when he pushed into me. Even now I felt I could not resist him; it was impossible. He pushed, and his cock, wet from my cunt, thrust into my ass. I moaned. He grabbed my shoulders and held me against him as he rolled over, taking me with him, so that now we were both on our sides on the bed, still with him behind me. We were nestled like spoons.

Again his hands clutched my breasts. His fingers dug in until it was painful. His cock pushed deep into my ass, with fast, deliberate movements. I tried to reach behind me, to touch him and feel him, but I couldn't. I just lay there on the wide, regal bed and let him use me for his pleasures, and gave my body to him. And finally he came, grunting and pushing and gripping me fiercely till his orgasm was over.

At last, then, he relaxed his hold on me. I turned over and freed myself. I stared at him, panting for breath and feeling a little crazy. I was tormented by conflicting emotions. I had been taken and *used,* and it was what I'd wanted, and yet it was something I never let any man do to me. I worshiped Zenya and at the same time I abhorred him. I needed him, I wanted him. And yet I recoiled now at the idea of his touch.

He lay there, calm and inscrutable. Slowly I reached out and touched him, his warm, strong, smooth body. "You shouldn't . . . you shouldn't have done it to me like that," I said.

"It was necessary." His voice contained a kind of tenderness, almost regret.

"What's that supposed to mean?" I still felt in awe of him. I still couldn't begin to understand what went on in his mind.

He stroked my hair. I had to stop myself from pulling away from him; but this time his touch was gentle; he was not trying to hold me or use me in any way. I even felt he was admiring me.

"You must have the capacity to give," he said.

"I don't understand."

"If you are to be my follower."

"What?"

"Stella has not the capacity to learn, to understand, to give. You are to take her place."

Just like that, there in the big old room, on the big four-poster bed, in the moonlight. It was my fantasy suddenly becoming true. And yet it wasn't my fantasy at all.

I had imagined Zenya inviting me into his world and sharing his power with me, as an equal. He the king, I the queen.

What he was suggesting now was different. Any ideas I had about equal status were my ideas, not his. And in a way, I could see, that was reasonable: he was the one who had the special talent, the knowledge, whatever it was that gave him the capacity to make contact with other realities that I had never even believed in before.

But . . .

"I'm not like Stella," I said slowly. "I won't be *used*. I have my own identity. My own self-respect and pride."

"I know." His voice sounded absolutely understanding, confident as always. He sat up and took hold of me, his hands gripping my upper arms. He drew me to him till my breasts were pressed hard against his chest. His lips touched mine, and I realized there was still no way I could hold back. Despite my mixed feelings, I couldn't resist this man. His mouth fastened on mine and I let my head fall back and let my lips open. We kissed, and his tongue pushed in, invading me as his cock had done just a little while ago. I couldn't stop it. I didn't know if I even wanted to.

After the kiss, he held me to him with one arm around my shoulders. I was almost in tears, with emotions I couldn't name.

"You see," he said quietly, "I do understand you, Christina. I understand it all."

I laughed shakily. "That's more than I do."

"Your will and your identity are important to you, in the life you have lived. But here, they have no place. For I am the teacher and you are the student. If the student refuses the teacher—if the student says what must be done, and how it must be done—how can the student ever learn anything? How can there be anything more than a useless clash of wills?"

I rubbed my hand over his wide, strong, smooth chest. I ran my fingers up to his shoulders, his neck, his face. I touched the wiry hairs of his mustache. I ran my fingers through the thick black hair of his head. A magic man, I thought; but if I am to have him, I have to become someone who isn't me. I have to let him take control, in a way that no man ever has before.

Or maybe . . . maybe, I thought, I could let myself go almost all the way but keep just a little hold on my old sense of identity, so that a little part of me, secretly, remained objective and in control. I could *seem* to give myself. . . .

The idea made me feel panicky. It seemed dangerous to try to deceive a man like Zenya. I almost believed he could be reading my mind.

"Are you serious about Stella going and your wanting me instead?" I asked.

"Of course I am serious. You are a remarkable woman, Christina, and I sensed that as soon as you walked into my home. I have already told you: I sense how much spirit you have. The vital energies are alive in you. All you must learn is that it is not shameful to submit to the will of a teacher. It is not humiliating to learn how to control those energies inside you, under my guidance."

"I see."

"Stella . . . she was one of the servants in this building when I bought it. She helped out in the kitchen.

Like all the domestic staff, she stayed with the place when I moved in. At first my only interest in her was physical. We had an affair. At the time I was still groping at the edges of the knowledge that I now have. I didn't try to bring Stella into the spiritual world I had discovered until quite recently. It has never been a success, and she knows that. She tries not to accept the fact, but really, she knows it."

I thought of the harsh words I had overheard outside the white door, and the scream from Stella. I tensed involuntarily at the thought of that ever happening to me.

Zenya felt the tremor in my body. "What are you thinking?" he asked me.

"I'm thinking I'm scared." I looked up at his face. I wished I could see him more clearly. "I don't trust you. Sometimes you seem quite evil."

He said nothing for a while. "All I have done is offer you a choice," he told me at length. "It is the same as when I telephoned you at your hotel room. I did not, then, tell you what to do. I gave you the knowledge I had gained and left you to decide how to use it. That is how it always has to be."

"Take it or leave it, right?"

He nodded. His hand caressed my back. "I think you worry too much. You are overanxious because everything seems strange. Quite soon it will no longer be strange to you."

That was what I was afraid of, I thought to myself. I could lose my judgment completely here. Zenya's will was so strong, and his powers were so great. And yet . . .

I knew if I passed up this chance, I would always wonder what I had missed. How could I say no?

"I am honored that you've invited me to be your . . ."

Your what? "Your student," I said finally. "And I'd like to learn all that I can from you."

That was it; it was said.

"Good." His tone was as measured and decisive as ever, as if he had known what I'd say. "Tomorrow, probably, I will show you my rooms, and I will tell you of my other studies, and all that I have discovered. You will move into the room that Stella has been using."

"Just like that? What about her?"

"She will be leaving the castle tomorrow."

"Does *she* know that?" Suddenly I was feeling worried about the girl whom I'd despised just a few hours ago.

"It was her choice to leave," Zenya said. "I told her that I could no longer teach her anything, and she felt too embarrassed, by what she saw as rejection, to go on staying here."

That made sense, I realized.

"Also," he went on, "I think there will be more people coming to the castle, Christina. My contacts with the world beyond are not made only when I convene the Circle. That is the most powerful way; but at other times I make contacts in different ways. I have been learning much; I have made more phone calls; I think curiosity will bring people here, in some cases."

"But how long can you keep this up?" I said. "How many people can you afford to entertain? The upkeep on the place must be astronomical."

"I have no shortage of money."

"Is your father a sheikh or something? How many oil wells does he own?"

"I prefer not to talk about my personal background, Christina."

His tone was suddenly very firm. I felt he had just given me an order. That was the side of him that frightened me. I couldn't imagine what he might do if his orders were disobeyed.

"Whatever you say," I said uneasily.

"Right. It is almost time for me to return to my room, Christina. It would not be good for us to lose sleep. We need to conserve our energy."

He looked down at me. His eyes seemed to be appraising me. I felt that awful mixture of emotions again—wanting to please him, wanting him to want me, and at the same time hating the way he acted as if he owned me.

His hand dropped down to my left breast and grabbed hold of it a little roughly. He squeezed the flesh, then let go, then stroked his fingers across the nipple till it stiffened in reflex. I tried not to feel anything, but it was hopeless—with him holding me and touching me, I couldn't stop myself from getting aroused.

His hand moved down to my thighs. He trailed his fingers over the skin. He went on watching my face. I felt he was toying with me. His fingers moved up to my cunt, still wet and sticky from where he had fucked me a little while before. He touched my clitoris, rolling it from side to side under his fingertip. Still he watched my face and saw the effect his touch had upon me.

Finally he took his hands away from my body, held my face between his palms, and kissed me briefly on the mouth.

"It is good, Christina," he said. "Together we will both learn much."

He turned away then, got off the bed, and stood up. I sat there, my whole body throbbing with the fresh sexual feelings he had aroused. I couldn't think of anything to say.

"Good night, Christina," he murmured. "Sleep soundly."

I didn't answer. I just watched him as he turned and walked to the door, moving swiftly, silently. He opened the door, and then he walked out and the door clicked shut behind him.

Only then did I realize how tense I had been. I slumped down in the bed and found that I was trembling. I rubbed my face with my hands and then hugged myself. All my perceptions came back to normal in a rush, as if I had been able to see and hear and feel only Zenya while he had been with me. Now, I noticed, my body was sore where he had violated me, my breasts were tender where he had held them roughly. I was sticky-wet between my thighs, and at the same time my skin was flushed and tingling with the arousal he had created just before he'd left. The sheets were wrinkled under me. My hair was tangled.

I didn't know what to think. Did I want to go through with this? But how could I turn away from it? And hadn't he been testing me, in a way, to gauge my capacity for giving myself?

I rolled on my side and pulled up my knees, feeling alone and afraid. He knew so much, he had so much, that was the trouble. If he had come back into the room at that moment and had wanted to have sex with me all over again, I had to admit that I would have been unable to refuse. And that made me angry—at him and at myself as well. "I hate you for what you're doing to me," I whispered, as if somehow he could hear me, wherever he was.

"But I don't want it to stop," I added a little later, as my eyes closed and I found myself drifting off in a bed that felt empty now that he was no longer in it beside me.

CHAPTER NINE

I slept restlessly and soon started to dream. It was a nightmare of the worst kind, where everything shifts, nothing can be trusted. I was back in Los Angeles; I was driving my car. The sun was bright and it was hot and I had the window open. There was someone sitting beside me, but for some reason I couldn't turn my head to look at him. I just felt his presence. I wanted to know who had ordered things so I wasn't allowed to look. And then, before I could step on the brake, I drove over a big pothole in the road, and the car jerked under me. I lost control of the steering. I felt myself spinning. I wasn't sitting in the car anymore. I was sitting in a kind of restaurant booth, except that we were still spinning, and all around the booth was some kind of discotheque. The music was loud and I wanted to put my hands over my ears, but now I wasn't allowed to move my arms. The music kept getting louder, till it hurt, and the disco lights were flashing, and the person who'd been in the car was sitting opposite me, but his face was a featureless black mask. "What happened to your face?" I tried to shout, but now I wasn't allowed to move my jaw. I strained, and my muscles hurt with the effort, and then I was running through London, down Oxford Street. There was no one else around, it was dark, I was alone, but I could hear someone ahead of me. I was running from one street to the next, and always the footsteps were ahead of me but out of sight around the next turn. I tried to run faster, but I couldn't. The person was forever just out of sight, and I knew I needed him to help me. Then I looked around, and there was a bus right behind me—I don't know how it had got there without making any noise, but it was about to run over me, and I knew my only hope was to fall flat and let it go over me. I leaped, and I seemed to fly a long distance; then, when I hit the ground, I slid as if I were gliding across black ice. I was on my back, and the bus was driving right over me, and then a whole succession of traffic. I didn't understand how they could keep coming one after another; surely they must stop soon, the traffic lights would make them stop. But then somehow I saw the traffic lights, and they were broken, they were on fire. Then I heard another noise—it sounded like a helicopter. It was; the helicopter was coming down from out of the black sky. I don't know where all the traffic had gone at this point, it was all very blurred. I thought the helicopter would put out the fires that were springing up everywhere, but instead, it just caught fire itself and started crashing down toward me. I was wearing my gray dress and I had some crazy idea that it was like an asbestos suit, it would protect me from the heat. Then I looked down, and I realized I wasn't wearing it after all, I was naked. I started running, but now I wasn't allowed to run, I had to stand there absolutely frozen. Then the fire touched me, but it wasn't hot, it was cold. And all the stars came down out of the sky at me, growing bigger and bigger, into a glaring white mass, and they were cold, too. I thought I was dying—

Someone's hand on my shoulder jerked me out of it. I opened my eyes and felt immediately relieved that I wasn't trapped in the nightmare anymore. I found myself stretched out across my bed at an angle; the covers had fallen on the floor, and I was cold. It was still dark. I peered up to see who it was that had touched me.

"Christina?" said the figure standing beside the bed. "Are you all right?"

It was Nick Weston's voice. "What are you doing in here?" I asked, sitting up and dragging the sheet and blanket back onto the bed. I shivered as I wrapped the covers around myself.

He sat down on the edge of the bed beside me. "I couldn't sleep. I kept dozing off and having nightmares that woke me right up again. I thought you might like a bit of company."

Company, yes, that was all I needed. "I don't know, Nick," I said. "I'm feeling pretty rough. I just had a horrible dream myself."

"Well, it's all right now. We can cuddle up together and keep the nightmares away."

I tried to think of an excuse, to get rid of him. I wasn't up to any more erotic scenes, not for a while, after Zenya. "Nick, I just want to sleep," I told him. "I'm sorry."

"Oh, that's all right. I didn't mean to imply anything else, Christina. I mean, whatever you say."

I almost felt like laughing. Nick was so polite, so obliging and anxious not to offend. After Zenya taking me, using me in whatever way pleased him, it was quite a contrast. I sighed. "You mean it, Nick? You won't expect anything of me?"

"I just don't want to go back into my room on my own," he told me, and he sounded shaky and unsure of himself.

"All right, come in and join me." I shifted over to make room for him in the bed.

He'd been wearing a flannel robe—the kind of thing the British call a dressing gown. He took it off, draped it over a chair, and climbed in beside me.

"Christ, you feel even colder than me," I told him.

"I've been up for a while. Just walking around the house. Actually, I didn't want to wake you. But in the end I didn't know what else to do."

He sounded so miserable, I felt sorry for him. He seemed to have been more affected by the most recent séance than anyone else. "Give me a hug," I said. "That'll warm you."

He felt for me in the dark. I turned around so that my back was to him; I didn't want to get him aroused. I felt his body slide closer. He was bony and lean, compared to Zenya. And where Zenya's chest and legs were completely smooth, Nick's had hairs that tickled me.

He lay nestled up against me, his chest pressed to my back. His hands tentatively circled around me and hugged me. I felt his cock nudge against my buttocks.

The position reminded me uncomfortably of the way Zenya had lain behind me just an hour or two ago, when he had taken me from behind. I didn't want to be reminded of that. I rolled over on my back so that my side was against Nick.

The way I turned resulted in his hand covering one of my breasts. He didn't move that hand away. In fact, he shifted his palm so that it cupped my breast more firmly. And then I felt his cock starting to stiffen, nudging against my thigh.

He pressed closer to me. He kissed me on the cheek, very lightly. I felt his breath on my neck.

"Getting warmer now, Nick?" I said.

"Yes. Yes, definitely."

I reached up and placed my hand on his chest. I started pushing him firmly away. "Then you won't need to hold me so close, will you?"

"Oh." He just lay there as I separated myself from him and moved away to my side of the bed.

Then: "Christina, I . . ."

"What?" I was beginning to get angry with him now.

"Christina, I need you. I really need you rather badly."

I realized there was only one way I was going to get any peace. "What do you need, exactly?" I said, keeping my voice flat and uninterested.

"I need to make love to you."

"You didn't say that to begin with."

"I know. I was afraid you'd tell me to leave you alone. But, Christina, I mean, you really understand me, I just need to feel close to you, that's all."

Well, I thought, at least this is a man I know how to handle. I turned in the bed and shifted so that I was propped up on one elbow. I looked down at Nick's face. He was lying on his back, his hands by his sides. Moonlight still struck through the window, where Zenya had drawn the drapes aside. In the pale light I saw Nick's face looking up at me. I bent my head and brushed my lips across his fleetingly. He made as if to reach for me and hold me, but I quickly held his arms down. "You just lie there," I told him quietly.

"Whatever you say, Christina."

"Yes, whatever I say." Part of me realized then that I wanted this scene with Nick in order to reassert myself over a man—any man—after submitting so totally to Zenya. I wanted to feel in control.

But I wasn't going to think about that. I turned my head first one way, then the other, trailing my long silky hair across Nick's bare neck and shoulders. I lowered my body till just my nipples touched his chest, tantalizingly. I shook my shoulders so that my breasts quivered, and he felt the warmth and softness of my skin. I kissed his cheek, his forehead, his neck. I licked around his ear with just the extreme tip of my tongue.

My body shifted under the crisp linen sheet. The

moonlight was bright enough to cast my shadow on the ruffled white feather pillows. In the shadows of the room, on the walls, the oil paintings of long-forgotten ancestors looked down at us. The canopy of the four-poster bed hung above us like a soft silver cloud.

I took hold of Nick by his short black hair so that he couldn't move his head. I lowered my face to his, and our lips touched, parted, then touched again. He struggled to raise his head, to kiss me harder. I tightened my grip and held him down. Knowing his weakness for dominant women, I thought that that would arouse him, and it did. It turned me on, too, to feel him so much in my power. I twisted my fingers in his hair till he winced and made a little cry. "Now, be still," I told him softly. And then I kissed him thoroughly, exactly the way I wanted to, running my tongue lightly around the insides of his lips, then pressing my mouth hard onto his.

By the time I finished kissing him, he was breathing quickly and his eyes were wide, staring up at me with desire. "May I touch you now, Christina?" As he spoke, his hand moved to my breast.

I grabbed his wrist and wrenched it away, letting him feel the edge of my fingernails. I think he'd wanted me to do that, and certainly it only turned him on more. I rolled on top of him, holding him down with my weight. I reached down and found his cock; it was very big and hard and ready. I opened my legs, straddling him, and quickly put his cock inside me. I wriggled down, sitting on his cock so it pushed all the way up into me.

"That's what you wanted, isn't it?" I said. "That was what you wanted all along."

"Yes."

I placed my hands on his shoulders, then slowly raked my fingernails down his chest, hard enough to redden the skin. "And that, too. You wanted that, didn't you?"

He nodded helplessly, as if he could no longer speak.

I started fucking myself on him very quickly, to see how fast I could make him come. I leaned forward, grabbed him by the hair again, and pulled his head up so I could kiss him hard. He was quite overcome. He kissed me back with total submissive need.

The old bed creaked. The moonlight faded as a single cloud passed across the sky. Our breathing sounded loud in the total stillness of the old castle. Somewhere outside, an owl screeched; then there was absolute silence once more.

I let Nick's head fall back onto the pillow. I let myself fall down on top of him. My breasts squashed against his chest. My buttocks rose and fell, rose and fell, faster and faster. I kissed Nick again, with more passion now. His body stiffened, his back arched, and he clutched at me. I reached down behind him with both hands and grabbed his ass, digging my fingernails in suddenly. He cried out. He writhed. Then he came, moaning and gasping.

Suddenly I felt very tender toward him. I had vented all the aggression that I had been left with after Zenya had visited me. I knew Nick had *wanted* me to be a little dominant, a little rough with him, but I still felt a slight pang of remorse. I hugged him to me and rolled off him, onto my back. His arms went around me. He laid his head on my breasts and buried his face into their softness.

I stroked his hair, then ran my hands down his back. "I hope I didn't hurt you," I whispered.

"Oh, no."

"I'm sorry if I was rough."

"Don't say that, Christina. Don't ever apologize. That

spoils it. Please. I need to believe you did just what you wanted to do."

"I did," I told him truthfully. "I did just what I wanted."

"I needed it so much." His voice was becoming muffled and drowsy. I realized he was already drifting off to sleep.

And I hadn't had a chance to come, myself. Well, it hardly seemed important right then. I stared up at the canopy of the bed and thought about the crazy events in the castle. Not one of the people I had found there seemed remotely normal sexually. I remembered Zenya saying, "Soon it will not seem strange," and once again I felt frightened that we could all go crazy here without realizing it, cut off from reality. I could see myself getting sucked into some decadent scene with Zenya, first as his student, then as his slave; and then, when he wasn't abusing me, I'd be taking it out on Nick. And Alexandra would be twisting Masterson around her little finger. And at the same time she'd be wildly jealous of my being Zenya's mistress. And there'd be an ugly scene with Stella, too, if she didn't leave the castle as planned.

Gently I shifted Nick off me and laid his head on the pillow beside me. I wriggled down under the covers and made myself comfortable around him. He was sleeping like a little kid.

As I drifted off to sleep myself, I realized that the only thing I was certain of was that I couldn't possibly guess how things would develop next.

CHAPTER TEN

We both slept late the next day. When Nick finally woke up, he obviously felt embarrassed about what had happened during the night. He started into his upper-class-apologetic routine—"I do hope you believe I'm not the kind of man who *often* does that kind of thing, Christina"—and I had to reassure him that it was quite okay, and it was also nothing to be ashamed of, that he enjoyed taking a submissive role in sex. Eventually I couldn't cope with his awkwardness and insecurity any longer, so I shut myself in the bathroom and took a long time showering.

When I emerged, he had gone. A sweet man, but it was clear he was going to be hard to cope with if I let him become too hung up on me.

He wasn't down in the dining room, either; out on his morning walk, I guessed. And there was no sign of Masterson or Alexandra. I asked Jenkins if he had seen them.

"Not a sign of them, Miss Van Bell." He walked arthritically around the dining table, minutely straightening each chair in its position, and then he consulted his pocket watch. "I trust they won't be wanting breakfast at this late hour."

He put the watch back in his waistcoat, then hobbled over to the fire and poked at it with a giant pair of wrought-iron tongs.

I finished my own meal, wondering what decadent

delights Alexandra had introduced Masterson to during the hours of darkness.

"What about Stella?" I asked Jenkins just before I left the dining room. "Have you seen any sign of her?"

He turned his pale old eyes my way and regarded me steadily for a moment, as if considering what he should tell me. "She has left Downton Castle," he said finally.

"What? You mean for good?" I tried to sound slightly surprised.

"She has left, madam. That is the extent of my knowledge."

So Zenya went through with it, I thought. I felt a pang of anxiety, but at the same time I felt a little thrill of anticipation. I turned to walk out of the room.

"Incidentally, Miss Van Bell," Jenkins added suddenly, "I think we are to expect a new guest sometime today."

I stopped at the door, turned, and looked at Jenkins. Of course, it was impossible to read anything from his impassive face, but I had the impression he knew more than he let on and was trying to tell me something.

"A new guest?" I asked.

"Yes, madam. Another young lady, I believe. So Mr. Zenya has told me. Sometime this afternoon, perhaps."

"How does he know?"

"I can only tell you what he has told me, Miss Van Bell." His voice was dry and matter-of-fact.

"Well, that's interesting news. Thank you." I walked out of the dining room then. It occurred to me that adding new members to our little group could act like a brake on whatever strange tensions and involvements were building. I didn't want anything to interfere with the psychic explorations of our Circle. On the other hand, I was still nervous about losing my perspective and my identity and all my self-control in some dangerous relationship with Zenya. The idea of a new woman at the castle, who would be objective and uninvolved, made me feel a little safer. I would at least have someone to talk to if things became dangerously weird.

I went back up to my room, thinking that since I was going to probably stay several more days at the castle, I should unpack more of my clothes and make myself more at home. When I opened my door and walked in, I found Stella standing in front of the window, waiting for me.

For a moment, neither of us said anything. As soon as I recognized who it was, I became wary. For all I knew, she had come to take revenge on me for stealing her man away. I paused by the door. "This is a surprise," I said finally. "Mr. Jenkins said you'd already left."

"I have already left. I just came back to warn you."

She didn't sound vindictive. She sounded shaken and tired. I closed the door behind me, but I stayed close to it, just in case. "Warn me?" I said. "What about?"

"Can't you guess?" She sat down on a Victorian armchair by the window. She looked unsteady, and I wondered if she'd been drinking. Her makeup was smudged, and though she was still dressed in white, the clothes looked wrinkled and dirty. "You think you can handle him," she went on. "But you can't. I thought I could, too." She sounded dejected and exhausted.

I decided there was nothing to fear from her. She hadn't come to attack or assault me. I walked over to her. "You look all in," I said, keeping my voice neutral.

"You would be, too. Or should I say, you will be? You know, I hated the sight of you when you turned up here, because I could tell right away he wanted you.

I could see it. All he wanted was to fuck you. And there wasn't anything I could do about it. But you know, I think now perhaps it was all for the best."

She was rambling, talking to hear the sound of her own voice. "You're better off away from Zenya, is that right?" I said.

"I think so. But it's only fair to warn you, that's all."

"Warn me?" On one level, I didn't take her very seriously. It was too obvious that she was making herself feel better by telling herself it was just as well she'd been booted out by her lover. But on another level, I was already uneasy enough about what might happen between myself and Zenya. The last thing I needed was someone playing on those fears.

"He's insatiable, you know." She stood up and wandered around the room vaguely, as if she didn't know what she was doing. "He wants sex all the time. If I ever refused him, he used to hit me."

"If it was that bad, why didn't you leave?"

"He wouldn't let me."

"But you were on your own some of the time, surely. He didn't keep you locked up."

She shook her head. I saw her blond hair was all tangled. There were circles under her eyes. "You don't understand. He didn't stop me leaving *physically*. He stopped me *mentally*."

We stared at each other. "He put a spell on you or something?" I laughed.

She went on staring at me, deadly serious. "He controls people's minds, you've got to understand that."

There was something crazy about the way she was staring at me. It gave me the creeps. Her whole presence was making me feel uneasy. She was so intense, it was hard to ignore what she was saying. She *believed*. "Well, I . . . I'll look out for myself," I said feebly.

"You think you can handle him. That's what I thought."

"No, actually . . . actually I'm not sure I can. I don't know what I'm getting into. It scares me. But I can't resist tasting the forbidden fruit."

She nodded slowly. Then she walked over to the door. She paused and looked at me. "That fruit is poison," she said flatly. Then she walked out.

Nice, I thought. Very nice. Just what I needed to make me feel better. At the same time, I was worried about the girl. I suddenly wondered if she had anywhere to go. The castle was out in the middle of nowhere, and I doubted she owned a car.

Cursing my own softheartedness, I left my room and went quickly to the stairs. Stella should have been only a second or two ahead of me.

As I reached the stairs, Jenkins was laboriously climbing them.

"Did she just come this way?" I asked him.

"Who, madam?"

"Stella. You must have seen her."

He paused, and as always, his face was inscrutable. "She has already left Downton Castle, Miss Van Bell. I apprised you of that just a short while ago."

Oh, Christ, I thought. Either I've started hallucinating or Jenkins is playing strange games with me, or . . . maybe there was a simple explanation, like back stairs, an alternative way to the ground floor that I didn't know about.

". . . was just coming to fetch you, Miss Van Bell," Jenkins was saying.

"What's that?" I dragged my attention back to him.

"A telephone call for you, madam. From America, I think."

"Why didn't you say so?" Quickly I pushed past him and ran down the stairs. At the same time, I was silently cursing Mel—if it was him calling—for picking such a bad time. My thoughts were running off in all directions. I could hardly even remember when I had last spoken to him, or what it had been about.

I went into the little room where the phone was and picked it up. "Hello?"

"Christina!" He sounded relieved. "I've been hanging on the line here for at least a couple of minutes."

"I'm sorry," I said vaguely. "The servant . . . I think he has arthritis, he can't climb the stairs very fast."

"What?" There were the usual crackling noises on the line.

"Nothing. It doesn't matter. Anyway, what do you want?"

There was a pause. "What do you mean? You asked me to call back."

I tried hopelessly to sort out my thoughts. "I did?"

"About the lawyer guy you wanted me to check on. Schmidt."

"Oh! Of course! You mean you have some information?"

"Not exactly. All I can tell you is that if Schmidt did wrong by you, you're a unique case. That guy is as clean as anyone can be. No dirt anywhere, not even by implication. As for the actual details of your sister's inheritance, and then her own will, it's hard for me to get anything detailed without power of attorney from you. But I've checked what's on public record, and it looks absolutely clear. There's nothing in any way suspicious."

He stopped talking. I stood with the phone in my hand wondering what to say. I still couldn't really concentrate on all of this. It no longer seemed very relevant. I didn't need evidence from Mel to prove to me that I had or hadn't made contact with the spirit of my dead sister. It was beyond proof now, as far as I was concerned.

"Christina, are you there?" He sounded worried.

"Yes. Of course. Look, thanks, Mel, you've been wonderful to take all this trouble for me."

"Too bad it didn't pay off. So when are you coming back home from your world of the supernatural?"

There was a patronizing tone to his voice, and that irritated me. "There's nothing *supernatural* here," I snapped at him. "And you couldn't possibly understand what's been going on."

Another pause. "Christina, you don't sound like yourself."

"Who do I sound like?"

"Like some kind of fanatic."

I managed to concentrate and get myself under control. I took a deep breath. "Mel, everything's fine. I'm sorry, you just happened to call at a difficult moment. There's all kinds of interesting people here at this place, and the man who runs it is . . . is very interesting, and I've been quite involved. Involved in the social scene here, I mean." Christ, I thought, if he has any intuition at all, he'll know from that that there's group sex here, at the very least. "I guess I'll stay on a couple more days," I added hurriedly. "You know, I never used to believe in, er, powers of the mind, that kind of thing, and it's been an eye-opener, that's all. I'll be back soon."

"If you *don't* show up soon, I'm coming out there and get you," he said, and laughed unconvincingly.

I laughed too, as if that were a great joke. Actually I just wanted to get off the phone. "You must be calling me before work," I said. "It's early, where you are."

"I tried to get you last night."

"Well, I guess we went to bed before you called.

Anyway, you must be wanting to get dressed and go to your job. I won't keep you."

There was a pause. "I'm missing you, Christina," he said.

It jolted me. Already it felt as if it had been years ago that Mel and I were lovers. "Well, I've missed you too," I replied automatically. "Of course, you know how it is when you're in a group of people—that takes your mind off it."

"Sure," he said. "You're still at this castle? Downton Castle?" He was very careful to pronounce the name clearly.

"Right. Look, Mel, I must run. I'll see you soon."

"Okay if I call you again in a day or two?"

"Sure, anytime."

"All right, Chris. Lots of love."

I finally managed to put the phone down. I turned around to walk out of the little room.

Zenya was standing in the doorway watching me.

I was already confused and on edge. The sudden sight of him made me jump as if I'd just touched a hot stove. "My God, I wish you would make some noise or something instead of just *appearing* like that," I said.

He smiled faintly. Once again I felt as if my words were being ignored as meaningless small talk of no interest to him.

"Your American friend is concerned about you," Zenya said.

Obviously he'd heard my side of most of the conversation. "Yeah, Mel doesn't know what's going on over here," I said.

Zenya walked toward me. He was dressed as usual in his golden robe, with all the mandalas and signs and mythological creatures and strange forms woven into it in multicolored thread. It rustled and shimmered as he moved. It made him seem even taller than he was. I looked up at him as he moved close to me, and I couldn't help but feel intimidated by his presence, no matter how hard I tried to be cool and casual.

He took one of my wrists in each of his hands and held them lightly. He bent his head and kissed me firmly and decisively. At the same time, he moved my wrists behind me so that his arms circled me. And while he still kissed me, he pressed me back against the wall.

His long black hair was around my face. His mustache was tickling my skin. His lips were pressed hard onto mine. His tongue pushed into my mouth.

He continued to hold me backed up against the wall with the weight of his body. He took his hands away from my wrists, leaving my arms still pressed behind my back. He moved his hands up to my breasts and grabbed them, squeezing them. In my mind was a wild jumble of conflicting desires—to give way to him, to fight him, to have him make love to me, to scream, to yield. I felt dizzy, as I had before last night's séance. At the same time, I heard Stella's voice telling me, "He's insatiable." I didn't know, I simply didn't know what was happening to me.

He broke the kiss but kept hold of my breasts through the thin cotton of the dress I was wearing. His grip was almost painful, and I was still trapped by him against the wall. His hips rubbed close, and I felt his cock press through the fabric of his robe, against my groin. "So, Christina," he said, watching me as if he were savoring my helplessness and confusion. "Have you changed your mind since last night?" He smiled as if mocking me.

I avoided his eyes. I didn't think I could speak in a level voice.

"Have you, Christina?" His hips pressed harder against me.

I shook my head quickly.

"Good. Then it is time now for you to come to your new room, and time for you to see some of the things in the east wing of this castle."

CHAPTER ELEVEN

He ushered me ahead of him up the staircase. I felt his presence behind me very vividly, as if I were being followed by some animal of the jungle. He moved silently, but I knew exactly where he was.

We reached the white door. "It is not locked now," he said. So I reached out and turned the polished brass handle. As I did so I glanced back at him, and for just a moment I saw past him, across the upstairs hallway, to the entrance to the west wing of the castle.

For just an instant I caught sight of a face there watching me. It was Nick's face. He was almost out of sight, peering across at me, as Zenya ushered me into his private part of the building. And then Nick saw that I had seen him, and retreated quickly out of my view. But I had had time to observe his expression. I didn't know whether it was jealousy, or what; but his face had been contorted with strange emotion.

"Go on in, Christina," said Zenya, not understanding what I had seen and why I was hesitating.

"Oh. Sure." I walked in through the white doorway. But Nick's face was still bothering me. He had looked anguished. At the same time, he had stared at me for that moment with the helpless eyes of a boy being deserted by his mother.

Well, I wasn't Nick's mother, and I didn't intend to be put in the position of having to act that role.

Zenya shut the white door behind me. To my right was the little black séance room that I had come to know so well. Ahead, the corridor was long and wide, with more doors off it at intervals.

"We will go to my study," said Zenya. He placed his hand on my shoulder and walked me along beside him. Our feet passed over thick carpeting. No oil paintings hung on the walls of the corridor; it had been redecorated in pure white, without any ornamentation. And all the doors off it were white, also.

He escorted me to the door at the end and opened it. He ushered me inside. "This is where my work is carried on," he said.

It was a huge room, with tall, narrow windows in rows at each end of the space. The stone walls had been painted flat white, like the hallway. Modern lighting had been installed—track lights and fluorescents—and the parquet floor had been sanded and repolished till it glowed with a rich luster.

In this huge space, like an artist's studio, were all manner of obscure and magical and arcane objects. Zenya took me by my upper arm. His grip was firm. "I am a collector of primitive artifacts of relevance to studies of the mind," he said. "I will explain some of them to you. Here, for instance . . . an astrolabe." He showed me a giant latticework of brass, shaped into a sphere, atop a pedestal. The brass strips and bands were engraved with legends and symbols. There were disks representing the planets.

"An early attempt at understanding the movements of the heavenly bodies," he murmured. "Inaccurate, for it was based on a pre-Copernican model."

"It was, huh?" I looked up at him and smiled.

He didn't smile back. He gave me such a withering look that I felt immediately embarrassed.

"Here," he went on, pointing to an exquisite embroidered wall hanging. "An even earlier attempt by man to discover and describe the world he lived in. The known surface of the earth seen as a disk carried on the backs of elephants. Charming and quite poetic, but only of historical interest as a curio."

"Of course." I tried to sound noncommittal.

"Here . . ." he moved on. "The periodic table of the elements, as used in chemistry today. Scientifically valid. Beside it, quite a different form of science. An alchemical table of formulae. You realize, I hope, that alchemists were quite methodical and scientific in their studies. They were the first men to investigate the way in which chemical reactions took place—and why. By no means all of their studies were fruitless."

"I thought they spent most of their time trying to turn lead into gold," I said.

"Many uneducated people think that." He said it casually, but it was like a slap in the face.

"I've got a college degree, you know," I said. "You don't have to behave as if I'm a high-school dropout."

He looked at me thoughtfully. "It makes no difference," he said after a little consideration. "I am sure that where the mystic arts are concerned, you are quite naive."

I shrugged. "Maybe so."

"But you have curiosity and intelligence and, most of all, you have the spirit," Zenya finished up. "Very well, you will learn. Here, now, is an orrery—the successor to the astrolabe over there. And here, in this corner, my own alchemical laboratory." It was a confusion of glass lab equipment, brass pots and containers, earthenware jars, and metal tubes, on two benches either side of the small furnace.

"And over here, my desk; and here, most important, the orgone box from which many energies are derived."

It was a large wooden cubicle, like an oversized coffin stood on end, with a hinged door that was standing half-open. "What does it do?" I asked.

"I thought I had asked you to read the works of Wilhelm Reich."

"Well, yes, and I did start—"

"It was his belief, confirmed by my own experiments, that there is an orgone energy in the universe. This energy provides the drive in us that we identify as the sex drive; but it is also the energy that sustains our creativity, our labors, our aspirations, and our emotions. It is life itself. Sexual arousal is a way of tapping that energy. You saw, last night, in the Circle, the effectiveness of that technique."

He stared at me steadily, as if daring me to deny what he said. Of course, I couldn't deny it and had no intention of doing so. The experience was still frighteningly vivid in my head.

"The orgone box," he went on, "is an attempt to tap and channel the orgone energies of the universe into the person who sits within."

I peered into the little cubicle and saw a seat inside it.

"Perhaps it would be good for you to spend a little while in the box now," said Zenya, "before we proceed further, and test your latent powers."

I hesitated. "Really?"

He simply opened the door wider, for me to get into the thing.

I glanced around, at him in his golden robe, and his vast room packed with occult and mystic and arcane devices and charts. It smelled of chemicals and of incense. The bright lighting glinted on dozens of brass and silver pieces of equipment. I felt like the sorcerer's apprentice. I was amazed at how much this man must know about things I had never begun to understand.

"Will I have to stay in this thing for long?" I asked, pointing to what he called the orgone box.

He shrugged. "Ten minutes."

"All right. But I suffer from claustrophobia."

"You will not feel that," he said, confident as always.

I got into the box. Though it was of paneled, polished wood on the outside, inside it was lined with some kind of silvery metal. My own blurred image looked back at me from the three walls. I sat down and he shut the door, which was also metal-faced, completely enclosing me.

I had feared it would be a dark, airless box. But the top was of some translucent material—a crystalline substance. It let in a diffuse, eerie light.

I sat on the little hard seat and wondered what I was supposed to feel. I was nervous in case this might become a frightening, intense experience like our contacts with the world beyond, in the Circle. I didn't like being cut off from Zenya's authority.

So I sat with all my muscles tense and my ears straining to pick up the slightest sound.

Seconds ticked by, and nothing seemed to happen. I didn't know if that was because there was something lacking in me or because the box really didn't work.

Then, just as I was ready to write off the whole thing, I thought I saw a change in the intensity of the light filtering down onto me.

My first reaction was to be afraid that it was going to get dark inside the box. But I realized that this was not what was happening. The light was not just fading; it was changing hue.

Slowly it segued from white to a pale blue; and then a darker, richer color, almost a purple. And as this happened there was a deep humming that slowly grew in intensity, till I felt enclosed by it and could hear nothing else.

It was a droning noise, and yet it was not an ugly sound, or even a boring tone to listen to. It was as if there were other noises behind it or inside it somewhere, just beyond my capacity to distinguish them. My eyes started seeing sparkly little patterns, perhaps because of the persistent purple light. And my skin began to tingle and feel warm, as if I had just had a couple of large brandies. But there was none of the fuzziness that alcohol would have created. Just the opposite: my thoughts seemed to speed up, as if they were racing around under extra nervous power. There were flashes of fragmentary ideas, visions, long-forgotten memories. My whole psyche was going into high gear.

When Zenya finally opened the door, I was reluctant to get out.

"It felt *good,*" I said. "Is it electrical? Did you plug it in or something?"

He took my hand and helped me out of the box. "There is no electricity—not as you understand it, anyway. The only power is the psychic power that I described to you, the orgone power. The box traps it; you radiate and absorb it; the specially insulated walls hold it and multiply it."

I frowned. "It sounds like . . . like a greenhouse." I looked at him nervously, afraid that he would scorn me again.

But he didn't. He looked pleased. "A greenhouse. Yes, that is very true. The greenhouse absorbs and holds heat; the orgone box, orgone energy. Yes, you understand well."

I felt like a little girl being congratulated for giving the right answer in a science lesson. I didn't like being reduced to that level of naiveté—but why try to deny it? I *was* at that level, where psychic knowledge was concerned. And the only way to learn was to admit my ignorance.

"Now the test," he was saying, "although I already know what the outcome will be. It is more to prove to you yourself that your powers are real. Here . . ." He gestured to his desk. It was an old oak piece with a leather top. His own high-backed leather chair stood behind it; he had placed another chair on the opposite side. In the center of the working surface lay a pack of cards. "Sit down, Christina." He indicated the chair on my side of the desk. And he walked around and seated himself opposite.

I looked at the cards. They had featureless black backs. He picked up the deck and turned them over. The reverse sides were white, printed with bold black symbols.

"These are basic cards used in testing telepathy and precognition," he told me. "There are twenty-five cards. Each card has one of five possible symbols on it." He showed me the symbols: a cross, a circle, a square, a star, and some wavy lines. "I will look at the cards one at a time. You will shut your eyes and try to picture in your mind the symbol that I am staring at. We will do this for each card. If you guess more than five correctly, that is a better-than-average score. If you guess more than, say, fifteen, the odds are millions to one against it occurring purely by chance. Guess more than twenty, and the odds are billions to one against."

I sat on the chair, still feeling strangely turned on and alive after sitting in the metal-lined box. I looked at him across the desk and my mind was a jumble of images: his eyes, his body, his forceful taking of me in my room last night, his hands that had gripped my breasts just half an hour ago, his apparent control over me. He stared at me as if he were evaluating me all the time. Up here in his sanctum, so full of marvels and strangeness and wonder, I desperately wanted not to make a fool of myself. I wanted to do well. I wanted to prove to him that I was worthy of being invited into his world.

"We will begin," he said. He shuffled the deck, without looking at the cards. His eyes were still on me, and I felt hypnotized. He turned the deck facedown and picked up the first card, carefully, so that I could not possibly see its design. His eyes shifted focus for just a second, and then stared back at me as soon as he had registered the symbol on the card in his hand. He waited.

My mind was racing, but through it all I saw the five different patterns, and one of them seemed to fluoresce in my vision, like an afterimage, hanging between myself and Zenya. It was a circle, and I said "Circle" before I even thought about it.

His expression didn't change by a fraction. He simply put the card facedown on the desk, to his right. "I cannot tell you anything until the test is over," he explained, picking up the next card. "For if I confirm that any of your guesses are right, that informs you, by subtraction, how many other cards of that design may be left in the deck. And there must be absolutely no possibility of cheating here."

I nodded blankly. If he thought my mind was capable, at that moment, of counting cards, like some bridge player, and working out odds and making mental math calculations, he was crazy. I could hardly even keep track of where I was.

He was already holding the next card. "Lines," I blurted, not even knowing why. Again he placed the card facedown to his right, on top of the first one.

"Cross," I said, to the next. This time he put the card facedown on his left on the desk. I realized one facedown pile was of correctly guessed cards; the other pile was of the strikeouts. But which pile was which?

The guessing went on. I became dizzier, with concentration and desperation and my hopeless attempts to actually see the symbols in my mind. The pile of cards to his right grew large; to his left, just a few accumulated. That upset me, because I had decided the ones on his left were the ones I had identified correctly. As the game went on, I became more dispirited and fatalistic. I started giving my answers faster and with less thought. The pile on his right grew bigger and bigger.

Finally he had been through all twenty-five cards and he picked up the pile on his left and counted through them methodically, not looking at me. I squirmed in embarrassment.

"There are only seven cards here," he told me at length. Well, I thought, at least that's a *bit* above average.

"That means there must be eighteen cards in this other pile," he said, picking up those to his right. "I confess I am surprised, Christina."

"I could try it again," I said.

He stared at me levelly. "If you wish. But I doubt you could do better. Eighteen is a very high score."

Then I realized he had been playing with me. The eighteen were the *correct* guesses. He laughed then—the first time I had heard him laugh. It came from deep in him. He stood up, walked around the desk, took my arm, and pulled me up beside him. "Yes, Christina, eighteen out of twenty-five. On your first attempt. Do you want to look at the sequence of symbols and check it with your memory of the sequence that you called out to me? Or do you believe now that the power exists, that it can be used and shared between us?"

He put the cards in my hands. I looked down at them. I couldn't concentrate. There was no doubt in my mind, anyway.

"Later you can test yourself, on your own," he went on. "To guess the next card to be turned over, and measure your powers of precognition. I'm sure you will do as well there, also."

At that moment, anything seemed possible. Why not? This man had just told me—shown me, *proved* to me beyond mathematical doubt—that I had telepathic ability.

"Come with me, now. To the room where you will be living henceforth."

Not *staying,* I noticed. *Living.*

I went with him out of his study, to the next door along the hallway. It opened into a small but pleasing room, all renovated and painted white like the rest of the east wing that I had seen so far. There was a built-in closet, a dressing table, a modern bed, and a small private bath. I had half-expected to find traces of Stella's staying in there. But no: the room was as clean and anonymous as a modern hotel room. The only hint of character of the castle was the stone window frame, though it too had been painted white.

Zenya laid the deck of cards on the dressing table. He pointed to a shelf of books. "You will read these. You will learn. We have only just begun."

I nodded dumbly, still in a euphoric daze.

He took me by the arm and pulled me to him roughly. He embraced me fiercely and kissed me with a kind of savage, careless pleasure. He seemed just as pleased as I was that I had shown psychic ability and was therefore worthy of him.

He paused, looked at my face, then reached out with one hand and opened the door of the built-in closet. Only one garment hung inside: a full-length pure white dress. He pulled it out and held it up for my inspection.

When I saw it more closely I realized it was not a dress, but a robe like the one he wore himself. Except that it was all in white; even the embroidery—which was exquisitely detailed, consisting of symbols and forms such as those in his own garment—even this embroidery was all in white on white. It seemed to be silk; it felt soft and fine to my touch. I remembered that Stella had always worn white, but nothing regal and beautiful like this. I wondered what Zenya's thing was about dressing his women in white, but at that moment I didn't care.

"You will put it on now," he said. "I have been waiting for someone such as you to wear this."

I was out of my clothes within seconds. Vaguely I realized he was watching me with hungry eyes while I stripped myself naked, but I didn't care. I took the white robe and pulled it around me; I tied the belt at the waist; I looked at myself in the mirror. Indeed, now, I was his princess.

"You will wear it at all times, in my private rooms of the castle, and downstairs also," he said.

"It's beautiful," I told him. I stood before him, under his appreciative eyes. Then I kissed him long and deep.

He took my face between his hands. He studied me, touching my cheeks, my nose, the curve of my brow. Finally, lightly, he ran his finger around the insides of my lips. And at the same time I felt his cock swelling and pushing up where our hips were touching.

"You will please me now, Christina," he murmured.

"Yes," I whispered, totally under his spell.

His finger circled my parted lips once again, and then pushed into my mouth, to my tongue. "You will please me well," he said.

Slowly I got down on my knees. I parted his golden robe, with its embroidery of scarlet dragons, alchemical symbols, astrological signs, and mythical beasts. I reached up and took his cock in my two hands. He folded his arms, looking down at me, watching me. I opened my mouth and kissed the head of his cock, then drew it very, very slowly between my lips, licking and sucking.

The very act of going down on him was arousing me. I felt giddy and high. I took his cock deep, opening up my throat and engulfing him. It was an incredibly erotic act for me. My whole body seemed alive. I was conscious of my clitoris, swollen and aching, and my nipples seemed to crave to be touched. All my sexual energies were humming, humming like the tone that had enclosed me inside the orgone box.

I slid my hands inside his robe and grasped his hips. I pulled myself to him until every inch of his magnificent cock was sucked into me. Then I commenced moving my head away and back again, taking him in and out of my mouth as fast as I could. With the tips of my fingers I caressed his balls and the insides of his thighs. I reached behind and ran my hands over his buttocks. I stroked my hand across his prostate, then cupped his balls tenderly while I sucked insistently and insatiably.

He came very quickly. His cock swelled until I could barely take it and my jaw ached and I felt as if I were suffocating. And then the semen gushed out, and I swallowed hungrily, draining his essence and taking it into myself.

When it was over I released him from my mouth reluctantly, and stayed kneeling on the floor, gasping for breath. My mouth was full of the strange sweet taste of him.

He stooped, put his hands under my arms, and lifted me to my feet. He embraced me loosely. "Very beautiful, Christina," he murmured. "Very fine."

I was so horny and hot I felt like raping him. I pressed hard against his body. I touched his penis tentatively. "Are you going to be able to . . . can you . . . ?" I was remembering how quickly he had regained his erection during the night.

"In a moment." He drew me to him and kissed me very deeply. His lips seemed more yielding than I remembered. Together we shared the taste of him that was still in my mouth.

His hand ran over my skin, under the white robe that I was wearing. His fingers caressed my belly, spreading warmth and little bursts of tingling sensation that ran down to my groin. I felt myself getting wetter and wetter inside.

With his other arm he held me more tightly to him, squashing me against him. He could be frighteningly strong when he chose to be. And still he kissed me.

Then his caresses moved from my belly, lower, till his fingers were brushing through my pubic hair. I made a little involuntary noise and parted my thighs as much as I could, standing there pressed against him. His fingers crept down and touched my labia; I shivered with excitement. I was breathing fast now, and aching with need for him. He stared into my eyes while he went on touching me.

His finger crept into my vagina. He smiled faintly as he found how hot and wet I was. He pushed two fingers into me and I gasped; my knees felt wobbly and I had to cling to him for support.

"Ah, Christina," he murmured. "You are very lovely." And he started rubbing one fingertip over my clitoris, very lightly at first, and then more and more firmly.

I felt my breath coming in short little sobs as he went on and on touching me, insistently, undeniably, while he stared into my eyes. I felt self-conscious, being watched by him, as I lost all my self-control and surrendered to the sensations he was producing in me. My face was flushed and my hair was disheveled and I was trembling, not far from orgasm.

"I want you to come now, Christina," he murmured,

still staring at me. His finger pressed harder on my clitoris, and moved faster, in a little frenzy of insistent motion. His other arm still encircled me, holding me against him. His hand clenched on my shoulder as he spoke. "Come. Come for me."

Part of me wanted to resist him. Part of me didn't like being so open and vulnerable and easily aroused by this powerful man. But that part of me was fighting a losing battle. He knew just how to tantalize and tempt me. He knew how to make me feel helpless.

I moaned and slumped against him. The desire was building to the point where it felt unbearable. I had to have the release. His finger on my clitoris, and the waves of sensation, became the totality of my awareness. I moaned again and my hands tightened convulsively where I was clutching him. And then the tension broke and the orgasm swept over me and I think I screamed with the passion and pleasure of it. I writhed against him. I looked up at him and saw him watching me, with ironic detachment. He smiled as I gasped and shook and finally lay trembling against his firm, strong body.

He kissed me lightly on the forehead. "Very sweet. Very beautiful." He finally took his hand away from between my legs. He hugged me to him for a moment, then he guided me over to the bed at the side of the room. Shakily I sat down on it.

He sat down beside me.

I was still breathing hard and my pulse was racing. I could feel where my thighs were wet with juices from my vagina. My whole body was hot and pulsing with each heartbeat.

He kissed me on the forehead again, and then on my cheeks and chin and all over my face, while he held my head in his hands. Finally he kissed me on the mouth, long and slow. It all felt good, but I was in no condition to be really aware of what was going on. I was dazed and dizzy with the power of the sexual feelings that this man had aroused in me.

He took my hand then and guided it inside his robe. I touched his cock and found it big and hard. Evidently he had gotten aroused again merely by watching me have my orgasm, at his command.

I stroked his penis, running my fingertips lightly up and down it, but I don't think I was doing it in a very coordinated or purposeful way. I still felt too shaken. And I wasn't sure exactly what he wanted.

My uncertainty didn't last long. He quickly made his intentions obvious.

"Lie back on the bed, Christina," he told me.

Slowly I did as he said. My embroidered white robe rustled against the bedcover. He reached for the robe and opened it to either side of me, so that my whole body was laid out naked for his enjoyment. I saw his eyes take in everything. His dark, impassive face hardly altered its expression, but I sensed he liked what he saw.

He shifted on the bed so that he was stretched out beside me, propped on one elbow, looking down at me. He ran his hand over my body, and circled his fingers around my left breast, savoring its fullness. His grip was firm, almost painful. I felt as if he were asserting some kind of ownership of my body, as if to say: You are mine now, and I can touch you anytime, any way that I wish. My head was a mass of conflicting emotions, not knowing whether to be flattered by his wanting me or angry at his assuming he could do what he liked.

He bent his head to mine and kissed me hard. At the same time, his grip shifted on my breast, till he held the nipple between his finger and thumb. While he went on kissing me, his grip tightened, pinching my nipple. It started hurting. I struggled and freed my mouth from his. I cried out.

He only relaxed his hold slightly. "It hurts, Christina?"

"Yes. Stop. Please stop." It was a sharp yet diffuse kind of pain, more like an ache, really, and though it didn't hurt very much, it scared me. I reached for his wrist, to pull his hand away from my breast.

He stopped me. He rolled onto me, pinning me. "You will learn to savor every sensation with me, Christina," he murmured. His other hand twined in my hair until that, too, gave me just a little moment of pain. "Every expression of desire, every surge of the libido. You will savor it all, as pure sensation."

And then suddenly he reached down and guided his cock to the mouth of my vagina, and in one motion he thrust into me.

I cried out again, more in surprise than anything else. Suddenly he was fucking me, very hard, and he was no longer pinching me or tugging at my hair. His arms were around me. His hips were slamming down against mine. The bed was shaking under us.

His body felt incredibly strong—so firm and rigid, and untiring. His cock thrust deep, so deep. I had thought I was completely sated by the orgasm he had given me a few moments earlier; but no, already the sensations were building again, and I was hungry for more. Perhaps the little twinges of pain really had turned me on, or made me ready for more. I didn't know and I didn't care.

He clutched me up against him and I felt as if he were bending me like a supple tree in a storm. My breasts rubbed across his chest. My thighs opened wide to take him as deep as I could. I locked my legs around him, urging him inside me. I gasped with each thrust of his cock, and I squirmed against him and clutched at him and lost myself completely in the sheer passion of the act.

He shifted slightly, moving up a bit so that the top of the shaft of his penis rubbed harder against my clitoris. It doubled the sensations that were pulsing and surging from my groin. All my muscles began knotting up as I came close to orgasm.

He sensed my arousal. He moved back a little and slowed his thrusts, preventing me from coming.

"Don't stop," I gasped. "I'm so close." I squirmed my hips, trying to take him deep again.

He kept his cock moving, just enough to sustain my passion, but not enough to take me up and over the edge into a climax. He looked down at me with a kind of hungry, passionate expression, savoring his control of my responses. I sensed he was holding himself back from coming, at the same time he was holding me back, too.

He reached down between our bodies and brushed his fingers over my clitoris. I gasped and flinched.

"You want it, Christina?" he murmured. "You want to come?"

"You know I do."

He toyed with me again. "Are you sure?"

"Don't play with me," I told him.

He smiled faintly. Suddenly he started pulling his cock out of me. "I am the one who gives . . . instructions here," he said.

Suddenly I hated him for his attitude. I wanted to tell him to go to hell. And yet . . . and yet, I wanted the orgasm more. I was caught again between my need to feel an independent, self-willed woman . . . and my crazy desire to surrender to him totally, and be used by him, and give him everything.

I closed my eyes. "Just fuck me," I said. "Please fuck me."

He pushed the length of his cock slowly back into my body. It felt so incredibly good. I arched my back and cried out.

"You want that," he whispered. His mouth was close by my ear.

I nodded helplessly.

"You want more of it," he whispered. He moved his hips insistently.

"Yes," I gasped.

"Tell me you want more. Tell me . . . tell me you want it so much you would beg for it, Christina."

I didn't know where I was. I only knew my need. "I want it so much . . ." I mumbled.

"Say it." His voice sounded tighter now, and he was breathing harder. I think the words were turning him on. "Say, 'I beg you to fuck me more.' "

And he paused in his movements, as if he were ready to pull out of me again and leave me empty.

I couldn't bear that. I would have said anything. It didn't mean anything, it didn't matter. "I beg you to fuck me more," I told him.

And then, finally, he released his self-control. He started fucking me wildly, with abandon. He panted and groaned and clutched at me. He moved in a frenzy. His cock jammed into my body so hard it was almost painful. He kissed my face. His hands groped at my body, as if he were a blind man, searching. His cock seemed to grow even larger. His passion was frightening. At the same time, it turned me on fantastically. I gasped and screamed as suddenly my orgasm swept over me—fulfillment at last!—and I think that seeing me come was what finally made him come. He gave a great shout of passion and release and fell down upon me, grinding his hips against mine. His cock spurted inside me, and I could feel every little movement, every spasm. It seemed to go on and on forever.

I lay there on my back under him, with my arms and legs wrapped around him, and I never wanted to let go.

Gradually our passion subsided. Gradually our breathing slowed and we returned to reality.

Finally he disengaged himself from me.

We both sat up on the bed. There was a different look on his face that I hadn't seen before. He actually looked kind of pleased, not so stern and impassive. I felt I had gotten through to him in some way and had broken some of his rigid self-control. Maybe he was even a little embarrassed by having exposed his spontaneous desires to me.

At the same time, I was embarrassed by what he had made me say in the moments of my greatest desire and passion. I wished I could forget the words, but I could still hear myself, all too clearly, begging him to fuck me more.

"That was very fine, Christina," he said. He kissed me.

I responded uncertainly. "I'm not sure you should have made me . . ." I began. "I mean, I don't normally ever say things to a man, like . . ."

"I just needed to know that you desired me as much as I desired you, my dear," he said, watching me carefully. "If the woman does not give of herself totally—if she does not have the courage to admit to her vital need—then how can the man give of *him*self?"

We looked at each other. Under the influence of him, there, with his charismatic presence exerting its magic on me still, his words seemed to make perfect sense. Later, I realized that what he said amounted to: You have to beg for it before I'll give it to you. But that was later—much later—and right then, sitting beside him, I had no doubt in my mind that he was correct, and that I was privileged to have been given so much attention from him. In fact, I even felt ashamed for having complained about what he had made me say.

"It is all part of what we are experiencing and learning here," he went on. He ran his fingers lightly over my smooth, soft skin as he spoke, and his eyes savored every contour. "To give, to tap the fundamental energies, to go further than one has ever dared to go before, into worlds of pure sensation and worlds that can be reached *only* by tapping those primal, sexual energies. Christina, we have only just begun. As the days pass you will find that you experience more and more levels of heightened fulfillment, quite beyond anything you have known before. At the same time, in our gatherings of the Circle, you will gain the courage to travel further, and harness these primal, vital energies."

His voice sounded hypnotic. His caresses, too, were putting me in a kind of trance. It all sounded so right; and I felt so pleased to have been allowed into this incredible experience, as his chosen partner.

He embraced me gently and kissed me. He was back in complete control of himself now, and every little word and movement seemed to be made with complete assurance.

He stood up slowly and gathered his robe about his magnificent body. He stretched, moving his shoulders. "I think, Christina . . . I think it is time for me to go down to the reception room. I think a visitor has arrived."

I blinked. I was still in a blissful, satiated, sensual trance. "A visitor?"

"Someone has arrived by car, and Jenkins has admitted her."

"Her? You mean you know who this is?"

"Possibly. She has come here out of curiosity, just as you did."

For a moment I felt a sudden stab of possessive, insane jealousy. At that moment the last thing I wanted was to have some new woman turning up at the castle and competing with me for Zenya's attentions. And then I realized: I was feeling what Stella must have felt when I had come to the castle originally.

I touched my fingers to my forehead. It was all too much to cope with. I was beginning to lose touch with my real self; I couldn't keep perspective. "You're going to welcome this new guest downstairs now?" My voice was as level and measured as I could make it.

"Yes. Soon, then, it will be time for our dinner."

Dinner? Was it that late? I realized we had spent quite a lot of time in our lovemaking.

"Well," I said carefully, "maybe I should, as your . . . your student, come and meet this new person with you now." I hoped my voice didn't reveal any of the jealousy and insecurity that I felt.

"You wish to?" He sounded thoughtful.

"If I may."

He seemed to reach some private decision. "Very well. Come, Christina."

So I went with him down the white hallway and out through the white door, in my white gown, into the rest of the castle. My skin was still flushed and my body felt exercised, sated, totally fulfilled. My mind was dizzy with all that I had seen and experienced—the smell of Zenya, the symbols on the ESP cards, the feel of his cock inside me, the hum of the orgone box, the pressure of his mouth on mine. I didn't know where I was anymore, but it didn't matter. I walked down the stairs with him, feeling like a queen in the robe he had given me. A mystic queen, chosen by the man who worked miracles.

CHAPTER TWELVE

We went into the reception room where I had originally met Zenya myself. It made me feel even dizzier to imagine that day, and how I had felt and acted then. I was quite dizzy enough already, so I chose to block it out of my mind.

We entered the room quietly. Zenya stopped just inside the doorway, and I stood beside him, waiting. Our guest was pacing nervously at the far end of the room, by the windows. She was dressed oddly, in a crocheted shawl over an oriental blouse, with American Indian jewelry and other ornaments around her neck, and gypsy-style earrings. From the waist down she wore faded Levi's whose cuffs had been unraveled into a decaying fringe. On her feet were clog-type sandals.

She looked up suddenly and saw us standing watching her. She had a round, pink face; I gauged her to be in her mid-thirties. She wore wire-rimmed glasses and her hair was frizzy and unkempt. She saw Zenya and beamed at him. Quickly she stepped across the room, her hand extended.

This woman is a kook, I thought to myself. This, the woman who I imagined might help me keep my sense of reality if I got in too deep. She had obviously lost her own sense of reality ten or fifteen years ago—probably around the time she started taking acid and casting the *I Ching*.

Zenya shook hands with her with even more reserve than usual, I thought. "You are Margaret Burke," he said quietly.

"You know!" she exclaimed, with a wide, blissed-out smile. "I thought you would. It was inevitable."

"I am Zenya," he said. "And this is Christina, my co-worker."

So I was a co-worker now.

Margaret Burke turned her sunny, radiant face my way and bobbed her head. "How wonderful," she said, and looked back at Zenya. "It's all just as I visualized it."

I realized I had seen women like her rooting around in health-food stores, gathering obscure herbs and roots and nuts and vitamins, and carting it all away in "Save-a-Tree" burlap bags. Well, I thought, at least she's no competition where Zenya's affections are concerned. I sensed in fact that he had been thrown off balance by her. She was shaping up to be as much of a psychic—or would-be psychic—as he. And this was no time for a crackpot amateur astrologer tarot-card-reading Ouija-board dabbler to turn up in our Circle.

"You really think you can put me into empathetic contact with Ruth?" she was saying to Zenya. She turned to me before Zenya could answer. "Ruth was my dearest friend. She only passed away a month ago. It was a tragedy."

"I'm sorry," I said. "Our Circle has had amazing success, though, in—"

"You will speak with Ruth," Zenya interrupted me. "It is possible."

"Really! Oh, how wonderful! When can—?"

"Christina will show you the guest room in which you will be staying while you are here," he cut in. "You have luggage. Please bring it in now."

"Of course! How kind you are!" She bobbed her

head and then bustled out of the room, her wooden shoes going clonk-clonk on the tiled floor in the hallway.

We followed her out. Then Zenya touched my arm, restraining me. "You will find out all you can about her," he murmured to me. "You will put her in the guest room that you yourself were using. I have already given instructions for your possessions to be shifted from it to your new room. It will have been done while we have been down here talking."

Instructions? When? But it was no use pursuing those kinds of questions. "Can we cope with this person in the Circle?" I asked. I could see her totally fouling the mood.

"She will be as one with us. You will see." There was, as usual, no doubt in his voice.

Margaret Burke was already coming back into the hall, carrying an old string bag full of secondhand clothes, and a knapsack over her shoulder. She had left the front door open; through it I saw the car from which she had just removed her possessions. It was a new Rolls-Royce. The woman might be a kook, but she was a rich kook.

"I'll show you the way," I said to her.

"I will be meditating until dinner," Zenya told me. Quickly he stepped ahead of us, up the stairs, and out of sight through the white door, which he shut firmly behind him. I took Margaret's knapsack for her and escorted her more slowly up the staircase and into the west wing.

We entered the room that, until now, had been mine. Sure enough, every single possession had been removed. The bed had been remade with clean sheets. The place looked immaculate.

"Why, it's just perfect," Margaret exclaimed. "It has such good vibrations about it," she added. "So does he. Zenya. I can't believe the good things that happen to me." She set down her string bag full of ragged garments and turned to look at me. "And you, my dear, I have an especially good perception of you. Show me your hand."

I did as she asked.

"No, no, your *left* hand! Whatever were you thinking of?"

"I'm sorry," I said, "I guess I'm used to shaking hands with people, and I forgot."

She didn't hear me. She was already studying the lines. "Have you ever had a Kirlian photograph taken, my dear?"

I thought fast. "Of course," I said.

"And what did it show?" She stared up at me with eagerness. Her eyes were strangely bright behind her steel-rimmed glasses.

"I have pronounced telepathic empathy," I said firmly, in the knowledge that this, at least, was true.

"How wonderful." She still had hold of my hand. She drew me toward her. "I just have to embrace you."

There was no time to think of an elegant way to refuse. She grabbed me in a bear hug, and I winced, imagining she was creasing my lovely silver-white robe.

"One should be able to express human love, don't you think?" she said, still holding on to me. "The love that links all *aware* people. Oh, and you are so lovely, it makes me feel wonderful to touch your beauty." As she said this, her hand stroked my cheek.

"Miss Burke—" I began.

"Margaret! Please, I'm Margaret!" She sounded suddenly upset.

"I'm sorry. Margaret. Please excuse me if I'm assuming anything, or being tactless, but I must tell you that I'm not gay. I only have relationships with men."

Her blissed-out smile didn't waver, but her startling eyes searched over my face as if looking for the source of some troubling little detail. "No, my dear," she said with the assurance of higher knowledge. "No, you're like me, inside. You love *all* humanity. It's only your social conditioning that causes you to draw imaginary lines and build walls where there should be none." Her face moved closer to mine. She had a strange smell—herbal shampoo, perhaps, or some kind of vitamin-E skin ointment. "I can help you, my dear. Just by looking at you, I know you've never been Rolfed. Do you have time? You can lie down on the bed and I can find the nodes that are out of alignment. The points that correspond to your life's traumas. Shall we do it now?"

"No," I said, "I have to go now." I started to struggle free.

"It's natural to resist the force that will open your psyche," she said reflectively, still beaming at me. "Freedom can be frightening. But have courage, my dear. Perhaps later?"

"The Circle meets after dinner," I said. "And really, Margaret, that is far more important."

"The Circle!" She seemed to test the word in her mouth. "How absolutely wonderful!"

"It *is.*" I gave her a hard look. See how your junkheap of secondhand fads and half-baked mystic crap compares to that ultimately real experience, I thought to myself. Assuming we would be able to shut the woman up, of course.

"I must leave you now," I said, trying to regain some of my regal posture. "You'll probably want to use the bathroom before dinner."

She didn't answer. She just clasped her hands and beamed at me some more, as if projecting some kind of well-being into my head. Trying to convert me into a replica of her, I realized. I turned quickly and walked out.

Approaching me along the hallway were Masterson and Alexandra. I paused, taking in their expressions: Masterson looking embarrassed but secretly rather pleased with himself, and Alexandra showing an almost supercilious self-satisfaction.

"I haven't seen you two all day," I said. "Have you been hiding in your room, Alexandra?"

"I've been hiding Harry in my room," she said and looked at Masterson. He turned red and started to say something in the way of an explanation, but Alexandra went on: "But I haven't seen you either, Chris. And what's this new outfit?"

"Zenya gave it to me," I said as casually as I could. "Stella has left, you see."

Watching Alexandra's face was a delight. She went through a succession of emotions—amazement, jealousy, anger, and finally resignation. "Well, congratulations," she ended up.

"The same to you," I said with light irony, and walked on down the hallway, feeling very pleased with myself.

I knew Alexandra was still watching me. And I couldn't resist flaunting my status to the limit. So I walked straight to the white door into the east wing. I was sure it wasn't locked; I hadn't heard Zenya lock it after he had gone in there a few minutes earlier. I turned the handle. Sure enough, the door opened. I walked casually in, glanced back at Alexandra and gave a little wave, then shut the door behind me.

I proceeded along the corridor, planning to go to my new room and sort out the possessions of mine that had been shifted there by Zenya's staff of servants.

But something made me pause. I listened and heard a rustling noise and then a man's voice moaning.

I knew that Zenya valued his privacy. I knew I should not intrude on any form of meditation. And yet my curiosity was insatiable. I crept along the corridor. The noise had come from a door on the right, just before the way into Zenya's study at the end. I moved closer and saw that the door was not quite closed. There was a thin crack where it was hinged.

Holding my breath, I tiptoed to that crack and peered through it. I saw a little room, all in white, like the rest of Zenya's rooms. A white, soft cushion was on the floor, so big that it virtually filled the space. There was no other furniture.

Zenya was stretched out facedown on the cushion. He seemed to be moving oddly, though it was hard to tell, since he was dressed still in his golden robe. He twisted and squirmed, and for a moment I thought there might actually be something physically wrong.

And then he moved to one side and I realized. He was not alone. A naked figure was lying prostrate under him.

My heart seemed to stop as I felt a surge of intense jealousy. I clenched my fists. And then I saw: the prostrate figure was a man. It was Nick Weston, stretched out naked under Zenya's body.

I stared until there was no possible doubt. Then I turned and ran to my room, and shut the door, and sat down on the bed. Too much, my head was telling me, too much of everything—too much sex, too much surprise and uncertainty, too much confusion, too much craziness.

But still, I knew, there would be more.

CHAPTER THIRTEEN

During dinner I sat at Zenya's right, where Stella used to sit. Nick, as usual, sat on Zenya's left. So he and I were opposite each other.

He looked his usual respectable British self, in a three-piece blue pinstripe suit, white shirt, and college tie. I kept stealing glances at him and wondering if his homosexual scene with Zenya was just a one-time impulse, or if it had been going on for some time. And who had started it?

Nick, I am sure, was filled with equal curiosity about me. My new role as Zenya's mistress clearly unnerved him. He avoided my eyes through the whole meal, and I kept remembering the lost look that I had seen on his face when he had observed me going in through the white door with Zenya, earlier.

Conversation might have been strained, were it not for Margaret Burke. She had dabbled in every cult, every therapy, and every branch of the occult. She told us about astrology, est, Synanon, vegetarianism, Scientology, Buddhism, and a dozen different Indian gurus. Zenya sat through it all with a faint smile. Even when she asked him direct questions, he said absolutely nothing in reply. This treatment didn't embarrass her, however; she seemed incapable of being embarrassed.

Dessert was just being served when the phone rang. Jenkins went out to answer it. I looked at my plate, feeling uneasy, *knowing* that the phone call was going to be for me, and that there was something ominous about it. When Jenkins finally hobbled back to the dining room and told me that the call was from America, for me, I found myself trapped in a déjà vu: I anticipated every word the old servant spoke, I felt trapped consciously in the actual flow of time, and totally helpless to alter the sequence of events. The uneasiness became genuine dread; I *knew* that this phone call was going to mean bad trouble in some way, and I sat there trying to think of something to do to evade the future.

"Are you not going to go to the phone, Christina?" Zenya asked me finally. I started, realizing that Jenkins was still standing in the doorway waiting, and everyone at the table was looking at me.

"If . . . you think it's all right," I said to Zenya.

He gestured casually to the door. "Go."

So, trusting his judgment more than my own, I went.

It was Mel, of course. "Just called to see how you're doing," he said in a tone of forced casualness.

"We were just eating dinner," I said.

"All right, I won't keep you. But is everything okay where you are? *Really* okay?"

"Of course, Mel. I thought I told you . . ." Yesterday? Or had he called the day before? My mind hunted around in circles, trying to figure what had happened when. But all of the past few days was a jumble of disconnected images and events. ". . . when you last telephoned me," I finished weakly.

"Yeah. So this guy who owns the castle, what was his name, Zenya? You think he's for real, huh?"

"He's completely sincere." I looked down at my white robe. I stroked my fingertips over its designs. I felt so cut off from Mel, so totally distant. Nothing he had to say seemed of conceivable interest.

"Have you, ah, paid him any money?" Mel asked.

I frowned. "What?"

"Is he collecting tithes, that kind of thing? You know, some of these gurus, they—"

"He doesn't even charge anyone for food and lodging, Mel!" I felt angry now. "He's a rich man, and in any case he's got more important things to think about than . . ." I realized I was almost shouting. I stopped abruptly.

"Okay, okay." Mel still sounded cool and easy. "You know, Chris, I was thinking, whatever you're into over there must be kind of interesting, to keep you there."

"It is, Mel. It's one of the greatest things that has ever happened to me." There, I thought: that should show you how much more important this is than you realize.

"How would it be if I came over?" he went on.

For a moment I tried to visualize it. It seemed impossible. I was in a present time of intrigue and discovery and mystery and wonder. Mel was . . . was outside of all that. He was out *there,* from back *then.* How could the two things coincide? "I don't think it would be a good idea," I said slowly.

"Why not, Christina? You know, I've really been missing you, and since there isn't as much work to keep me here as I thought, I could just come over for a couple of days."

I realized he must be testing me in some way. Perhaps to find out if I was already involved with some other man. I didn't know what to say. "No, Mel," I blurted in the end. "Please don't come here. I'll be back soon."

"This guru guy—this Zenya—I thought he's open to visitors."

"I . . . I don't know. Perhaps not. Trust me, Mel. I have to go now. And please . . . please don't keep calling."

"Okay, Chris." He still had that artificially casual tone of voice. "Take it easy." And he hung up.

I put the phone down slowly. I still had a horrible feeling of dread. I knew something was going on, beyond what Mel had said. He knew something, or was planning something, or . . . I couldn't imagine it.

I went back to the dining room. As I walked in, I heard Zenya talking. He was briefing Margaret Burke and the rest of the group on the function of sexual energy in the Circle. I quickly looked at her face to see if she seemed shocked; but of course not. She was beaming, nodding, taking it all in. "Why, that sounds absolutely wonderful," she said when Zenya had finished. "I sense . . . so much love here, in this place. You are all such warm people." She turned to each person, radiating her own unstoppable enthusiasm.

Love, I thought. Well, that's one way of describing it. I seated myself discreetly beside Zenya.

"You do not look composed, Christina," he murmured.

"My American boyfriend. Mel. He wanted to come here."

"And you told him . . . ?"

"I said no."

Zenya nodded. "It is as well. We cannot admit any more new people to the Circle for a while, I think. We must develop our knowledge in a closed group."

He made it sound very rational, as if the fact that Mel had recently been my lover had nothing to do with it at all. Well, maybe in Zenya's mind that's the way things really were.

He stood up then. "It is time for the Circle to meet," he said. He extended his hand to me and helped me up from my chair. That was a nice moment; it made me feel so special and unique. "Tonight," he went on, "we will go further, even, than in our last meeting."

I couldn't visualize that, and actually didn't believe it—which shows how little I knew.

Zenya led us upstairs. Once again the black room had been slightly rearranged; the candlestick had been moved from the center and placed in one corner, and the cushions had been gathered together in the middle of the room instead of being arranged in a circle.

We filed into the little room and Zenya shut and locked the door. "While you were speaking on the phone, Christina," he said to me, "I explained to our newcomer, Margaret, the intimate nature of our Circle. And I suggested that this evening we should begin by tapping as much of the orgone energies as possible, as directly as possible." As he spoke, he unbelted his robe and let it fall casually open. In the flickering candlelight his bronze body was just visible between the folds of the robe, his cock hanging limp but large, half in shadow.

Then, in one movement, he shrugged off the golden fabric and stood naked, tall and dignified. He surveyed the other people in the room; they all began undressing. Margaret Burke had stopped her incessant talking; her eyes seemed as round as her face, and she was staring at Zenya's body as if she were hypnotized. Nick, on the other hand, seemed to be avoiding looking in that direction, as if he were embarrassed.

I dropped my own silver-white robe, reluctant to let go of it, but at the same time happy to show off my own body.

Zenya waited until everyone was naked. Then he turned to me and wordlessly embraced me in front of the others. I can't deny that I enjoyed the exhibitionism of it. And I also liked it when I felt his cock beginning to swell, pressing up against my groin.

After he had hugged me, he released me and turned to Alexandra, who was standing on the other side of him. He embraced her next; and we realized what he intended. Everyone was to embrace everyone else, to cut through the unconscious mental barriers to physical contact, and to bring to life the physical excitement that was latent in the group.

I turned to Masterson, standing beside me, and I hugged him, not letting myself judge his body, just embracing him as a fellow human being. Then I went to Margaret, who of course was only too ready to hug anyone; and then I went to Nick, who was obviously nervous and seemed to want me not to touch him.

By this time Zenya had knelt down on one of the cushions, and we joined him. I knelt on his right, Masterson beside me—the same circle as before, except that Margaret grabbed for herself the place that Stella had once occupied.

Zenya extended his arms to the middle of the group. Everyone else followed suit, so that all our hands were together and touching. Zenya leaned forward and ran his hands up and down the arms of some of the other people—men and women alike—and soon everyone was pressing close, touching, rubbing, caressing one another.

Quickly Zenya reached behind him to his robe, extracted the little golden box he had used the previous night, and took out a large pinch of the powder in it. He sprinkled it into the candle flame burning in the holder in one corner, and the aromatic scent filled the small room. It tickled my nose, and this time, I was sure, I felt myself grow more sharp-eyed, more aware in every way, as a result.

Zenya rejoined the group. He was thoroughly aroused by now, his magnificent cock standing out rigid. In a way, I didn't like the idea of the other two women seeing him and touching him. But I realized that this group sharing of physicality was quite different from moments when Zenya and I were alone together.

He started touching me more than the others in the group. Seemingly by accident, his hands started moving more over my breasts. Then his fingers rubbed my pubes, dropped lower, and caressed my thighs.

I felt my skin start to glow with an inner warmth. I felt so close and accepted in that circle, and at the same time, so special, as Zenya's mistress. I was filled with benevolent, happy emotions. I found myself fondling Masterson, beside me; and then it became hard to sort out who was touching whom.

Our breathing, and the gentle stroking of skin on skin, were the only sounds. We sprawled more carelessly on the group of cushions. All the men had hard-ons and were stroking the women's genitals. I got that familiar feeling that the black walls of the room were simultaneously receding to infinity and closing in to the point where the room was like being in my own head. I touched Zenya and was overcome by a shameless need. I took his head in my hands and kissed him deeply. Around me, I sensed others following my example. We were one body, six people united, kissing, reaching, touching, probing. And then Zenya pushed me onto my back and entered me. I made a little whimpering noise—I had wanted this ever since our short sex scene earlier in the afternoon. Masterson was close by me; I reached for his hips and pulled him to me and took his cock in my mouth while Zenya fucked me with long, slow strokes, and someone else kissed my breasts. I have never felt more beautiful and more desired; I lay on the black cushions in the flickering candlelight and felt myself awash in erotic sensations—beautiful and languid and at the same time very strong—pulsing through me. Zenya was surely right: this was the primal energy, the force that pervaded us all, and the universe around us.

Zenya's hand moved between my legs as he worked his penis in and out. He touched himself, touched the warm wetness of my juices, and then rubbed my clitoris gently with one fingertip. I looked up through half-open eyes and saw him watching me. I arched my back, pulled my knees up more to allow Zenya deeper in me, and felt myself getting close to my climax. At the same time, I resumed licking and sucking on Masterson's cock. He groaned with the pleasure of it, he stroked my hair, he ran his fingers over my face. And somewhere very close by us, Nick and Margaret and Alexandra were in a scene of their own; I couldn't tell who was doing what, but it didn't matter, we were just one glorious physical unit, flesh upon flesh upon flesh.

Zenya took my hips in his hands and lifted them. He pushed in as deep as he could, till I cried out. He fucked me with hard, decisive strokes, and his finger worried at my clitoris at the same time, and suddenly I came. I shut my eyes, but I had a series of vivid visions, of stars and space and physical forms. The orgasm seemed to last forever, but even when it was finally over I still wanted more, more touching, more sex feelings, more of this wonderful group energy.

Somewhere I heard Zenya saying, "We will chant." As I embraced another person—Alexandra, I think—and felt new fingers exploring between my labia, I started whispering the word, then speaking it, in unison with Zenya. Everyone else joined in, and soon it seemed as if every caress and movement was in rhythm with the chant. The chant was all around us, and in us. The Word described the force, the desire, the need. I felt soft skin against my cheek; then body hair under my hands; then other thighs against mine; then breasts against my back; then hips pushing against mine. And through it all, the chant grew, as if it were the noise that our sexual energy made by itself.

"There will be a sign," said Zenya, and the candle extinguished. We had all grown to expect this, of course. But Margaret Burke was caught by surprise, just as I had been on my first visit. She screamed—as I had screamed—and I felt for her in the darkness, held her, and pressed my mouth over hers. The chant went on around us still. She struggled in my arms. I desperately wanted her to be calm and not make a fuss. I couldn't stand the thought of her disrupting our Circle and its slowly spiraling energy. She tried to speak, but I kept on kissing her. I reached around her with one arm and pressed her very close. With my other hand I stroked her small breasts.

Finally I lifted my lips from hers. "Oh, I'm so scared," she whispered in the darkness. The other voices of the multitude had taken up Zenya's chant now, and I suppose it *was* scary. The unseen nameless crowd were all around us and above and below us, chanting, chanting. It was totally dark and the noise was growing ever louder. But the point was *not* to think about it, not to allow fear. The point was to feel it, to be it.

I felt Zenya beside me then, in the total darkness. His hard, hairless body was unmistakable. He touched me lightly on my shoulder, as if to say: I'll deal with this. And then he lifted Margaret Burke out of my arms and embraced her so strongly she couldn't utter a sound. Within seconds he had calmed her; by then I was already cuddled close to someone else, kissing one pair of lips, while another pair ran up the insides of my thighs and someone's tongue probed up into my vagina. It was warm and close in the room, as if our sexual energy were generating its own form of heat. And the chant became overlaid with the steady singing note that we had heard the previous night, until my head was full of it and I truly didn't know what I was doing any longer.

The singing note grew shrill, a vast operatic crescendo that went on and on. Flesh, flesh all around; body smells and the smell of the powder in the candle flame; a roaring in my ears; wave upon wave of desire and erotic excitement; the taste of skin and perfume and juices and other mouths; the feel of total oneness.

"Is there one we know?" Zenya cried, his voice almost lost in the storm of sound. "We seek one . . . one we know . . ."

"Christina!" The voice was deafening. It was so close as to sound *inside* my head. "Christina, do not trust the one who speaks across the sea. Do not trust! He means to take away all that you have found. He means to separate us. He does not believe. He poisons with his limited vision."

My mouth was open in amazement. It was chilling to hear her, so real, and so close and coherent this time. "Where are you, Fran?" I cried. "Can I see you?"

Her voice hesitated. "I wish . . . perhaps . . . there are others . . ."

"Speak, whichever others are here," Zenya intoned.

"Dad!" cried a voice, as if it had been holding back a desperate need to communicate, to the point where it was painful. It was Masterson's son; I recognized the voice from last night. "Dad, I want you not to worry, not to blame yourself, not to care. And stay with the Circle. So each night we can bridge the gap. I have sensed Mother, and she is all right, you're needed more here, don't go, Dad."

"I . . . I'll do whatever you say, son," Masterson was saying, but already another spirit voice was among us.

"Alexandra!" The voice was deep, old, weary. I think it was Alexandra who was in my arms at that moment. I felt her stiffen with excitement as she recognized her father's speech. "Alexandra, after so long, so very long. Come to me here again, and be true, be trusting, Alexandra. Speak and act truly, do not deceive those around you. . . ."

I wondered what it meant, but there was no time to find out:

"Nicholas! At last, Nicholas! I see you, my son. I see how you wonder and worry, but you must be patient. I can tell you . . ." The voice became garbled by other voices speaking over it.

"One! We would speak to just one of you!" Zenya cried. But it was escalating out of control again, as it had the previous night. The voices rose in a tumult, hammering at our ears. And then in the blackness I saw something new and terrifying, quite different from the patterns in my eyes that I had seen in the past. This time, a misty luminous shape was taking over the center of the room above us. Green-blue and swirling, it pulsed and grew as the roaring of voices grew. And I cried out in recognition—it was just like the luminous form that Nick and I had seen hanging over the castle when we had been out in his car on my first night. And now here it was penetrating down to us.

In the swirling misty form I saw half-formed faces. We all saw them, I think, and we all became frightened. One minute, we had clutched one another in passion. The next, we were holding on to each other in fear.

The luminous shapes grew brighter and brighter. I realized in panic that I could actually see the other people of the Circle around me, their faces and bodies picking up the ghostly hue.

The din of the voices rang incessantly in our ears. The floor seemed to tremble under us. The touch of the bodies around me now felt cold instead of warm. The air seemed to be freezing over my face. And it sounded as if the spirit voices were no longer speaking to us merely to make contact out of love. They were shouting a warning. Whatever it was in the center of the room, glowing and swirling, was dangerous. I saw hideous shapes in it—contorted faces and broken, tortured creatures. It pulsed brighter and brighter, and moved lower.

Suddenly Zenya was on his feet. He was stumbling, scrambling, leaping for the door. I felt a rush of panic; I really thought I was going to die. I opened my mouth to scream, although any sound I made would have been drowned in the bedlam of voices and noises and a roaring that was building up in the air like a constant explosion.

Then Zenya reached the door, turned the key, and flung the door wide open.

Light from the white corridor flooded into our little room. Simultaneously there was a horrible, ethereal howl and a searing flash of green fire that was everywhere at once; and then the noises were gone, the luminescence was gone, and there were nothing but the afterimages in our eyes and the ringing in our ears.

CHAPTER FOURTEEN

No one said anything. Not a word. In the total silence, Zenya walked to the corner and relit the candle. He then returned to the door of the little black room, and for a horrible moment I thought he intended to start the ritual all over again.

But he merely pushed the door almost shut, and didn't attempt to lock it. He remained standing there, and surveyed us with his dark eyes.

We were sprawled naked around the room. I was still dazzled from whatever had seemed to blow up in my face. The shadowy candlelight was mundane and reassuringly familiar. The feel of the cushions and the stone floor was real and vivid. I ran my hands over my own body, as if to restore my sense of my own separate identity. I discovered my skin was in goosebumps, and I was trembling.

"The bridge we build to the world beyond," Zenya said, "is open to any who choose to cross it." His voice was low, as if all energy had been drained from him. "The spirits of those we know and care for, they can cross the bridge and come to us. But others, other forms we do not even understand, perhaps alien to our planet—they may reach us, also. It is the risk we take, in our exploration. And yet, as you see, the bridge is fragile, and can quickly be destroyed when there is danger. When the Circle is broken, and the integrity of the space is broken—merely by opening a door—and when our concentration is broken by sudden white light from the everyday, real world . . . then the bridge is broken. Without the bridge, the world beyond *cannot* reach us." He stared slowly around the room, at each person in turn. "I hope you all understand."

I shifted uncomfortably. I was still frightened, and cold, too—the temperature change had not been imaginary. Whatever it had been, phosphorescing, invading our space, it had sapped everything: heat, vitality, all forms of energy.

"You're, ah, in no doubt about this?" It was Nick speaking.

Zenya shrugged. He spread his arms. "You saw yourself. We lost contact in a fraction of a second."

"What if you, ah, hadn't been able to get to the door in time?" Nick sounded polite, as always, but his voice was more high-pitched than usual. All of us were still completely unnerved.

"I do not say 'what if,'" Zenya told him. "I say, 'what *is.*' I deal in certainty, not possibility. I am certain of being able to safeguard our Circle from the world beyond. That is all." His voice had regained its strength. He surveyed us again, more sternly now. He stooped, picked up his robe, and put it on.

Clearly the meeting was over.

"I didn't even get to hear my friend's voice," said Margaret Burke. She sounded as if the experience had touched her only superficially. She was like someone asking for her money back because the movie wasn't as advertised.

"Few of us make contact with our lost ones on the first visit to the Circle," Zenya told her.

"But you told me it would happen."

"I told you it *will* happen, Margaret. And it will. Tomorrow, or the night after that, or after that."

"I don't rightly know I've got the inclination to try one more of these sessions," said Masterson, wearily getting up and searching around for his clothes. "I don't know as how I need so much excitement, at my age."

"Remember the words of your son," said Zenya. "Whom you are only now beginning to be able to speak to."

Masterson paused reflectively. He shook his head. "Well, I just don't know."

"The choice, of course, is always yours," said Zenya.

Everyone now was getting dressed. I wrapped my white robe around my body, but it seemed to offer little warmth. Personally, I trusted Zenya; he had moved quickly, had done exactly what had needed to be done. But I felt, with each new meeting of the Circle, the stakes were getting higher. We were making better and better contact with the world beyond; but that could bring fear as well as fulfillment.

I stood up and walked to Zenya. "You have my faith," I said.

He stroked my hair. "I expected no less, Christina."

He opened the door out of the room then, and it was clear to the other members of the group that it was time to leave.

"I will rest now," Zenya told them. "If you wish to talk more about our Circle—any of you, or all of you—we can meet tomorrow in my library downstairs, in the daytime. I think we have discovered much. We have made a vital, wonderful link with the ones we wish to reach out to across the grave. We shall learn more. I bid you good night."

One by one they filed out past him, out of the little black room, and out of the white door that was the dividing line between his private world and the rest of the castle. Masterson went first, still looking unhappy; then Alexandra, taking his hand as if to reassure him. Then Nick, avoiding looking at either myself or Zenya, and then Margaret. She paused before she left. "It was a most interesting experience," she said, looking up at Zenya. Her bright eyes were cheerful again. Her round face was beaming again. "Quite wonderful."

He just stared down at her, waiting patiently for her to leave.

"If I might make a suggestion," she went on, "about the food tonight. Could you consider using more whole grains? The purity of the nutrients we take in has a direct correspondence to the chemicals of life that sustain us, even sustain our thoughts. Perhaps—"

"Tomorrow," he said. "Talk to me tomorrow." For the first time, I saw him becoming overtly angry.

It didn't touch her, of course. She just smiled and nodded. "Very well. But please think it over."

And then, finally, she was gone. Zenya went and shut the white door and locked it, and I was alone with him in the east wing. I felt some of my energy and spirit returning, and I felt delighted to be with him, away from the others. "Do you need to rest?" I asked. "Do you need to be alone?"

"I need to think," he said. "But you may lie with me. Come. To my sleeping quarters."

I followed him down the corridor. He opened a door that I had not been through before, and switched on the light.

The room was, of course, pure white. One wall was paneled completely in huge mirrors. There was a large bed draped with what seemed to be genuine zebra and llama skins. Books were everywhere, lying on the thick-pile white carpet, on the bed, and on a table by the window. Most of the books were open, or marked with notebook pages covered in handwriting that, I realized, was in Arabic.

Zenya dumped some books off the bed and onto the floor, and stretched out. Cautiously I joined him. I lay close, feeling just a little out of place in this room that seemed so totally his own. I touched his arm. "Are you all right?"

"Yes." He stared at the white ceiling. "It was close, you know, Christina. I did not tell them how close. I have to be careful next time."

I shivered. "Don't scare me."

"Do you not want to know the truth?" His eyes challenged me.

"I . . . guess I do."

"I offer to share my knowledge, Christina. If you refuse that, you refuse the role I have allowed you. You must be strong."

I sensed the implied threat, that if I didn't measure up, I'd be kicked out just as Stella had been kicked out. "I understand," I said calmly.

"Good."

"What was it," I asked, "that came to us tonight?"

He shrugged. "There are things that even I cannot know, for we are moving now where no one has ever been before." He sat up, and I saw his fists clench, as if in a dedicated determination. "You realize? *No one* knows what we are now learning."

"I see."

"But what worries me . . ." He lay back down beside me. His arm circled my shoulders. "What worries me is that I might not have been quite quick enough tonight."

That struck a frightening chord. "What do you mean?"

"Whatever reached us—perhaps some of it is still in

our space, our continuum. Just perhaps. It is a chance." He looked at me suddenly, and very intensely. "Mention none of this to the others."

I swallowed hard. "All right."

"Anyway, we will know soon enough. If it is with us, its presence will manifest itself, one way or another."

I squirmed restlessly on the bed. I touched him. "What do you mean? I saw it—whatever it was—I saw it vanish."

"Perhaps, perhaps not. Anyway, Christina, it is pointless to speculate. This is not some barbaric myth we are talking about. It is not a matter of hanging garlic around the room to keep away the vampires. It is an unknown thing. It is not limited by laws of space as we know them. It is not matter as we know it. It does not think, and is not in any sense alive. Our only defense"—and he smiled faintly—"our only defense is our *spirit*. For we know that the negative force that invaded our space tonight is just the opposite of the positive force of the libido, which we generated so powerfully."

I thought about that. "You mean the stronger our sexual and spiritual energy, the safer we are?"

"That is my guess. So you will stay in this room, in this bed, with me, tonight. We will share our energy, and sustain it, against the unknown."

That sounded right by me. I felt free now to reach for him and hold him, as if I had been given permission. I pressed my body to his, and my silver-white gown rustled against his gold one. We kissed, and I felt faint stirrings of sensuality.

It was not as easy as before, though. And I remembered my premonition of dread that had accompanied Mel's phone call. And I remembered the spirit voice of my sister, Fran, warning me not to trust Mel. It was all so complex and mysterious. All I had to go on, ultimately, was my intuition.

My intuition told me to beware. There was still an ominous, formless threat in the air. I clung to Zenya, but even his strength seemed insufficient to fight the unseen menace that had descended upon the castle.

CHAPTER FIFTEEN

"I know what you are feeling," Zenya murmured to me. "You are thinking about what happened to our Circle tonight. You feel a coldness, a premonition of danger here."

I nodded. My arms were still around him. My head was on his shoulder. I was finding it hard to let myself relax and become aroused.

"You must narrow the focus of your awareness," he told me. "Until only you and I are in your thoughts. Then, together, we can generate the positive energy to drive out all the coldness and fear that is encroaching on you now."

"You'll have to help me," I said. My voice sounded small.

"Very well." He got up from the bed, walked to the door, and turned off all but one small light. Then he walked to the windows and drew the drapes, shutting out the night. The fabric was gold, like his robe—embroidered with the moon, the sun, the planets, the astrological symbols, and the other signs I did not understand.

I lay on my back on his bed, waiting for him. He undressed and walked to me. He bent down and lifted me—he seemed amazingly strong. He held me in his arms and kissed me; at last I felt more secure, more protected. He pushed back the zebra and llama skins covering the bed and laid me between sheets that were so delicately soft, they had to be pure silk. I was still loosely wearing my robe; he took it from me and laid it aside.

Then he covered my naked body with his. Warmth flowed from him, that special warmth he always seemed to have. His broad chest pressed down upon my breasts. He took my head between his hands and kissed me; the kiss went on and on, and the longer it lasted, the more I was able to do as he had said, and forget everything else but the two of us.

"You see," he said finally, "you can do it."

"With you I can." I ran my fingers up into his thick mane of black hair. I ran my mouth across his cheek and touched my lips very delicately to his neck, up behind his ear, then down to his throat. He continued to lie over me. I ran my hands down the sides of his muscular body, caressed his ass, his hips, and then pushed one hand between us and closed my fingers around his cock. He lifted his body a little so that I could touch him more easily. His penis was thick and heavy. I stroked it, savoring the anticipation of it thrust into me. I tickled around his balls. I opened my legs. I held his cock and rubbed its head between my labia. Already I was wet and ready for him. I pulled gently on his cock. He lowered his hips and I guided him inside me.

He embraced me. His muscular arms circled me and held me tightly. I felt enclosed by him, protected by him, warmed by him. He kissed me hard and worked his cock deeper into me. I sighed with pleasure and soaked up the delicious sexy feelings. I gripped his shoulders. I buried my face in his neck; his hair fell around me.

For a while he barely moved, holding his cock deep and grinding his hips against mine. We both took it very slowly, allowing the passion and the need to build.

Then he lifted himself on his elbows, and then on his

hands, so that he was supported over me with his arms stretched out straight, two columns of muscle and golden skin. He watched my face, and I felt as if I were posing for him, as if the beauty in my features was what was arousing him. I touched his arms and felt their strength. I brushed my fingers across his chest.

He began moving his cock in and out of me, a little farther each time, and every thrust grew stronger.

"Lift your legs, Christina," he said.

I pulled my knees up.

"No. Farther," he said. "Draw your knees up to your breasts."

I did as he asked.

"Now, rest your heels over my shoulders," he told me.

I did that. I was totally vulnerable to him now. I felt open, exposed, and powerless to prevent him from taking me in any way he chose. It was a scary feeling, but I wanted it. I wanted to know that I was holding nothing back, and was not able to defy his desire in any way.

He pushed his cock deep. With my legs up, he was able to penetrate me to the limit. "I don't know if I can take you all the way in like this," I gasped. "You're so *big.*"

"Just relax," he told me, still watching my face. "Relax all the muscles and allow it to happen to you, Christina."

I shut my eyes and tried to obey. Again he thrust in, a fraction farther than before. And then again, deeper; and again, reaching to my very core. I cried out, but not in pain. I reached down to his buttocks with my hands and urged him to do it to me more. He embedded himself totally, and I felt totally his.

With my legs drawn up, my thighs sandwiched under his body, my calves up over his shoulders, I wasn't able to move much. I just lay there and looked up at him as he began fucking me in earnest, with long, deliberate strokes of his cock. I felt the soft silk sheets under me. I heard his heavy breathing, and the warmth of it touched my face. I heard the wet noise of his flesh penetrating mine. I felt him trembling with the exertion as he held himself over me and fucked me harder and harder. He was gasping now, grunting with the effort and the ecstasy of taking me this way.

Each thrust into my body took me higher. I reached up and touched his face almost worshipfully. I'd seldom been able to give myself so totally to a man—I'd seldom known a man who deserved it.

He closed his eyes and clenched his jaw. His movements became almost desperate. His hips thudded against me insistently. I felt myself losing touch with reality. The white room receded. The gold drapes across the windows were a blur. The bed rocked under me and I felt as if I were flying on a magic carpet with this Middle Eastern man. I let go of the last of my self-control and clenched my fists and curled my toes and arched my back and shouted as I came; and the orgasm went on and on. Zenya came, too, with perspiration beading his brow and filming his chest. The waves of sensation ran through me like a surge of pure energy and life.

When we were both fulfilled, he finally lowered himself onto me and lay there panting, with his cock still inside me. It took us a long time to come back to reality. I stretched out my legs; we lay beside one another, embracing.

"That ought to keep the demons away," I said very softly.

He didn't answer. He regarded me for a moment with his serious, dark eyes, then kissed me on the forehead and drew the bedcovers up over us. "It is time to sleep," he said.

"Fine. I'm ready." And I was.

Nestled up against his strength and his warmth, I drifted off, totally at peace and feeling that all my fears had been erased.

I woke with my mouth dry and my skin in goosebumps. My pulse was racing. My breath was coming in little shallow gasps. All my muscles were rigid and I was trembling. I was instantly, fearfully awake.

What the hell was that? I thought.

And then: What the hell was *what?*

I didn't know what had roused me from the blissfully deep sleep. I hadn't been dreaming. One instant I had been unconscious; the next, I was clutching at the covers with my eyes wide open and my heart thumping in my ears.

The room was dark. That was odd—we'd gone to sleep with one light still on.

But what . . . what had disturbed me? There was no sound, absolutely nothing. My imagination? Or . . . some sixth sense? My whole body shuddered in a strange reflex. My skin prickled all over.

I tried to swallow. My mouth was too dry. I had to have a drink of water. And I had to turn the light back on. The darkness was pressing in on me.

Hesitantly I reached out and touched Zenya. He was lying quite close to me, breathing slowly and regularly. I wanted to wake him. I wanted him to hold me and make everything all right again. But I didn't dare wake him. I suppose I felt ashamed of my nervousness. I didn't want him to think I was weak and foolish.

I slid out of bed without disturbing his regular breathing. I found my white robe and wrapped it around me. I groped for the drapes and opened them a little, allowing just a trace of moonlight into the room. I picked my way over to the small table lamp that had been on while we made love.

I clicked the switch. Nothing.

Now I felt really uneasy. There was no reason—no *logical* reason—that I should be scared of the dark. I never used to be scared of the dark. I laughed at people who were scared of the dark. But now darkness meant something new. Darkness was the little black room where we heard voices from another world, a world beyond. Darkness was as big as the universe, but as claustrophobic as being trapped in your own skull. Darkness was panic and noise and a blue-green swirling luminous thing that came out of nowhere and seemed to draw the very life out of you.

I ran across the room to the light switches I had noticed by the door. If the bright overhead lights came on, they would wake Zenya, but I was no longer so concerned about my pride. I had to have light. I clicked the switches.

Nothing.

I bit my lip. I hesitated. And then there was a noise from somewhere, a long, calling noise, half-moan, half-scream. I jerked in fear. And then I desperately told myself not to be ridiculous, it was just an owl screaming out in the night.

Again I tried to swallow. My mouth was so dry it was painful.

Be rational. Be rational, I told myself. There's been a power failure of some kind. If there were anything really dangerous, any real cause for alarm, Zenya would have woken. Listen to him, sleeping so soundly. Doesn't that make you seem ridiculous?

Sure. But I was still in a panic, still scared of the darkness.

Then I thought of the candle in the little black room.

I could get that and light it. That would be enough. I quickly opened the door out of Zenya's bedroom.

The corridor was in total darkness. I felt as if I were staring into a bottomless pit. I clenched my teeth and picked my way along the corridor with my hands outstretched. My fingers were trembling. A shiver ran down the back of my neck, as if there were something right behind me.

I turned my head quickly. Darkness, everywhere. Just a faint rectangle marking the open door of Zenya's bedroom, where a trace of moonlight filtered in.

My heart was still racing. I took a few more steps forward. I reached what I was sure was the door into the black room. And then I realized I didn't dare open it. I was scared that if I did, I would see that thing, that blue-green glowing shifting shape in there.

I hesitated. Finally I grabbed the handle of the white door that would let me out into the rest of the castle. There were candles down in the dining room, weren't there? That would be better.

The white door was locked, but it was the type of lock you can unlatch from the inside, without a key. I fumbled with it; my fingers wouldn't work properly. The end of the corridor where I stood seemed horribly small, closing on me in the dark. I broke a fingernail, cursed, finally wrenched the handle and got the door open.

It swung against the wall with a *bang* that echoed away through the castle. I stood breathing hard, clutching myself. The stairs were to my right, leading down to the ground floor. A tall window was to my left. Moonlight was flooding through it. Here, at last, I could see where I was.

Still there were shadows—deep shadows everywhere. I needed the candlelight. I ran to the stairs and hurried down them, clutching the banister rail.

The downstairs hallway was dark. I stumbled and fell. My knees hit the stone tiles. It hurt; a stab of pain shot through me. And I was getting cold, so cold.

The noise again! The scream, the moan, whatever it was. It echoed horribly. It wasn't from outside the castle. It was somewhere inside the building.

I ran. I blundered into the wall. I found a doorway, groped my way through. My hand searched desperately beside the door frame for a light switch. I found it. I turned the switch. Nothing.

I blundered on. This must be the dining room. Yes, it was, and more moonlight was filtering through the windows. Here was the white-clothed table, the silver already laid for tomorrow's breakfast. And there, on the wall, in the holders, were candles. And embers still burning dimly in the fire in the giant fireplace. I grabbed a chair, stood on it to take a candle from its holder, then ran to the fire and thrust the end of the candle against a heap of glowing embers beneath a half-burned log.

At first nothing happened. Then, at last, the delicate, feeble little candle flame flickered into life.

I cupped my hand around it protectively. It cast giant dancing shadows around the room, as if all the furniture were alive and moving.

The screaming, moaning noise again. Christ, why didn't anyone else hear it and wake up and do something? Where *was* everyone?

I needed to be with Zenya. I needed his wisdom and protection. Carefully, carefully I stepped out of the dining room, protecting the candle flame from stray currents of air. I walked slowly, my numb feet padding silently across the icy stone floors. I looked around me as I went. My eyes checked every corner, every shadow. My hands were trembling. But I was determined to get back upstairs to Zenya.

I made it to the hallway. The black-and-white-tiled floor stretched away like an infinite chessboard. The oil paintings towered over me in the gloom. I looked up at the staircase. The sound had seemed to come from up there. I didn't want to go up there. Maybe if I shouted, Zenya would come down to me. But I had left the white door closed as I had left the east wing. I doubted my voice would carry all the way through to where he lay in the bedroom.

I put one foot on the bottom step of the stairs. I forced myself to start forward. I was shivering now, and yet at the same time my face was burning hot, feeling dry like my mouth. Each step up those stairs was an effort of blind faith and mindless willpower.

I was halfway up when I thought I heard a sound from behind me.

My head jerked around. I saw a movement, like something coming at me. I opened my mouth to scream. I shifted my weight to run up the stairs away from whatever it was. I lost my balance. My legs were tangled in my long white robe. My arms flailed. The candle went spinning out of my grip.

It was extinguished instantly. I was falling. I couldn't see, couldn't keep my balance. I had an instantaneous impression of stairs knocking against my shins, then my arm smashing painfully against something, and then my head—and then I was unconscious.

CHAPTER SIXTEEN

When I woke up, I found myself stretched out facedown on the tiled floor of the hallway. I was so cold and numb, I could barely move. My muscles were stiff and my hands and feet throbbed and hurt as if they had been immersed in ice water.

My head gave me horrible shooting pains as I moved it. I felt up and ran my fingers over a big bruise where my forehead had banged against the stone floor after my fall down the stairs.

There was very faint gray light filtering down from the window on the upstairs landing. Dawn, I realized. I felt an incredible sense of relief that the darkness was over. And I was still alive, and . . . and all my fears had been an illusion?

I saw the candle lying where it had rolled across the hallway after I had dropped it. Obviously it had gone out when it hit the floor. Nothing supernatural about that.

So what had I sensed behind me that had made me turn in such panic? I looked around at the barely visible outlines of the hallway, and now that I could see, everything looked so safe and normal and mundane. The thing that I had thought was coming at me—it could have been just a dancing shadow from the candle.

Slowly I stood up. I waited for my head to stop its stabbing pains, and then I walked back in the direction of the dining room. There seemed to be yellow light coming from there. I walked through the first of the intervening rooms, and sure enough, the light was on. I remembered groping for the light switch beside that door frame and turning the switch on.

So there had been a power failure during the night. And now the power was restored.

I was beginning to feel very stupid, having panicked so badly. I went into the dining room, climbed on the chair, and replaced the candle in the holder from which I had originally removed it. I put the chair back in its position at the dining table.

Outside the windows I saw a faint trace of dawn cracking open the deep, dark grayness of an overcast sky.

I sighed. I touched the bruise on my head again. I tried to recapture what it was that had so much upset me in the night. I couldn't. My mind was too full of conflicting images: the faces of the people in the Circle, Zenya holding me, the fright I had felt in the black room, the ecstasy I had felt before that in the group-sex experience, the ominous sense of doom that had preceded Mel's phone call. It was too much. My nerves were shot. No wonder I had panicked. And the noise I had heard in the night—maybe it *had* merely been an owl.

I walked back to the stairs, and up them. I wanted to creep back into bed with Zenya before anyone else in the house was around. I wanted to try to pretend that everything was quiet and normal and safe, and nothing to worry about.

I climbed to the top of the stairs. I stopped then. The white door into the east wing was standing wide open.

That almost destroyed the new sense of rationality I had just been trying to cultivate within myself. For I knew, beyond any doubt at all, I had left that white door closed when I had walked out of the east wing in the dark. I had seen it closed when I was climbing back up the stairs holding the candle.

Who had opened it now? Had Zenya gotten out of bed in the night and come looking for me? If so, he hadn't looked very far—he should easily have run across me stretched out unconscious in the hall. And he, too, would have left the door closed. He always closed it.

Slowly, I peered in, along the corridor that ran the length of the east wing. The door into Zenya's bedroom was standing open, near the end. Inside, lights were on. I realized they were on because I had tried the switches before leaving the bedroom during the power failure.

But if the lights were on, they must have woken Zenya. Even if he were a sound sleeper, the bright overhead lighting would have disturbed him.

With a renewed sense of trepidation I walked into the corridor and along it. I moved absolutely silently. As I reached the doorway, I crept very slowly. I glanced behind me; then I proceeded, my eyes and ears alert for the tiniest sight or sound of someone or something alive or moving in the castle.

I reached the bedroom. I peeked in.

Zenya was lying in bed; I saw the familiar shape of his body under the covers. Under the glaring lights, he still seemed fast asleep.

I switched the lights off. My eyes readjusted. There was some gray dawn light filtering in between the drapes, where I had opened them a little way in the middle of the night.

Daring to feel a little more confident again, I walked into the bedroom and shut the door behind me. I was still terribly cold. I remembered the warmth of Zenya's body. That was what I needed. I walked over to the bed, shrugged off my robe, and slid under the covers.

He had the covers pulled completely over his head. I guessed that was why the light hadn't woken him. Maybe he always slept like that.

I hesitated. Then I decided he wouldn't mind if I woke him now. I was still shaken and dizzy. I needed human contact and reassurance.

I turned the covers down so that I could embrace Zenya and kiss him awake. My hand touched his shoulder, and then in the faint gray light of dawn, I bent my head and pressed my lips to his cheek.

It was . . . wrong. Something was wrong. It was all slimy and cold and horrible. It wasn't Zenya's cheek. It was wet and sticky, and it came off on me.

I recoiled. I scrambled out of bed. I jerked the drapes open to let in more light. I stared at what I had uncovered in the bed.

Zenya's body lay there serenely. But his head was a ghastly pulpy mess of blood. Blood everywhere. On me, too: my hands, where I had touched him; my mouth, where I had kissed him.

I clutched at myself and screamed.

Later—how many hours later, I'm not sure—they calmed me enough so that I very nearly stopped trembling. Alexandra, Nick, Masterson, and Margaret Burke—they sat around me in the library downstairs. Nick and Alexandra were holding my hands. Margaret was sitting close by, studying me with a kind of alert concern. Masterson was slumped in a chair farther away, staring at me with a tired, haunted expression on his face.

"We'll have to tell the servants soon," Nick was saying. "They'll be preparing lunch for us, and I expect they probably go into Zenya's wing of the building in the afternoon to do chores in there, wouldn't you think?"

"You ought to know," I said in a low, shaky voice.

He gave me a wary glance.

"It's no time for secrets, Nick," I said. "I'm well aware that you and Zenya were . . . involved in some homosexual way. You're no stranger to the east wing."

His face turned pale. He looked for a moment like a hunted animal. Then he managed to get control of himself. "I see," he said in a small voice. "I didn't realize Zenya had—"

I shook my head. "He didn't tell me. I caught a glimpse of the two of you together. I wasn't supposed to see, I'm sure."

Nick looked down at my hand, where he held it in his. Then he glanced uneasily around the room. "May I prevail on everyone—that is, I would appreciate it very much if nothing could be said about my . . . liaison . . . with Zenya. If only for the sake of my career."

I looked at his pale, worried expression. I burst into brittle laughter.

His head snapped back to face me. "What's so funny?"

"Your career! Christ, Nick, you're involved in what looks like a murder here, and you're worried about your career!"

His face twitched. "Well, you don't imagine I *killed* him, do you?"

My laughter died as quickly as it had started. I felt hollow and drained and dead. And already I missed Zenya's presence. "I don't imagine anything," I said.

"After our experience last night," Margaret spoke up, "it seems silly to pretend that Mr. Zenya must have been the victim of a physical attack."

I looked at her and could see, as far as she was concerned, it was odds-on that Zenya's skull had been smashed by an evil presence. The thought, of course, was on all our minds. I think we all realized it was insane to believe such a thing. But at the same time, we all were, if it came to that, prepared to believe it.

"I think that we should phone the police, Christina," said Alexandra. "Now that you're feeling calmer."

I sighed. "Sure. What does it matter?"

"The police cannot possibly understand what has been happening here," said Margaret. "And wouldn't it be an awful thing for someone to be accused of the crime, when in fact *no one*—no one *alive*, no person—is guilty of having done it?" She stared from one of us to the next, her expression intent, her glasses glittering.

"What do you suggest, then, Miss Burke?" said Masterson, speaking slowly.

"I suggest that we form the Circle," she answered promptly. "Then we can ask the spirits who committed the crime. *Then* we can think about dealing with the police."

There was a horrified silence. What she suggested actually made sense to us all, insane as it sounded. But the idea of reconvening the Circle . . .

"I can't," I said. "I simply can't. I'm too scared. What if that . . . that apparition that we all saw in the black room last night—what if it comes again, and Zenya isn't here anymore to help us?" I started up out of my chair. "Don't you see, we can't cope. None of us can cope!"

My voice was becoming shrill. Nick and Alexandra held me back in my chair and tried to calm me. I realized then I had been getting hysterical, and I deliberately slowed my breathing and tried to ease the knots out of my muscles.

"We could adopt a logical outlook instead, ma'am," Masterson said to Margaret. His tone was remote; he obviously didn't like the woman.

"Just what do you mean?" She turned her bright eyes his way.

"We should consider who had any *reason* to kill our teacher and friend."

"Oh, God," I said, "if there's going to be interrogations, let's let the police do it."

He regarded me in a kindly but authoritative way. "I assure you, Christina," he said, "it will be no more of a picnic dealing with them. Just think, now. We should be clear in our heads, as clear as we can, under these circumstances. Did Zenya, as the saying goes, have enemies?"

We were all silent. "Stella," I whispered.

Masterson nodded. "Quite so."

"It wasn't clear whether she'd really left the castle or not," I went on. "Jenkins said she had. But then she turned up in my room—the guest room I originally used—and warned me Zenya was evil, and told me all kinds of things he'd done to her while she was his mistress."

"I think we should also think about the servants," Masterson went on. "Did any of them know about Zenya's activities? Most of them, as I understand it, had worked here for years under a previous owner. Perhaps some of them were superstitious, were uneasy about the goings-on here now, and even imagined Zenya was evil in some way. Who can say?"

"Yes, who can say?" I took up from him. "Because if *that's* reason enough to have killed Zenya, then any one of us could have done it. You yourself, Mr. Masterson. You've said you had a religious background. Did *you* think Zenya was the devil? Or Alexandra, you were jealous of me being chosen to be Zenya's new mistress, weren't you? Did the séances make you crazy enough to kill him for it? I mean, just how crazy *are* we? How can any of us tell?"

"Please!" Alexandra was squeezing my hand. "Please be calm, Chris. Please don't shout."

"Well, answer me, then!"

She nodded. "All right. Yes, I was jealous." Her eyes looked at me steadily. "But not so jealous as to do something insane. I admired Zenya. I wanted him to live."

It sounded right. She sounded so sensible. But none of us was really as sensible as we seemed. "I believe you," I said. "But at the same time, I believe any of us could have done anything, and not even be sure of our memories."

"Including you, Christina," said Masterson. "You seem, I agree, to have less motive for Zenya's murder than others of us. But you *did* have the *opportunity*. You alone were with him in the locked east wing."

"But I've explained that already!" I said. "I woke in the night, unlocked the white door, fell, and lay unconscious, and by the time I revived, Zenya was dead. The person who killed him had several hours, then, to walk through the unlocked door and do it."

"We only have your word for all of that," Masterson remarked.

I stared at him. He stared at me.

"I still say we should convene the Circle," said Margaret.

"That will not be necessary, madam, if you'll excuse my interrupting," said a new voice. Everyone's head jerked around. It was Jenkins, the old servant, standing in the library doorway.

"Good God, man," said Nick, "have you been eavesdropping?"

Jenkins regarded him for a moment without speaking. Then he shrugged. "The servants in a house such as this, sir, often know more about the goings-on than they are given credit for. Also, I would remind you that we have been employed by Mr. Zenya, sir, and now that he is dead, our loyalty is no longer required.

Every man for himself, so to speak. But this is all by the by. The police have arrived, and wish to be admitted."

We were all staring at the old man. For a long moment no one spoke.

"Did you telephone them?" Nick asked finally.

"No, sir." Jenkins blinked. "They seem to have come on other business." He coughed. "Perhaps it would be best if you ladies and gentlemen all came to the front door, to decide what should be done."

We looked at each other. Slowly we stood up. I don't know how the others felt, but I was scared inside. The castle had become such a closed, complete world to us all. And now it was being invaded by people who could not possibly understand or believe what we had come to know as a reality.

We filed out and walked to the front door. Jenkins opened it.

Outside, it was gray, cold, and wet. There was a cruel wind. Two police officers in their neat military-style British uniforms were standing on the doorstep, wincing at the gusts of icy rain blowing in their faces. As soon as the door opened, one of the cops stepped forward. "Mr. Zenya?" He looked inquiringly from face to face.

Other people were in front of me; I was at the back of the group, and my view was blocked. But I caught sight of a third man, in plain clothes, walking toward the castle across the forecourt from the police car that stood parked out there.

"Mr. Zenya can't come to the door right now," Masterson was saying carefully.

"I have a warrant for his arrest, sir," the cop answered very politely, but with an edge to his voice. "I also have a warrant to search these premises, and must demand the right to do so immediately."

Masterson shrugged and stepped aside. The police officer walked in, followed by his assistant.

And then the man in plain clothes stepped into the hallway as well. He saw me, and I saw him, and I seemed to feel the whole universe shift under me, as if reality were realigning itself. I blinked, and I was taken back a week, to before I ever entered Downton Castle.

"Mel," I said, and the word seemed odd in my mouth.

He stepped over to me quickly, caught me in his arms, and hugged me close. "Thank God you're all right," he was saying. "Is the bastard still here? Or has he run off?"

"Who?" I didn't understand him. He seemed like a stranger, and yet so familiar, I clung to him as if from blind, unconscious instinct.

"Your friend Zenya. Where is he?"

"Why? What are you doing here? How—?"

"He's an extortionist, and I look forward to proving it in court."

"No." I was so dizzy now I had to concentrate hard to keep track of the few things I knew were true. "No, Mel, that's not true. And he's dead. He's dead and it's all over."

And then, for the first time, I really understood that it *was* all over. There was a sense of crippling loss; and at the same time, immense relief.

I clung to Mel, my emissary from the real world, and started to try to understand.

CHAPTER SEVENTEEN

Coming back to the real world was hard, and for a while it was cruel and cold and miserable, too. I don't even like to remember it too vividly, so I'll skip the little details.

The gist of it was this. As soon as the police found Zenya's body, everyone was under arrest. The guests, the servants, *everyone*. Within a couple of hours there were more cops than civilians in Downton Castle. There are not many murders in Britain, and violent crime is even rarer outside of cities. We got the impression that this was the biggest thing to hit Herefordshire in the last half-century.

In the end, all of us, including the servant staff, were locked up in Hereford police station and questioned individually while the cops searched every inch of the castle and Mel ranted and raved about habeas corpus and that kind of thing and demanded my immediate release. That was sweet of him, but he needn't have worried; within a matter of hours after taking statements from everyone, the police uncovered evidence at the castle that made it clear who'd killed Zenya. The cops found all kinds of records and information; among them, precise details of a blackmail game that Zenya had been playing with Nick Weston. Nick had been handing over large sums of cash; in return, Zenya had agreed not to reveal Nick's homosexuality (and he had ample documentary proof of it, because he himself had been homosexually involved with Nick for some time).

Poor Nick, getting screwed in every sense! As soon as he saw that the police knew, he confessed the rest. He had believed in Zenya, as we had all believed. He had been under Zenya's spell, like the rest of us. But more than that, he had felt a slavish helplessness. Nick had played a submissive role in his sex with me. That role was amplified a thousand times in his dealings with Zenya.

Nick had seen me as salvation, somehow. He had had many failed relationships with women, and he was miserable about his homosexual life. He fixed on me as the answer; and then I became Zenya's mistress. It seemed to him, at that point, that Zenya was pure evil, and the only way Nick was ever going to free himself was by killing the man. He didn't plan it well. He lured me out of the east wing by turning all the house's electricity off at the fuse boxes and making creepy noises. He saw me conveniently knock myself unconscious. Then he killed Zenya, using the giant tongs from the fireplace in the dining room.

He was so horrified at what he'd done, he covered up Zenya's corpse; and then I revived and staggered back upstairs, so Nick didn't even have a chance to root around in the east wing and find and destroy the blackmail material that Zenya had hidden away.

So Nick confessed, and the rest of us were released after a lot of time spent hanging around in concrete-floored prison cells and answering endless questions from the police.

But there were still a lot of other questions. In particular, how Mel, my savior, had happened to turn up like that.

This was how he explained it. He'd been disturbed by my weird voice when he'd first called me, transatlantic, at the castle, and he'd decided I had lost my grip on reality and was becoming a victim of some kind of cult. Knowing that cults need money, and take it freely from their rich believers, he'd checked with my bank in New York. Sure enough, they reported receiving a phone call from me ordering a transfer of funds to a British account.

Now, I have a friendly relationship with my New York bank. They handle large sums of money for me. They have had every reason to get to know me on a personal basis, and one of the officers knows me well. In fact, he swore that it was my voice he heard on the phone from Britain. He was so certain it was me, he agreed to transfer a hundred thousand dollars if I would send written verification right away.

Of course, I have no recollection of making that phone call, or of writing the authorization that turned up a few days later—after Mel had intervened, and Zenya was already dead.

As soon as Mel picked up his information from the bank, he called me, asked me if I'd given money to Zenya, and naturally became even more concerned when I denied it. He took the night flight to London, arrived at six in the morning, telephoned ahead to the Hereford cops, and convinced them of the importance of the matter. He told them to go and get a magistrate out of bed to sign a warrant, while he grabbed a rented car at the airport and made his way to Wales himself. By the time he got to Hereford, the police had their paperwork done and he came with them to the castle —just like that.

The police discovered some other interesting things when they searched the place. Some items that were disillusioning, to say the least.

Zenya's little black room was wired for sound. There was a large loudspeaker in the base of the black candlestick. There were more loudspeakers behind fake stones in the walls, up where no one could reach to touch the surface. There were even loudspeakers inside the cushions we sat on, and a giant infrasound unit under the floor, powerful enough to make the whole room tremble. There was an ultrasonic unit that could be focused at the candle—the ultrasound was outside our hearing range, but it was powerful enough to blow out the candle on command. And the powder that Zenya liked to sprinkle on the flame was some sort of hallucinogenic. There were also large numbers of suspicious mushrooms found in the castle kitchens—it seemed our daily diet was contaminated by them—and other chemicals in Zenya's study. All of them were reality-distorting drugs.

As for the blue-green phosphorescence that I had first seen above the castle, that could only have been some coincidental electrical discharge of a natural kind; it was, after all, a stormy night, and there were reports of ball lightning not many miles away. And the luminous shape that had terrified us in the black room: that was created by evaporating liquid carbon dioxide through a hole in the ceiling and shining ultraviolet light on it, which was reflected in the visible spectrum. This and all the other black-room gadgets were remote-controlled by Zenya, using a tiny radio transmitter that he gained access to behind a false-fronted piece of "stone" in the floor, while we were chanting and out of our minds on sex and psychogenic drugs. The sound effects were all produced from a full-scale electronics setup in a hidden room next door, and were fed through the loudspeakers, giving that surround-sound effect.

I know all this, because Mel went out of his way to tell me. He searched the castle with the police, and then he finally got permission for me to inspect it, too, because he had to prove to me how I had been tricked. You see, at first I refused to believe the whole thing had been a fraud. My faith in Zenya had been so total; even when I saw the electronic gadgetry, I clung to the idea that perhaps Zenya had kept the gimmicks just in case one of the séances didn't work naturally, and he didn't want to disappoint us.

But Mel checked up further. He ran down Zenya's background. He'd been some sort of electronics genius at an American college, and the first use he had made of his knowledge was to learn computer language and codes, so he could tell the computer of one bank to transfer a lot of money to a computer at another bank (Zenya's bank) and not reveal anything about it.

They caught up with him on that, but a little too late. He managed to get out of America, where the deed had been done, and he resurfaced in England, with a new name and enough capital from his bank con to buy Downton Castle. There, he decided, it was ideal to set up his own commune of believers, with miracles that really worked, and a philosophy that conveniently made it necessary for him to have sex with all the healthy, beautiful women he recruited. Such as myself.

As for his methods of finding out facts about people that they thought no one could possibly know, he merely brought up-to-date the methods used by mediums and magicians decades ago. His knowledge of computers gave him access to data in various computer memories, in credit institutions, government agencies, and so on. He added to that some contacts of his own, and made mysterious phone calls (on a deliberately fouled phone line) to people like me, sparking their interest so that they had to come to the castle to investigate, and the whole thing seemed to be a matter of free will.

Then, once the guest was on the premises, Zenya recorded his or her voice. and computer-analyzed it. He used this two ways. First, he used his electronics workshop to produce another computer-generated voice that sounded *similar* to the person's voice, but older or younger. These were the "spirit voices" that spoke to us. There's always a family resemblance in speech patterns, and that was enough, with all the other sound effects going on as well, to convince us.

Second, he produced a replica of our exact voices, which he used in his phone calls to (for instance) my New York bank. Available technology was just about capable of providing this cybernetic speech, if you knew how to program it, which he did. That part of his research apparently cost him less than ten thousand dollars.

Mel told me all this, and as I say, I found it hard to believe. Because I had *been* there, I had *felt* everything. And Zenya had made an incredible personal impression, on top of everything else.

But in the end, I had to see reality for what it was, and I had to admit that I had been made a fool of. It took two days of "deprogramming" (as Mel insisted on calling it). And he and I managed to enlighten two of the other guests as well; both Alexandra and Masterson stuck around long enough to see the whole fraudulent setup exposed. (Nick was locked away, of course; and Margaret Burke was the type who would always prefer to believe a mystical explanation rather than a logical one. The last we saw of her, she was negotiating to *buy* the castle, because clearly it was a place with mystic powers.)

At the end of my "deprogramming" I was sadder, wiser, and indebted for life to Mel, who had sacrificed three days of his demanding law practice in New York just to come and put my head straight.

On the afternoon of the third and last day that he and I were in Wales, we had a little farewell lunch with Masterson and Alexandra at a small hotel in Hereford.

It was a congenial but sad occasion; I'd grown to like Alexandra, and it seemed a shame that we were going to go our separate ways. And there was still a question I had been wanting to ask her. At the last minute, when we both went to the ladies' room at the same time, I had my chance.

"I always wondered," I said to her, "why you passed over Nick Weston in favor of your Southern gentleman, Mr. Masterson. Did you have some second sense that Nick was hopelessly fucked-up? Because I certainly didn't."

Alexandra laughed. "Much simpler than that, Christina. As I told you when we first met, I'm the type of woman who has to live by my wits. I don't have an inheritance like you. Nor a career, either. At times, you know, I'm dependent on a man for his generosity. And given the choice between Nick Weston and Harry Masterson, I could see that Harry really had much more to give. Though it's only fair to add, I've grown *very* fond of him. You know he's promised to take me on a world cruise?"

There goes a survivor, I thought to myself as I watched her leave with Masterson. A girl who can look after herself—but, at the same time, can do it without hurting other people in the process. Because there was no doubt about it: Masterson was delighted with her.

Mel and I were left on our own together then. It was afternoon, and I knew he had to get back to his neglected work in New York.

"I'll have to take the first flight out tomorrow morning," he told me. He looked at me with a sort of restrained hopefulness. "Am I going to have a traveling companion?"

"Of course," I told him. "I can't wait to get back there with you."

"So we just need to find somewhere to stay overnight tonight," he went on. "And I've had it up to here with Wales. So how about . . ."

". . . a night at the Ritz?" I finished up for him.

"Definitely," he said.

And that's how we found ourselves back in London, in the plush but discreet and totally quiet luxury of the Ritz on Piccadilly. The room wasn't the same one we'd stayed in before, but it had the same atmosphere of elegance and old-world charm. It was the last stimulus I needed to reestablish my sense of identity and reality. It made it seem as if the whole excursion to the Welsh castle had been a dream, taking seven days out of my life and leaving me wondering how I could have ever acted in such a totally uncharacteristic fashion.

Mel and I went to bed, and I rediscovered him, too. It made me realize how totally I had subjected myself to my "guru," Zenya, at Downton Castle. That evil man—for indeed he *was* evil—had known exactly how to work on me to the point where I was no longer a free individual. I had lost my own identity, like poor Stella, and become a mindless follower who wanted only to sacrifice herself for the Great Man.

By contrast, with Mel I was *me:* an alive, self-possessed woman with a will of her own.

We lay together in the soft bed in the quiet room. The hotel was so well heated that we had been able to open the doors onto the balcony slightly, and a faint breeze stirred the moonlit drapes. Distant murmuring sounds of traffic on Piccadilly drifted in; it was very relaxed and very romantic.

At first we simply needed to rediscover each other. Lying under the quilt of pure down, facing each other in the faint light, we watched each other's faces for long moments. Then I gently traced my fingers across Mel's forehead, around his cheeks, and down his neck.

I ran my hand through his hair; I stroked my palm down over his shoulder and across his chest. Vaguely I remembered the hairlessness of Zenya's skin, and its dark honey color; I threw that memory aside. Mel was with me now, and Mel would be the only man I would think about.

His hand touched my cheek. He leaned closer and kissed me very gently on the forehead, then the end of my nose. Then his lips touched mine, tentatively at first. I closed my eyes and opened my mouth to him. The kiss deepened and became more erotic. Our tongues touched fleetingly. The slight roughness of his cheek brushed against mine. His hands held my head; he kissed me harder. I heard his breathing, gradually increasing in rhythm.

"It's good to have you back," he murmured, pausing in his kissing me. He nuzzled my neck, and nibbled at it, making me shiver. The tip of his tongue tickled at the lobe of my ear.

There were no words I could think of to express what I felt, so I just pressed myself closer to him. My breasts pushed into his chest. Already my nipples were stiff, and I think he felt them press against his skin. With one hand he reached down and caressed my ample rounded flesh. Then he trailed his fingernails across the sensitive skin, just enough to give me tingles. And then he licked his finger and thumb and rubbed them gently, insistently over one of my nipples.

"I want you, Chris," he murmured. "I want you a lot."

He didn't need to tell me. Already his cock was standing out hard, nudging up against my belly. I reached down and fondled it, feeling the softness of the skin, the veins, the contours of the flesh. I traced my finger around the glans, and touched the top, where just a little oily moisture had moistened it. I rubbed my fingertip through the drop of liquid, to and fro, to and fro. He made a little noise of pleasure.

Now that I was touching him, I wanted to see him. I pushed the covers back and looked at his strong, hard body. I reached up with both hands, ran my fingers from his shoulders down across his chest, and caressed him, savoring the feel of his muscles under the skin. Then I stroked all around his balls, and tickled my fingertips through his pubic hair and down the inside of his thighs. And then I kissed the end of his cock and ran the tip of my tongue down the underside of the warm, pulsing flesh. I kissed his balls and took them very gently between my lips and flicked my tongue to and fro. I kissed the insides of his thighs. Finally I opened my mouth and let his cock push in, in, all the way to the back of my throat. I sucked hard and insistently, sliding my hands behind his buttocks and pulling his hips toward me. He let out a sigh of pleasure.

I sucked him for a long time. Finally I felt his hands reaching down to my head, gently pulling me away from his cock.

"I want to kiss you," he was saying.

I wriggled back up in the bed, beside him. We kissed deeply, and his hand moved between my legs.

I opened my thighs as wide as I could. He pushed one finger into me, and then another, twisting them to and fro while he went on kissing me. Then he started massaging my clitoris and I really began to feel the desire building up in me. I held on to his cock with one hand, imagining how it was going to feel inside me. The idea made me impatient with anticipation; but, no, I held myself back. I wanted to take it slowly, so very slowly.

With his other arm he hugged me to him. I squirmed against him, rubbing my flesh across his. We kissed some more. I rolled half over him, with his fingers still busy between my thighs, and my hand still holding his cock.

Then I took his fingers away from me and guided his cock so it pushed between my thighs and nudged up against my cunt. I wriggled my hips and closed my legs, holding his cock between them. I squirmed around, and the top of his cock nudged tantalizingly against my labia. He arched his back and sighed.

With each of my hands I took hold of his wrists and stretched his arms out on either side, while he lay under me. "Play dead," I whispered in his ear. He smiled and closed his eyes.

Now I felt I had his body to play with, to please myself, for as long as I wanted. Or at least for as long as he could stand being tantalized.

I knelt over him, bent low, and trailed my nipples lightly over his skin. I squirmed lower, till my breasts rubbed down across his belly to his groin.

I pressed my breasts up together, then pushed them down onto his cock, so it thrust between them. I thought I heard him let out a stifled grunt of pleasure. But I chose to ignore that. It was too much fun playing with him.

I moved so that my breasts went up and down on his cock, engulfing it in their soft flesh. Then I held his cock in my hand and rubbed the head of it over my body, across first one nipple and then the other. His cock felt so hard and strong and alive; I loved touching it. I knew how much he liked it, too.

I poised my knees on either side of his hips. I brushed the tip of his cock through my pubic hair, to and fro. At the same time, I touched my own clitoris. And then I lowered myself, a fraction at a time, till his cock was swallowed up between my labia and into my vagina. And then I sank down suddenly the rest of the way, taking it all inside me at once. I started moving up and down on it quickly, bracing my arms against his chest. It was like scratching the most tantalizing, delicious itch. I kept up the urgent rhythm for perhaps a minute, while Mel still lay stretched under me, his eyes shut. Only his fast breathing gave away the fact that he was as turned on as I was.

Then I ceased my quick movements and laid myself flat out on top of him. I kissed and nibbled at his nipples. I kissed his neck. I nipped the skin of his shoulder between my teeth. I moved my hips slowly, tantalizingly, with his cock trapped inside me.

"Well," I whispered finally. "That was nice." I made as if to get up off him. "I think I'll go—"

"Not so fast!" Suddenly he wasn't playing dead anymore. He reared up under me and threw me around onto my back, with his cock still thrust deep. I giggled and pretended to struggle. He grabbed my wrists and held them down on the bed. "My turn," he said.

All his suppressed passion was out in the open. He started fucking me very hard, forcing my legs open wide. His hips thudded against me so forcefully I thought he must be bruising me—but I didn't care. I loved it.

Barely pausing in his rhythm, he shifted so his legs were outside of mine. I felt even more trapped and at his mercy now, with his hands still holding my wrists down and my legs trapped between his. Also, with my thighs pressed close together, his cock could barely squeeze into me. The sensations became so sharp and vivid, I couldn't hold myself back any longer. I suddenly felt myself letting go, and then I was crying out, overwhelmed by a powerful orgasm.

He slowed his movements.

"No, don't stop!" I gasped. "Go on! More!"

I felt as if there were no limit to how much I could take. I wanted him to fuck me for hours.

He was still full of passion; he didn't need any encouragement. His body pressed down onto me, hard and hot and moist with his perspiration. His lips kissed all over my face. His hips thudded against me. His cock plunged deep. I gasped, out of breath from my orgasm, and felt myself getting aroused all over again.

I wanted to touch him. I pulled my wrists free from his grip and grabbed hold of his head, pulling it down so that I could kiss him on the mouth, long and deep. Then I grabbed at his shoulders, and down to his plunging cock. With my fingertips I felt it sliding into me. I writhed and jerked my hips, matching his thrusts.

He was slowing down a little, getting tired. I shifted and pushed, and we ended up lying side by side. I pulled my knees right up, and he lay on his side between my legs. I started moving my hips as fast as I could, urgently, insistently. I wanted to come again, and I wanted him to make it with me.

All the covers were off us now, in a tangle on the floor. It didn't matter; we were generating our own heat. The bed swayed and bounced as we shared our passion. A faint breeze from the open window wafted across the room like a cool caress over our flushed skin.

"Fuck me," I whispered. And then, louder: "Fuck me, Mel, fuck me till it hurts."

We were both in a frenzy now, hands groping, hips jerking. We scratched and bit and fought with each other. All the emotions came pouring out, as if we were battling to possess each other. He kissed me violently; our teeth touched; he bit my lip. I dug my fingernails into his shoulders, and then again, harder, till he grunted in pain. I pounded my fists against his chest. I kicked my heels against his buttocks. "I want it," I was saying, half out of my mind. "I want it all, give me all of it."

And then he tapped some incredible last reserve of strength and threw me over onto my back and held me there, and fucked me harder than I think I had ever been fucked before. His hand closed over my pubic mound. His finger jammed down against my clitoris, while his cock pounded into me. I cried out. It seemed to incite him more. His breath was coming in great gasps. His body was slick with sweat. His whole body stiffened, and he arched his back.

I grabbed his hand and pushed it harder up against my clitoris, harder still, till it hurt. I grabbed his other hand and pressed it onto my breast. His fingers dug into the soft skin.

And then I came. It was so powerful it was frightening. I couldn't stop it, I couldn't do anything. I was helpless in the torrent of sensation, and it almost hurt, it was so strong.

Mel was coming too, shouting with the pleasure and release. He fell down onto me, and we clung together, shuddering and gasping and kissing.

And then we just lay there for a long time, gradually recovering from that amazing moment.

Finally he rolled off me and lay beside me. He was still perspiring. I could feel the heat radiating from his body. I felt dizzy myself, but I managed to prop myself up on one elbow, and leaned over him, and kissed the places where I had bitten and scratched him.

"That was quite a reunion," he said. He sounded shaken.

"I'm sorry if I hurt you," I whispered. "I got very carried away by it all."

He touched my cheek. "You didn't do anything to me that I didn't do to you. And neither of us did anything that the other person didn't want. Isn't that right?"

"I guess so." I kissed him lightly. I touched his cock, limp now, and sticky with the juices of our lovemaking. "You felt so good. . . ."

His hand ran over the swellings of my breasts. "You

too. I missed you in New York, Chris. It'll be good to have you back there with me again."

I lay down beside him. Then I realized I was getting cold, and I dragged some of the bedcovers up off the floor, over myself. I huddled close to him. "I'm sorry I acted so crazy, Mel, and got caught up, at the castle, in all that weird stuff, and wasted your time."

His hand stroked my hair. "It's okay. It's understandable. That guy had something. The ones who form cults like that, they always do have something, a kind of charisma. That, and all his electronic gimmicks. . . . You didn't have much of a chance."

He embraced me and we lay close without talking. All the confusion and weirdness of the past week had been thrown off somehow in the fierceness of our lovemaking. I had needed that violent passion. Now we were both left with a glow of simple shared affection.

"You know, I think I could go to sleep right here in your arms," I told him.

"Mmmm. I'm dozing off myself. But, Christina . . ."

I opened my eyes. His voice suddenly sounded very serious and important.

"What is it?" I asked.

"If the phone rings beside the bed now . . ."

"Yes?"

"This time, Chris, don't answer it!"

Well, Mel and I went back to New York, and we continued our affair for a while, but that's a whole other story.

Now and again I still receive postcards from Alexandra, mailed from various obscure parts of the globe. The last one I received had been sent out from Japan; seems she was out there with some new boyfriend, a rock-promoter millionaire, whom she hoped to collaborate with on some kind of business venture. It sounded like her ultimate, ideal affair: a rich lover who would make her a partner in the business operation.

I read a small item in the New York *Times*, reporting, very briefly, on Member of Parliament Nicholas Weston's trial for the murder of mystic Zenya—and the ten-year jail sentence that was imposed by the court. I guess it caused quite a scandal over there.

Otherwise, I never hear anything anymore to remind me of Downton Castle.

So the mystic and the occult are no longer a part of my life, and these days I'm just as much a skeptic about that kind of thing as I was before I ever heard Zenya's voice on the telephone line telling me about my dead sister.

On the other hand, of course, I'm a woman of great natural curiosity. So sometimes when I'm alone and I'm sure that no one else will see me, I take out the deck of ESP cards with the symbols on them. That deck was the only souvenir I took with me from the castle; after all, Zenya *had* given the cards to me so that I could practice with them and build up my ESP talents.

I deal out the cards one by one, and each time I try to guess which design will come up next. I take it slowly, working methodically through the deck. I concentrate. I really try to guess the symbols correctly.

And you know what? I score average—five out of twenty-five—almost every single time.